Praise for *A Cold Season*

'A scary read that will chill you to the bone'
CrimeSquad

'This is a very spooky story . . . Disturbing in a *Midsomer
Murders* kind of way'
Daily Express

'A thick layer of snow hides the sins of a creepy rural village
in Alison Littlewood's chilly debut novel . . . an itchy tension-
cranker of parental paranoia'
SFX

'Littlewood's first novel is an assured and finely crafted piece
of work, probably the best horror debut since Joe Hill's 2007
novel, *Heart-Shaped Box*'
Reader Dad

'An intelligent, sensitive book. Its chills
are delivered with precision'
Spooky Reads

'Littlewood's fiction is set in a world where the possible
and the improbable rub shoulders, and strange stuff creeps
through the gaps in out of the way places. She is the real
deal, a writer with a unique vision and the talent to make us
see the world anew through her eyes'
TTA Press

Also by Alison Littlewood

A Cold Season
Path of Needles
The Unquiet House

A
COLD
SILENCE

ALISON LITTLEWOOD

Jo Fletcher
BOOKS

First published in Great Britain in 2015 by

Jo Fletcher Books
an imprint of
Quercus Publishing Ltd
Carmelite House
50 Victoria Embankment
London EC4Y 0DZ

An Hachette UK company

A CIP catalogue record for this book is available
from the British Library

PB ISBN 978 1 84866 992 5
EBOOK ISBN 978 1 84866 993 2

10 9 8 7 6 5 4 3 2 1

Typeset by CC Book Production

Printed and bound in Great Britain by Clays Ltd, St Ives plc

This one is for Trevor, my dad.
Thankfully I have a good one . . .

I said I'd free him. I didn't say he'd stay free.

THEODORE REMICK, A Cold Season

THE FIRST CIRCLE

ONE

When the sound of footsteps began, Ben was already regretting his decision to walk. It had felt like the right thing to do when he'd started out – the name Kirkstall, in his mind, was always followed by the word Abbey, and he'd wanted to see it – but the evening was dark and cold, and the streets were interminably long.

He had been listening to his own steps for some time as they echoed back from row after row of red-brick houses, each looking much like the last. He caught glimpses through the windows: the shadows of families settling down to dinner, balancing plates on their knees while the television's blue light flickered. The front gardens were filled with ever-multiplying numbers of wheelie bins, upturned plastic tricycles, filthy tennis balls – all manner of broken and abandoned things. Above him the clawing arms of aerials and telephone wires sliced the darkening sky.

Ben could almost feel the presence of the abbey, which dominated this part of the city. The very idea of it was written into the street plan: Vesper Lane, Abbey Walk, Eden Mount. The whole place was underwritten by an older time, the traces still felt despite the abbey's ruin: fine arches and bright windows crumbling and shattered, the remnants of a once-proud church.

Ben had never been able to fathom why his mother had stayed here. She had inherited the tall, mean house a long time ago. It had been her father's, someone he could barely remember, at least in nothing more than the impression of a dark outline of a man looming over him, his expression stern, as if he didn't like what he saw. She and his dad, Pete, had rented it out for a while, and Ben remembered visiting it with her sometimes, checking on the heating system or the electrics or the contents. There was always someone new answering the door, a succession of faces he didn't recognise. Then came the divorce and the custody battle, and at some point along the way, before he'd even suspected the possibility, it had become his home.

It wasn't his home now and he was glad of it as he turned a corner and started up the hill. He heard the footsteps somewhere behind him, almost but not quite tracking his own.

He stopped dead when he heard them and did not know why. It wasn't so late that the streets should be empty – anyone could be about. Besides, he had spent years of his life in this place; he wasn't afraid to walk here then and he wasn't afraid to walk here now. And yet there was something about the sound of them, something that spoke of intent, but without the need to hurry. He could picture the person who would make that sound, their stride long and sauntering. In his mind's eye they wore a half-smile, though of course he couldn't picture their face. They knew they would reach their destination, that person; they would reach it soon, and whatever they found there would be – *satisfying*. That was the word that sprung to mind.

Ben shook the image away, amused by his own reaction. They were only footsteps, and anyway, they had stopped. He looked back the way he had come, seeing only houses, their gates closed against the world outside – and nothing else. No children played. Those hurrying home from school or college or work had already locked their doors behind them.

There was nobody there and yet when he began to walk once more, he could hear it, a steady *tap, tap, tap,* coming from somewhere directly behind him. He stopped under the pretext of wrapping his coat more tightly around his body, though it was already buttoned to the neck. Winter had passed and yet the night had drawn in quickly; there was a chill in the air and the darkness was close. He almost felt he could shrug it away like a physical thing, but the cold of it was still there, like a villain's last cackle. The whole city felt as if it were steeped in the last dirty dregs of winter.

There was silence again: no footsteps or anything else. The only sound was his own breathing, but somehow that only accentuated the stillness around him. He'd probably only heard the footsteps because of a trick of the architecture, channelling them from the next street. They might even have been his own, distorted and returned to him by the angled walls. They hadn't quite been in time with his, but that could have been an illusion too, couldn't it? Still, Ben couldn't quite shake the impression that someone was following him – trying, but not quite managing, to keep in step. Perhaps they were even doing it on purpose.

He turned and looked at the empty street. He smiled at himself. He wasn't afraid, not exactly, but there was *something*, a sense of things out of place, things that didn't belong. Now he could see that everything was just the way it had always been. Maybe the only thing that had changed was him – it could be that he didn't belong here any longer. He'd moved on and had been glad to do so, and yet he continued to be drawn back here by ties he could never sever.

The impression of the world having become at once familiar and strange stayed with him as he set off once more. He somehow knew that the sound of footsteps would be there to meet him, and it was, but this time it was closer. Louder. He whirled around and stared at the street. It remained empty and dark, wedge-shaped shadows demarcating each small front garden. He'd been so sure he would be able to see the source of the sound. He tried to remember if the houses had thrown back such distinct echoes when he'd been a child. He'd done a lot of his growing up in these streets. He'd run up and down them all, sometimes with his friends or his sister, sometimes alone. He tried to recall if they'd created illusions like this, ones that could be heard and not seen.

Everything was still. Only his heartbeat had quickened. He did not know why he'd thought the sound so odd, and of course it didn't matter. There was nobody there, no one to see him as he stood gawping at shadows like a frightened child.

He turned on his heel, walking more quickly. Soon he would reach the end of his mother's street. He would be at her door in moments and she would be standing there, smiling or staring at him; he wasn't sure which it would be this time. Either way, he would be glad to go inside and turn the key in the lock behind him.

He forced himself not to hurry. If he arrived out of breath and out of sorts, she would see it and demand to know why. She would create a fuss, one that wouldn't be forgotten all night. He wasn't going to do that because of a simple illusion. There was no one there. They were probably his own footsteps after all, distorted by the streets and the night and his own imagination. Still, his stride lengthened as he headed up the slope. The footsteps were closer than ever, though their rhythm hadn't quickened. In his mind's eye he saw the shape of a man cut into the night, keeping pace without difficulty, impossible to shake off.

There was the corner. He turned it without pausing. His mother's street was lined with back-to-back terraces that were taller than they were wide, most of them topped with the jutting evidence of loft extensions looming like watch-towers, their windows shining blankly down. The thought returned to him that he didn't know why she'd stayed, and with it came an unaccountable anger: if she hadn't, if she'd gone to live somewhere else, he wouldn't be here now. It wasn't as if she'd had to keep the place – there was nothing to keep her here, after all; she could have moved on at any time, as Ben had. He thought of his flat near the centre of Leeds, as shiny and new as the building it occupied. It was a place where the past didn't live, keeping pace like – *like footsteps*, he thought, and almost laughed, though he didn't know why. He was relieved he'd managed to keep it inside.

He imagined that dark figure reaching out an arm without even having to stretch, and taking hold of his shoulder. He suppressed a shudder. His spine was a cold line down his back, winter seeping its way into him after all, and as he walked, thin flakes began to float into his face.

He lifted a hand and swept his fingers through the greyness. He thought it was snow, but he knew that wasn't right, and then he saw what it was: ash, fine flakes of it, and he realised he could smell it too, smoky and acrid. It reminded him of the nights when he'd been small and had looked out of the window towards the abbey – too young to attend the events they sometimes held – and there had been fireworks. He hadn't been able to see the building itself, not from here, but sometimes he'd been able to make out a pale glow in the distance, and it had seemed to him then that the whole ancient edifice was burning.

He couldn't see a fire anywhere, but perhaps someone was burning waste. He walked onward, into the drift. The ash had carried along the streets, lifting and falling on the cold air until it found him. But that didn't matter, nothing did, because the footsteps were at his heels. His breath quickened, stirring the flakes hanging in the air and they parted around him, none settling on his clothes or on his skin. There were three houses yet to pass, nine wheelie bins ranked in the gardens, a collection of chipped plant pots where nothing grew but weeds, and a few crisp packets no one had troubled to pick up. There were more deep shadows that could be concealing anything, but it was at his back that he sensed danger; it was as if the night was coalescing and taking form.

He could see his mother's house. If he focused on it hard enough, he would resist looking behind him. The place loomed as tall as the rest, just like the other houses in appearance, and yet it shone like a beacon in his mind. A few more steps and he would be there. *Tap, tap, tap.* There was nothing else, only the night and the sound of his own breath and the blood rushing in his ears and two sets of footsteps walking, now, together.

He turned in at the gate and it clattered behind him and he knew that he should turn, that he should *see*, but suddenly he knew he was afraid after all, despite all his resolutions and justifications. He was afraid of seeing nothing once more, of what that might mean, and he was afraid of what he might see, but he did not turn; he went on and up to the door. He grasped the handle and turned it, and it opened because she'd left it open for him and he felt a rush of gratitude as he stepped inside.

It was only after he was over the threshold that he looked behind him. Everything was silent; the street was empty. Flakes drifted through the air, the only moving things in a frozen world, as if the night was really filled with snow; it was a scene so redolent of his childhood that it suddenly made him want to cry. There were no footsteps, probably never had been. He'd allowed himself to be spooked, just as if he was a child again. There was nobody there, nobody except the person he could sense standing behind him, the one who had left the door on the latch so that he could step inside.

He didn't know why he'd allowed an echo to trouble him so much. He didn't know why he'd even thought there was something wrong with it. Except he *did* know. The knowledge settled inside him and he pushed it down deep as he forced a smile onto his face and turned towards his mother. For a moment, the footsteps hadn't been following him at all. At the last, it had sounded as if someone was walking right beside him.

TWO

The terraced house was the kind that estate agents would describe as deceptive; the plot was hemmed in but the rooms were wide, the living space expanded by bedrooms crammed under the eaves and a small damp cellar hollowed out beneath it all. Despite the years Ben had lived here with his mother, it still surprised him – now that he had a flat with communal halls and spaces – that when he closed the door behind him he was already standing in the lounge, the heart of the home. At its centre stood his mother. Today she wasn't smiling, but as soon as she saw him focusing on her expression, she forced the corners of her lips upward. She did not look away from his face.

She had been drawing again. Ben could see new sheets of paper tacked up on the walls, some of them crooked, some overlapping the old ones that were curling at the corners. He never knew if it was a mercy that the wallpaper – brown and beige and seventies' old – had been covered over just a little more, or if he would rather rip all the pictures down. He saw that some of them were threatening to fall off anyway. One clung on by a corner, hanging loose over the top of the electrical fire, an ugly affair of faded wood and exposed bars. A sense of frustration, familiar and yet new each time he felt it, rose within him. He knew it wasn't a fire risk, not here, but the reason only compounded his irritation; his mother wouldn't put the fire on, not even if she were freezing. She wouldn't even think of it, not when it was just her in the house. It didn't matter how much he nagged at her to take care of herself. She didn't want to do that; she'd only ever wanted to look after him.

And his sister, he told himself, knowing all the time that that wasn't quite true.

But the pictures – at least they were something she did care about. He examined them more carefully. He found he still didn't want to see them, not really.

He focused instead on his mother's face. Her skin was taut and a little sallow. She was not yet fifty years old and on the thin side of slender. Her hair was touched with grey at her temples and ragged at the ends; she never could be bothered to have it cut. Was she thinner than the last time he'd seen her? Ben's frustration was replaced by concern as that forced smile flickered its way across his mother's lips once more.

'Sweetheart,' she said, in the low but intense way she had, the one that had always made him shift with discomfort whenever his sister Gaila was around, and she held out her arms, although she didn't come any closer. 'You're back.'

Ben nodded. He always came back. What did she expect? He hadn't been able to leave her alone, not for long. He never had. *Not like Gaila.*

He pushed that thought away and forced a smile of his own. 'How are you, Mum?' He stumbled over the word. He'd almost called her Cass, a contraction of the maiden name – Cassidy – to which she'd returned years ago, but he knew she preferred 'Mum'. Formally, she was known as Gloria Cassidy, though no one ever called her by her first name; few even knew what it was. She had lived to be a mum, always had. Even now that she was in a position to move on, to pursue any interests she chose, she didn't care for anything else. And it was that – her desire to support him, to do everything she could to help him – which had made it so difficult to leave, to do the things he'd wanted to do. If he pushed her, encouraging her to get out, to meet new people, she'd only point at those God-awful pictures, as if they were some sort of substitute for getting out and living.

She gestured towards them, as if she could read his thoughts – perhaps she could – and he was forced to look again. The impression he'd gained from the door wasn't dispelled by closer inspection. The subject matter was nothing new. She'd painted a series of white hills covered in snow, interspersed with sharp, angry jabs representing skeletal trees. A drawing showed a group of figures huddled together and yet alone at the side of a wintry lake. The next showed a black church spire looming over a grey, mist-shrouded valley. Others were blank save for deeply black shapes that looked like holes in the world, one with a single white circle in its centre. It was a little like an eye. He had seen these things before, many times. Each time she drew them they made him shiver. Ben had hated the snow ever since he'd been small. He didn't know why, just as he didn't know what had made her choose these things as subjects, and nor did he really care; he only wished that, just once, she would paint in a colour other than black.

But his mother wasn't showing him the pictures, not really. She was showing him that she was doing something, not sitting here missing him. She was showing him that she was fine.

'Very nice,' he said. 'Did you join that art class I found for you? It's not far away, and you could meet people—'

She shrugged. 'No point. It's not as if I'm any good.'

The frustration was still there, simmering, and Ben swallowed it down. 'You could try. You might enjoy it.'

'Oh, Ben.' She sighed. 'Why don't you sit down, love? Make yourself comfy. I got some of that tea you like. It's brewing, ready – I'll get you some.'

'*You* sit down, Mum. I'll fetch it.' He went through into the kitchen. It was cramped but orderly, smelling of pine cleaning fluid. Next to the sink was a small stack of washing-up that had been left to dry: one cup, one plate, one fork. He flipped open the top of the bin and saw the cardboard sleeve from a ready-made meal for one. A dose of guilt joined the frustration. But the reason he had come, the one that made it difficult to look her in the eye – didn't he deserve his guilt, really?

A teapot, barely big enough for two, sat on the worktop, the lid by its side. He removed the sodden teabags and binned them, then slid a tray from its place on top of the cupboards and added cups. When he carried it through, he found his mother perched on the edge of the sofa, as if she were the guest and he the host. This time, when she smiled at him, it was genuine, though her hands wouldn't keep still. They kept clawing at each other, as if she wanted to pick away the skin.

'This is nice,' she said.

He balanced the tray on the largest of her nesting tables and laid out the cups, pouring the tea, glad of something to do. She sipped at it at once, though it was too hot and he knew she didn't like the smoky blend she'd bought for him.

'So how's work?' She always asked, and he always answered the same way.

'It's fine, Mum.' He tried not to grimace. Work was as it had always been since he'd moved back here: routine.

'You're doing so well.' She paused. 'Not like—'

He started. He knew exactly what she was going to say and yet it came as a surprise that she had been thinking of it too.

'That poor girl,' she said. She set down her cup, rattling it against the saucer, and then couldn't seem to lift her gaze from the tray. She stared down at its faded design of roses, the chipped edge revealing bare wood beneath. 'We should have looked after her.'

'Jessica,' Ben said. 'Jessica Winthrop.' He felt the faint echo of a memory; saw the brief image of a little girl with long brown hair tucked back under the hood of her coat. She was holding a hand to her cheek. Blood seeped from it, the colour shockingly bright against her pale skin, and there was snow everywhere, at her feet and all around her . . .

And now she was dead. She had killed herself; died alone in an apartment in Darnshaw, the village where they used to live; the one Ben could barely remember, only in brief images that hardly felt connected to him. If it hadn't been for their occasional visits to see Jessica, he would no doubt have forgotten it entirely.

'We can't go,' Cass said, and Ben was shocked to see that her eyes were full of tears. 'The funeral's this Friday, did you know? But it's in Darnshaw, and you know how I feel about the place. We can't go. I forgot her once, let her down, and now I can't even say goodbye—'

He reached for her hand and Cass snatched it away. He sighed. It was always like this whenever he asked her to explain: nothing but silences and withdrawal. He never had known why they were supposed to take care of Jessica. He only knew that she was the daughter of an old friend of his mother's, someone called Lucy who had died back when they had lived in the village. Cass had made him swear never to revisit. Even their trips to see Jessica had taken place elsewhere, on neutral ground.

Ben couldn't remember how he'd met Jessica. When he tried to think of it there was only that image of a little girl surrounded by snow, as if her name conjured not just a person, but a place and a time. He could almost feel it, that snow – the cold flakes settling on his face, melting at once, leaving behind nothing but a chill spreading across his skin.

His mother drew a long sigh. 'I wish I could go, for Lucy's sake. I know that Jessica wasn't a child any more, that she was all grown up, but – I want to go, I know it's the right thing, but I really can't. It's not worth the risk.'

Ben sighed. Yes, Jessica had been grown up, was only a year or two younger than him, and she hadn't needed them to look after her any longer. And yet she had, hadn't she? She must have. He remembered the email he'd received a week before she climbed into her bath and opened her wrists.

Hey, Ben – long time no see. I wondered if you might be able to come over? Things are kind of weird here. I keep finding myself thinking of old times – oh, stuff I barely remember. Will you come? I heard you're back in Leeds, 'oop north' again, eh? Hope to catch up. I think it might help.

And he remembered the irritation he felt when he'd seen the comment about Leeds, the annoyance at having to travel all the way across the Pennines to see someone he'd barely thought of in years. He hadn't understood why they were supposed to look after her then and he hadn't wanted to look after her now. And so he hadn't gone, and then he'd heard the news, a short but to-the-point email from her aunt. He'd read the word suicide and hadn't been able to take in what it meant. All he could think about was how young Jessica had been: younger than him.

Old obligations, he thought. *Old promises. You think you can walk away, but they never really let go.*

He remembered what Cass had said about Darnshaw. Saying goodbye to Jessica meant breaking another promise, albeit one he'd been forced to make and never really understood. It was why he'd come to see his mother tonight, though he saw now it wasn't something he could ever discuss with her. Her feelings about Darnshaw clearly hadn't faded over time. Whatever had happened there to cloud her heart was as present as it ever was to her and as mysterious to him.

He frowned and looked up at Cass and found she was watching him. 'You remember,' she said. It sounded like an accusation.

And he did remember, quite clearly, though it had been back when he was small: it couldn't have been long after they'd left Darnshaw. 'Promise me,' she had said, her tone low and flat and without expression. 'You have to make a promise and you have to never ever break it.'

He had looked at her, startled, and her eyes were unblinking, the pupils wide and black and fathomless. 'You mustn't go to Darnshaw,' she'd said. 'I never want you to go there again. It's not a good place, not for you.' And then she'd added: 'On your soul, Ben.'

Now she reached out and caught his hand. Ben forced himself not to pull away. He could feel the bony strength in her fingers. Her skin wasn't warm, wasn't cold. He could also feel the rough patches on her palm that he knew were there, but didn't like to think about and didn't really want to touch. It was another sign of whatever it was that had taken root inside her. And like the promise she'd extracted from him, the day it had happened was clear in his memory.

She had been having one of her . . . *turns*, he supposed he could call them. There wasn't really a name for what she had. He didn't think any of his friends' parents ever behaved the way she did, though he hadn't asked them; he felt he knew this as truth. He hadn't fought it either. He'd simply knelt when she told him to kneel and listened to her talk about how he was *his father's son*, even though he didn't understand what she meant because it didn't seem to be Pete that she was talking about. She'd tell him to *be ready*. She told him he'd been *dedicated*. And he'd stand and the words would drift from him, like flakes of ash brushed from his shoulders. Except they hadn't left him, not quite, because she had been everything to him and she hadn't made sense, and she hadn't made him feel safe.

It wasn't long before Gaila was part of it too. It didn't seem to affect his sister the way it had affected Ben. She would simply sit there, barely old enough to follow the words, and she would smile. Ben could still remember the way her eyes shone. She hadn't had a choice and she hadn't understood, but it had somehow made Ben feel more alone than anything else. It had been Cass and Gaila together, dedicated, *ready*, waiting for this father who never came, until one day, it wasn't.

Gaila was older then, six or seven maybe, and Ben had entered his teens. Cass had been pacing up and down the kitchen, spilling confusion from her lips, not looking at either of them. And Ben remembered the fear, old and familiar, the taste of it in his mouth. He no longer believed that some long-lost father was going to come for him. What he feared was that his mother would be taken away.

But that time it was different. She'd started talking of the Devil and betrayal, and how everything was nothing but a lie, that it always had been. And then she'd said that Ben was good, that he was the only thing that mattered, the only thing that ever had. He remembered how Gaila's eyes had gone dark at those words. Then they had gone blank as his sister pushed her feelings down, her thoughts turned inward and hidden.

Cass had switched on the hob. Ben had known that was a mistake because they'd already eaten and she'd nearly finished clearing everything away. Still, he hadn't said anything. He had grown used to not responding to Cass when she was in one of her moods. He was used to not listening. He'd shut out the words until the hob began to hiss and Cass called out, as if she were speaking to someone who wasn't even in the room, 'I don't belong to him,' and she turned and pressed her hand down onto the hot surface and the hiss became louder and his head filled with her scream—

'Ben, love?'

He roused himself. He had no idea what she had been saying. She had relaxed her grip on his hand, though, and he was glad of that. He looked down at her fingers, still wrapped around his, and then she took hold of his hand and turned it over, staring down at his palm as if she could read what was written there. There was nothing, only an old scar, a thin white line across the pink skin.

It seemed his life had been full of promises; promises demanded and made and reversed. After his mother had burned her hand, things had changed. Instead of his mother and Gaila together, it was his sister who would sit alone while Cass fussed over him. Soon after that, Gaila had started to call him *Golden Boy*. Ben had only felt confused. He had never really understood what his mother wanted or why it even mattered, but he turned his hand over once more, hiding the mark on his palm, and he squeezed her fingers.

Her expression lightened and Ben felt nothing but relief. What did it matter if she didn't know about him attending an old friend's funeral? How much could one promise matter? All of that was in the past.

Something had cleared from his mother's eyes and that

was good. It felt a little like escape, as if the shadow of the past had touched them and then retreated once more, leaving only the present, where everything was known, understood: safe.

THREE

The long road from Huddersfield led straight along the valley floor through village after village, names that were half familiar, though Ben didn't know why: Milnsbridge, Linthwaite, Slaithwaite, following the line of the River Colne and the Huddersfield Narrow Canal. It wasn't the quickest route to the funeral, but that was fine with Ben. Besides, the memories he had of Jessica lay at the end of this road, in Marsden, the last of the villages before the open moorland began.

A light rain hung in the air like gauze, constantly dampening the windscreen. He'd borrowed a friend's car, since he had no need to own one and nowhere to park at his flat anyway. The wipers needed replacing and they squealed against the glass, the rhythm getting inside his brain, a constant irritation. He turned them off and the world smeared and blurred into a mass of blackened stone and grasping trees. He sighed, flicked the switch and the shrill squeaking started up once more.

He saw the church just after he'd passed the sign that told him he'd entered Marsden. It was tall and fine, its spire soaring upward from a dip in the valley floor, large enough to belong in a city rather than a village on the edge of the moor. He remembered his mother saying it was known as the Cathedral of Colne Valley. They had driven past it when he was a kid, on to where the canal walks began in the village. That was where they'd met Jessica and her rather silent aunt so that Cass could fuss over the girl, who had always seemed somewhat puzzled by the attention, as if she wasn't quite sure who Cass was. Afterwards he gathered that something odd had happened; that Cass had found the child wandering in the snow, that Jessica's mother had died and Jessica was alone, that she needed looking after. Ben remembered little of it.

He realised he was almost through the village. It ended with a large, permanent road sign with various snow warnings written in large letters, with lights next to them that indicated when the road beyond was closed. It used to make him laugh when he was young, seeing it there in the sunshine, as if winter was only a breath away even in the height of summer.

Rough grass verges gave way to the dull orange-brown and purplish-grey of dead bracken and heather. Sheep grazed right at the edge of the road, no fencing to keep them from wandering onto the tarmac. Ben barely noticed them as he drove on towards the summit. Ahead was a steep cutting, a cradle of sky held in its notch. When he reached it he felt he was entering a tunnel, dark shapes looming all around, and then he was through and the view opened out.

The road descended in a series of curves into a new valley. He followed it down. There were a few blackened stone cottages, a pub, the silvery flash of an improbable office building, and then they turned off in a new direction, tracking the course of a little river. Ben wondered if it was the same one that had run by the old mill where they'd lived, had a sudden image of boys splashing in the water, the flash of an acid-green millpond. He sat up a little straighter. He really might remember it after all. Perhaps he had been happy here; perhaps his mother had. That would be a nice thing to discover, something uncomplicated perhaps, unadulterated by her odd swings in mood and ideas.

Promise me, Ben.

He pushed the thought away. This would be for him and him alone. It needn't concern Cass. He found himself smiling, and he wound down the window to try and catch the scent of fresh water running through the valley, everything washed clean and smelling of the rain.

If the church in Marsden had been the Cathedral of Colne Valley, the one in Darnshaw was a dark squatting toad. It wasn't situated in the heart of the village. Instead, it clung to a steep slope, hovering above the lives below, its tower like a blasphemous finger pointing at Heaven. From up here, the valley appeared grey. There was the empty sky, the road, darkened buildings and, beyond, the heather smeared by distance and the constant rain, and all Ben could think was: *Mum's colours*. This was the church she had painted. He had recognised it at once, though nothing else in Darnshaw had looked familiar; if he hadn't seen the sign bearing the village's name as he flashed by, Ben might not even have realised he was home.

It was strange to think that this place had been so distant to him and yet so close all the time. Cass' paintings had captured the sense of foreboding carried in the old stone. Perhaps her dark pictures were nothing to do with her state of mind at all; it might just be that a part of her was still here, full of the memories of this place. But he remembered her words when she'd spoken of Darnshaw long ago; the way she'd refused to see Jessica unless it was somewhere over the moors. And he remembered the way she had made him promise never to come here. *It's not a good place, not for you. On your soul . . .*

He stepped out of the car and the cold found him at once. He tilted his head back, letting the water settle on his face, the weight of responsibility pressing down. It should have been such an easy promise to keep. There had been nothing to bring him to Darnshaw, and anyway, he had barely remembered that the place existed. He'd never had any desire to visit.

He turned towards the church and suddenly there was another image, sudden and vivid: Cass bending over him.

He had been crying. Something had frightened him, but he couldn't remember what it was. He almost thought it was Cass, but he knew that couldn't be right. They were standing in the church and someone else was there but that was all right; he couldn't see their face but somehow he knew they made him feel safe. The thing he remembered most clearly was the feeling of their arms folding around him, of being comforted.

When he opened his eyes once more, he caught sight of a huddle of figures dressed head to toe in black outside the time-worn door. He swallowed. He reminded himself that this wasn't a casual visit, wasn't about him at all; it was about a person – a dead person, someone who'd had family and friends, people who had loved her; most of whom he didn't even know.

The rain still hung in the air, coating everything with a fine mizzle. Ben wiped it from his face, but it didn't help, only made him more conscious of the moisture on his skin. It clung, viscous; but it was just rain, and this would only take a couple of hours, and then he would be gone. Soon the service would be over and he could leave. Cass would never have to know.

He saw that more people were gathering by the door. Some were already making their way inside, walking slowly, their heads bowed. He drew a deep breath, glancing once more towards the road before he followed after them.

*　　*　　*

The girl in the photograph was beautiful. The picture was propped in front of the altar, and it was oddly full of colour against the old stone and faded wood. It had captured Jessica laughing, her expression full of thoughtless joy. Ben thought he could see the shape of an arm around her shoulder and her own arm was raised, as if she'd been pictured with a friend. He had no idea who that could be. He had been her friend for a time, but it had been so long ago.

Jessica's hair was long and brown. Her shirt was yellow. Her jacket was pink. Her coffin was white. It too sat by the altar, half drowned in lilies. Ben could smell them from where he sat and he wished he couldn't. They were sweet to the point of sickliness and made him think of rot.

He shifted in his seat, feeling the pew hard against his spine. *A body*, he thought. *There's a body in that box.* And he glanced at the people around him, veiled and black-suited, and he thought: *Don't they know?*

He couldn't remember attending any funerals before this. He assumed he must have been at his grandfather's memorial, but he had no recollection of it, and other than that, he had few relatives. There was his dad, of course, and Gaila, who was younger: this was the year she'd turn eighteen. The idea of any of them dying was ridiculous. But the girl in the picture, though she must have been in her twenties, closer to Ben's age, looked little older than that. He couldn't take in the thought that she was now inside that plain white coffin, half buried beneath its sickly scented load.

He forced himself to look around the church. It felt old. It must have witnessed thousands of ceremonies in its time: christenings, weddings, funerals, beginnings and endings. Stolid pillars held aloft a grey and faded ceiling, punctuated by carved bosses he couldn't quite make out. Only the windows were bright jewels, shards of yellow and red and green. As he watched, the light brightened, laying a fall of brilliant blue across the coffin.

Ben remembered what he'd read of this place when he'd looked up the details of the service. He'd read that the current church was a replacement for an earlier building still, one that had been a less imposing affair. In the original church, the floor had been made of earth. It had been easier that way; the custom had been to bury the faithful inside their place of worship. He grimaced, wondering what that must have been like, to sit in a pew, hymn book in hand, knowing that the dead were interred beneath your feet. Apparently, they'd continued with the situation until it had become untenable. As the years passed, the pews emptying as faith and obligation declined, the ground had become full; eventually it had been so crowded, the bodies so near to the surface, they'd had to tear the whole thing apart and rebuild.

Ben shifted in his seat again, pushing the thought away. That was when he heard the voice behind him, someone speaking in tones that were at once hushed and urgent. He couldn't help listening to what they said.

'It had to be something she found there. I'm telling you, she got to the end.'

There came an answering voice, also a man's. This one was almost a hiss: 'I said it's stupid. I told you I don't want nothin' to do wi' it.'

'Well, her aunt said it was all right. She said I *should* visit one last time. She gave me a key. It would be wrong not to, under the circumstances, don't you think?'

'You did what? But that's— I don't even believe it.'

'It doesn't *matter* if you believe it. It doesn't matter if it's real. It's what *she* believed that matters.'

They subsided. Ben found himself listening for more and it took him a moment to realise that the vicar had stepped forward. The vicar began to speak and his voice at once turned to echoes, distorted and difficult to follow. Someone sitting at the front of the church had begun to cry; one of the girl's relations, no doubt. *The girl.* It was easier to think of her that way, not as someone with a name, someone he had known, someone he had played with in the snow. He passed a hand across his eyes, thinking of that brief flash of memory: whiteness stretching out all around him, covering everything. And he saw something else: a hillside, more snow, powder lifting from it on a light breeze, wreaths of it snaking across the smooth surface to where a young girl lay, her brown hair escaping her hood. Ben standing over her, something clutched in his hand . . .

Everyone shuffled to their feet. Ben started. He stood too,

flicking through the order of service as organ music swelled, banishing the silence and unwelcome thoughts. He found the words in time to join in singing, 'The Lord is my shepherd, I shall not want'. He'd sung the song before, during his schooldays in Leeds. It had confused him. It seemed odd to say that he would not want God as his shepherd; it was like something his mother would have thought, at least until the day she'd pressed her hand onto the hob. But then a teacher had explained what it meant. She'd said that, with the Lord, he would not need anything else; that he would not want for anything, no bicycle or teddy bear or the latest games console, because he already had everything he needed.

Ben had pulled a face at that, and he could still remember the teacher's expression when she'd seen it. But Ben hadn't pulled that face because he wanted the toys or games she'd spoken of. It wasn't out of desire for anything, not really, it was only that he was tired of such words, tired of his mother trying to drum things into him that shifted and changed from moment to moment.

Even though everyone was standing, he could still see that pitiful white box between the people in front of him. Had Jessica had everything she needed in her short life? It was painfully clear, looking at that photograph with her brilliant smile, the laughter on her lips, that she should have had so much more.

I think it might help, she'd said.

Music swelled around him, all the gathered voices blending into one. But he *wasn't* one of them. He kept on singing, but he felt like an impostor. He had barely known her and he didn't know why she'd contacted him. He thought of his mother extracting her promise, making him say he would never come back here.

He was hemmed in by people he didn't know. His mouth kept on moving but he'd lost his place on the hymn sheet, and anyway, the words were like something alien, written in a language he didn't understand. He was grateful when the hymn ended and he sank into the pew once more, sitting there hunched, staring at his hands clutched between his knees. He barely took in the rest of the service. The words washed over him until it was time to stand and file slowly outside into the cold and darkening air.

'Ben – hey, Ben!'

He was nearly back at the car when he heard the voice behind him. The rain had grown heavier, filling the world with white noise so that the voice echoed it, coming from everywhere and nowhere at once. It didn't seem real and that was more likely to him than that someone should really be shouting his name, here, where nobody knew him.

He turned and saw a man with pale, slightly sallow skin and dark hair pushed back from his forehead, limp and drenched by the rain. His features met with nothing in Ben's memory. The man was about his own age, and he wore a wry expression, as if he was in on some joke that Ben had yet to be told.

'Skirmish, Ben?'

That *did* chime with something in Ben's memory, but it still took a moment for him to get it. He had a sudden image of himself sitting in a circle with a group of boys, the light dimmed by the curtains drawn across the window. One of the boys, his long fringe hiding the look in his eyes, held out a glass. Ben took it and peered into the murky liquid. He wasn't thirsty, but his friend was waiting so he raised it to his lips, just touching them to the acrid-tasting drink. And later – they'd been playing Skirmish, *Street Skirmish*, the video game they used to like, bending over the controllers, intent on the television screen, lost in the light flickering over them.

Ben found his voice, the name only coming to him when he opened his lips: 'Damon?'

'The very same.' Damon grinned. 'I thought you'd forgotten. How the devil are you?'

They exchanged greetings, Ben speaking the words automatically. It was odd, being faced with another reminder of a past he could barely recall. Somehow, though, this seemed easy, like slipping straight back into an old and comfortable friendship. He could forget the rain that was darkening everything, the hills louring all around them, closing them in. He'd felt so far away from home and the people he knew when he'd come here, and yet the sense of isolation was retreating.

It's not a good place, not for you.

He shook the memory of his mother's voice away and said, 'You knew Jessica?' He gestured towards the church. 'My mother sent her best.'

'*Did* she?' There was something in Damon's expression, a curl at the corner of his lip, and then it passed. 'Actually, I did know Jessica. We stayed in touch when I moved away. We were – well, we shared an interest, shall we say. That's why I came back.'

'Back? I thought you must still live around here.'

Another smile. 'No, I moved on a long time ago. I'm in London. You?'

A thread of envy twisted inside Ben. He forced himself to nod with polite interest. 'I lived there too for a while, but I came back. I work in Leeds now. It's quieter, but it suits me.'

Damon gave a brief nod, then asked, 'How did you know her?'

'Well – I didn't, not well anyway. I mean, I did, some time ago. I'm afraid I don't really remember. Mum used to bring me over. We'd meet up now and then. Cass would have come today, if she could.'

'Ah. That's good of her. Very, very good of her.'

Ben shifted uncomfortably. He again felt irritated with his mother. She had always said they should take care of Jessica, but the way she'd refused to come back here – it was ridiculous. Now he was creeping about behind her back; she didn't even know where he was. Why hadn't she come to say goodbye? Surely that was what a normal person would have done. He pictured her pacing the walls of her narrow house, only those gloomy pictures for company, and he pushed away the thought.

'It's lovely here, isn't it?' Damon swept a hand around the hillsides. His sleeve was already dark with rain, but he showed no sign of wanting to move, to get under cover. And then he asked: 'Do you remember the snowmen?'

For a moment Ben couldn't, and then he did: rolling the cold whiteness into rough globes, patting them into shape, lifting the heavy mass in both hands. And other hands came rushing to help, lifting it into position to make a head. *Damon's* hands. They had been *best* friends, hadn't they? Practically family. It was odd that he'd forgotten that. Odd that he always felt he'd hated the snow when the memory had been a good one, hadn't it? But then, it wasn't so strange that he couldn't remember. He'd only been young after all, maybe seven or eight . . .

'Funny that any of us could tear ourselves away from this place,' Damon added, his voice wistful. 'Speaking of which—' he looked over his shoulder and Ben realised there was another man waiting there, not far away, standing in the rain. He was perhaps a little younger than them, though his posture was that of an older man, hunched as he was into his black donkey jacket; the owner of the second voice he'd heard in the church, perhaps?

'Listen, you should come with us. There's something I have to do – I need to call in at Jessica's apartment, but it shouldn't take long.'

'Oh – no, I couldn't do that.' It had been bad enough at her funeral. The thought of standing in the dead girl's home, trying not to look at her things – there was no way.

'You really should.' That wry smile was back on his old friend's face, his head tilted to one side, regarding him. 'It might bring a few things back. She lived in the same place you did – her apartment's in Foxdene Mill.'

He gestured out across the valley once more and Ben caught his breath. Everything was still smeared by the rain, but there was something else there after all, something that snagged at his memories: a glimpse of honey-coloured stone.

Damon was speaking again. 'Like I say, we won't be long. You don't even need to set foot in the door if you don't want to.'

Ben didn't answer. He met Damon's eye, but he was seeing something else: a grand old building, winter sunshine mellowing its glowing stone. It was the only thing that was comfortable to look at in a world covered with dazzling snow. The clarity of the memory was overwhelming. If he'd been asked, he wouldn't even have been able to name the place, but he found he wanted to see it. He wanted to be enveloped by its walls, lost in a past that surely must have been happier than the one he remembered. He found himself nodding before he could think. Damon snapped out words that half washed over him, and Ben only caught the end: that he should hold on a moment, then follow Damon's car. It was only after the arrangement had been made and Damon had walked away that Ben's stomach dropped.

I never want you to go there again. It's not a good place, not for you. On your soul, Ben.

But he was here already. A little further wouldn't hurt. He couldn't see Damon now – it wasn't as if he could grab his shoulder and explain why he had to leave. And he'd promised his mother so much, hadn't he? Cass had demanded so many promises over the years, followed by reversals of the same, so that at some points in time he'd entirely lost track. He had given up everything; left his job and his life in London. And here was Damon, with his no doubt fancy career, all set to go back to the capital because he could do that; he could simply walk away.

On your soul, Ben.

He looked around at the almost familiar hills. The place did make him feel like a child again, but this time he felt like a naughty youngster out past his curfew, his mother waiting on the doorstep, her face creased with anger at the lateness of the hour. But he *wasn't* a child, not any more. And he didn't have to be long. He only wanted to take a look, to see what memories returned to him. Cass never even had to know.

A steel-grey Audi pulled around the corner, headlights flashing. He caught a glimpse of Damon's wave; he was no doubt wondering why Ben was still standing there in the rain. He pulled the key to his friend's car from his pocket, triggered the lock of the little Fiesta, and hurried to catch up with his friend.

The slightly different squeal of Ben's wipers told him that the rain was easing and this time, when he switched them off, the screen remained clear.

It didn't take long to reach the turning that led down to the mill. Ben stamped on the brake. The car stopped at the top of the slope and he stared down at the old building. It was smaller than he remembered, but it still dominated this part of the valley. Its stone had darkened with damp to a rich gold, and it glowed even in the dull light. He couldn't stop gazing at it.

The promise he'd made to Cass felt more ridiculous than ever. The place was beautiful. Everything was perfectly proportioned, grand and yet welcoming. Its main door was large, painted a glossy red. Here and there, warm lights shone in tall windows. A tower crowned its slate roof and there was a white-faced clock set into it. He noticed it didn't have any hands, and that seemed appropriate somehow; it was as if this place was set in a time of its own, no need to hurry or count the passing seconds.

Ben realised he had lost sight of Damon's car – he hadn't waited – and the notion passed. He let the car roll forward, its nose dipping into the steep lane, and he found a parking space right outside the smart, shining door.

He heard Damon's voice as soon as he stepped out of the car, though he couldn't see him. He caught the words '. . . won't take long', and then Damon appeared from around the side of the building, digging keys from his pocket. Damon's friend – Ben didn't know his name – followed a few steps behind, huddled more deeply than ever into his coat. He didn't look at Ben but stared off into the distance, not focusing on the mill, or the row of cars out front, or anything else that Ben could see.

Ben was no longer sure that the man was younger than him. His hair was dark and slightly curling, in need of a cut and quite possibly a wash, but his face, though young in feature, was old in expression. Lines creased his forehead and his eyes were shadowed and pouched. His hands twitched at his pockets then away, as if he wanted a cigarette.

'This is Ashley Bolton,' Damon said. 'Ash.'

Ben and Ashley nodded at each other as Damon palmed the keys and tapped a code into a panel next to the door. A brief buzz told them the lock had disengaged and he yanked it open. There was a slight sucking sound, like a seal being broken. 'Onward,' said Damon, and he waited while Ben and Ashley stepped inside.

Ben's shoes tapped against stone flags. It was reassuring, as if he *knew* the sound, as if it was right somehow; his feet had remembered this place better than his mind. The stone was irregular, the unevenness worn into it over – how long? centuries? – and yet the place appeared new, recently refurbished. The postboxes set into one wall gleamed with polish. Several had letters sticking out of the slots. A bright-green Swiss cheese plant spread outward from a fat brass vase, one leaf jutting across the stairs, browned and worn where people had brushed past. Ben pushed it aside and put one foot on the first step, then indicated upward to Damon, asking a question.

'Not there,' Damon said. 'We're on the ground level.' He pointed to a door at the opposite side of the lobby. There was a print on the wall next to it – Lowry's *The Sea*, grey water against a grey sky, everything flat and yet infinite.

Damon went past them, pushed open the door and led the way into a wide hall that was lined with more doors. This place had not been refurbished. The carpet was thinning and greyed in the middle, deepening to its original crimson at the edges. Ben wasn't surprised when Damon strode purposefully along the hall, ignoring the doors to left and right. A part of Ben knew where he was going. He remembered the way, didn't he? That door, the one to the corner apartment – the very last, so that the rooms had views over the river but also across the back, over the millpond – that was the right one.

He reminded himself that he wasn't even on the right floor. His home *had* been on that same corner, but it was up the stairs, above this one. Number 12, wasn't that it? Still, Damon continued until he reached the door Ben had expected hime to go to – directly below the corresponding door in the flat he used to live in. This one – belonging to a dead girl, frozen for ever in a photograph – was number 6. The thought of her pulled Ben back to the present. It felt wrong, suddenly, to be here. This wasn't a nostalgic sightseeing trip. It was a person's home, someone who was now gone, leaving a hole in the life of those who'd known her.

He felt like an intruder. He knew he shouldn't have come and yet the memories were there, surfacing unbidden now that he wasn't trying so hard to remember. Damon rattled the key in the lock and turned the handle, and as the door began to open, Ben saw the ghost of an apartment, its structure sketched in by rough wooden beams and lintels, but there were no walls, not yet. Nothing was painted; all was grey, cobwebs hanging from everything as if building work had begun but then been suspended or forgotten.

Ben blinked. When he opened his eyes once more, it was worse. The floor, already grey with dust, was writhing. With horror, he realised it was covered with rats. Their bodies, small and grey, visible only because of their constant move-ment, were everywhere. He wanted to back away, but he was frozen. He forced himself to put a hand to his face and he rubbed at his eyes. This wasn't anything he'd ever really seen, was it? It wasn't *real*.

He felt Damon's hand on his arm.

Another image rose in his mind's eye. It was him, sitting on that filthy floor, but he was small, only a young boy. He was wearing pyjamas and his eyes were half closed, still half in sleep. He was letting the rats crawl all over him. He wasn't even responding to their touch. For a moment, he felt them: their light feet, their tiny claws. The sudden moisture of little tongues licking at his fingers.

Then Damon's face was up close to his. The door to the apartment was open and inside everything was not grey, but cream. There were walls in there, and they were painted, and pictures hung on them, as normal. He was looking at a short hall with more doors set into it. The carpet was a shade darker than the walls, and nothing moved; the place was empty.

Ben wasn't sure what Damon had said to him, but he forced himself to smile and nod before he stepped inside. Damon led the way. Ben followed and Ashley came after, shuffling, still trying to burrow his way into his coat, his expression hidden by his too-long hair.

The lounge was wide and sunlit. Light streamed in from two huge windows and Ben saw that the only thing moving in there was dust, motes of it turning and circling in the beams of light.

Two tasteful beige sofas faced each other in the centre of the room, a coffee table between them. There were no mugs there now, no rings to show where any had been. A flimsy pink cardigan was thrown over one cushion. It looked as if at any moment someone would come in and claim it, and Ben wondered why no one had put it away; then he imagined Jessica's aunt standing there, touching the soft material, unable to admit that her niece was never going to walk into this room and pick it up again. He squeezed his eyes closed. For a moment he tasted the dust that floated through the air, thought of it flowing into his lungs and inside him.

He took a deep breath. He didn't want to look at anything, but now he was here, he couldn't help seeing it all: the picture of a dandelion clock, half blown away, on the opposite wall; family photographs ranked on a shelf, people's smiles trapped behind glass; the television, its screen misted with dust; the desk in one corner, a laptop waiting, as if she had been working on something, had only just walked from the room.

Ben strode past all of it and went to the window. Damon and Ashley were speaking in low voices, but he didn't want to listen. Outside, the view wasn't quite as he'd expected. The angle was lower than the one in his memory and he found he couldn't see the river at all. The main thing he could see was the car park, thinned white gravel just visible between the cars. It wasn't full, but it was busy, Golfs rubbing shoulders with BMWs; Minis and Beetles suggesting a younger set. Someone had left a bright orange-and-pink plastic children's tricycle in one corner. Behind that was a set of swings, something that hadn't been there when he was a child, though no one was playing there now.

He remembered peering out of a similar window onto an empty space and wondering where everybody was. He had been promised there would be other children to play with, but there had been no one. Now that he was too old for any of it, they had found the place at last.

Behind him, Damon and Ashley continued to talk, their tones still low, but more urgent. He still didn't turn around. It wasn't any of his business. He kept staring out of the window, past the car park and up, following the line of the hills that hemmed everything in: the mill and the whole village.

Another memory came to him, unbidden and strange. He was sitting cross-legged in a lounge just the same shape and size as this, with his games controller in his hands. He had looked up from the screen and his eyes had taken a moment to focus, but in that moment, he had seen someone staring back at him through the window. It was a man, and his face was kind. It was his teacher, wasn't it? His teacher and his mother's friend, watching over them both. Remick – hadn't that been his name?

He frowned. The memory couldn't be real. He had lived upstairs and the rooms here were high, built for large machinery, for industry. No one could ever have looked in on them like that. He was trying too hard to remember things, inventing memories to take the place of the ones he had lost.

When he turned, Damon was leaning over the desk. He had pushed Jessica's things aside – her papers, a small calendar, a picture in a silver frame, everything except the laptop. Ashley stood by the desk but a step away from it, half turned away, and he stared at nothing, as if he didn't want to be there, doing this. Ben warmed towards him a little. He at least seemed to have a sense of respect. Damon on the other hand was brisk in his movements as he pulled the laptop closer, flexing his fingers over the keys.

Ben moved closer, wanting to see what Damon was going to do. He didn't care if his old friend had known Jessica better than him. If Damon started to rummage through her private files he would say something. It may not be his business, but it didn't feel right; none of it did.

He looked down at the picture. He had expected it to be of her aunt perhaps, but it was not. It was a smaller version of the picture that had been by the altar in church, but this one wasn't cropped and he could see it properly. As he'd thought, she was with a friend, a man; maybe even a boyfriend. Their arms were draped loosely around each other's shoulders. The picture had been taken on a day that was filled with sunlight. There had been laughter, too; he could see it in their smiles and the way their eyes shone. It took a moment to realise that her friend was Ashley. It was odd, seeing them like that, though Ben didn't quite know why. Perhaps it was simply that Ashley had appeared younger then, less careworn; though Ben couldn't tell if that was because the picture had been taken some time ago, or because Ashley had been smiling.

He wondered how well Ashley had known her, or indeed, how well Damon had. How close had they been when she died? He had thought Ashley taciturn, but perhaps he had every right to be. It was Ben who understood nothing of this. He glanced towards the hall and the door to the bathroom. That must have been where she had done it. With her things

around him, these recollections of her life, he couldn't imagine why she'd done it, gone in there and taken a blade to
her skin. He opened his mouth to ask if the others knew and
felt coldness creeping into him. He remained silent, looking
again at the photograph. It hadn't changed, but he wondered
now if he could see some trace of it in her eyes, some sign of
what was going to happen. There was nothing.

'We need to see what she was seeing,' Damon said, his
voice low, speaking more to himself than anyone else. He
peered into the laptop's dead black screen as if he could read
what was written there. 'I'm not sure if it's even switched off,'
he said, 'or only sleeping.' He pressed a button, once, and the
laptop began to whir.

'It'll 'ave a password.' Ashley's voice sounded dry, as if he
hadn't used it for a while.

'It doesn't.' Damon's voice held a note of triumph. 'It wasn't
even shut down properly. Look!' He shifted back a little so
that everyone could see. The screen was still black, but now
it was backlit, the colour not quite so deep. Ben narrowed
his eyes. Was there something there, slightly darker than
the rest? He wasn't sure. The screen was no longer blank,
not quite. It had the grainy, colourless quality of a darkened
room. He thought he could see the suggestion of bare walls,
paint peeling from them. Then it was gone, the subtle vari-
ations of darkness lost to him as white letters formed and
grew brighter, making everything else blend together.

'I told you,' Damon said. 'I told you she finished it.'

Shining in front of them, hovering like a mirage, was a single word:

END

Damon leaned forward and tapped a key, but nothing happened. 'There has to be a way back,' he said, 'so we can see what it was she found.' He pressed a combination of keys together, then swiped at the mouse-pad, and again more quickly. 'There must be.' He sounded angry.

Ashley shifted his feet. 'I really don't think—'

The word gradually shifted, its light merging and twisting into a logo or symbol. Then, with another whirring sound, the screen died.

Damon cursed and prodded at the keys. At first nothing happened and Ben thought, *at least we can go*, and then the light came back on and he saw that the symbol had vanished, giving way to something else. They all stared down at it. Damon's hands, on either side of the keyboard, curled into fists and his knuckles whitened.

A brief flash of memory: Ben playing the game he used to like, *Street Skirmish*, except this time he wasn't alone. Damon was sitting beside him, curled around the controller as if that was all that existed in the world. Ben wasn't watching the game. He watched Damon's fingers as they flew across the buttons, dealing out death, the boy focused on nothing else.

Ben blinked and read the words on the screen. This wasn't anything like *Street Skirmish*. It was like nothing he could have played as a child. His gaze went once more to the picture in its silver frame, the image of the dead girl, the smile on her lips and in her eyes, not knowing that her whole life was about to come to an end.

The word that had appeared previously had been replaced with a question.

PLAY AGAIN?

Ben shifted his feet. All he could see was his mother's face, the expression written there just the same as when he'd last seen her, the same pleading in her eyes. *It's not a good place, not for you.*

If Ben had kept his promise to Cass he wouldn't be here now, seeing things that were not his concern, not knowing what to do or how he could get away. He supposed he should simply make his excuses and walk out of this room, the apartment, the mill; he should get into the car and drive away without looking back. It wouldn't take long to clear the dust from his lungs. He could be out there on the open moorland, breathing deeply of its clean air, far away, perhaps before anyone had even noticed he had gone. But somehow he did not move. He didn't move and he couldn't speak; he couldn't bring himself to break the silence that had crept into the room.

FOUR

Ben caught one last glimpse of the mill in his rear-view mirror as he drove away. He had wanted to leave so badly, but now the place was behind him, so peaceful and beautiful in a sudden burst of sunlight, his visit seemed to be over too quickly. He followed the slight curve of the lane as it rose to the road that would lead him away, everything familiar now, as if he'd been driving this way for years. He turned his head at the top of the lane, seeing for a moment the hunched figure of an older man, wisps of hair clinging to his head, an old dog waddling along beside him; then it was gone, nothing but another memory, and he shrugged it away.

On impulse, he turned in the opposite direction to the one he'd planned; not the quickest route home but another road, one that led straight up onto a new section of the moor. He found himself comparing the valley to the green swathe of commuter belt that curved around the north of Leeds, all open fields, fast cars and designer wellies. This wasn't quite like that. It felt more like a place where families would have clung on for generations, bedding into it like dormice into their burrows, where their lives would have depended on digging and sowing and reaping.

There was a fleeting glimpse of a small row of shops – a post office, a butcher's, a store with a plate-glass window full of notices – and then he rounded a corner edged by smoke-blackened houses. He wondered which way Damon had headed. His old friend's manner had softened into affability when they'd finally left the dead girl's apartment, and he had clapped Ben on the shoulder, saying how good it was to see him, pressing him to keep in touch. Ben doubted they would – it was just the kind of thing that people said, after all, and then they went on, leaving old ties behind them. He'd swapped mobile numbers anyway before he'd set off.

He drove onward, ascending the steep side of the valley. A pheasant watched him go from its perch on a drystone wall. Something lifted from Ben as he went, all the weight of the day: a funeral he hadn't wanted to attend, his discomfort at being in the mill, and the old acquaintance he hadn't expected to make and hadn't been looking for. He wondered if something of the day would cling to him and he thought of his mother. Would she be able to see the knowledge of his broken promise in his eyes?

He reminded himself of the old adage, that what she didn't know wouldn't hurt her. He settled back into his seat.

Somehow it wasn't as comfortable as when he'd first set out on this journey. The back was too straight, too unforgiving, and he pressed hard against it. It didn't help; a dull ache was settling into his shoulders. He should adjust it, make it fit him, but there was nowhere to stop. The road was all S-bends and the single lanes were bounded by high stone walls. He ignored his discomfort and kept going, the sky ahead of him a mass of broken clouds revealing patches of watery blue.

Soon he was out on the open moorland. The old stone walls were replaced by verges of dry, tufted grass. Beyond that were brighter colours, russet and purple and green, the earth covered in low mounds for as far as he could see. There was nothing else. No other cars passed. There was nobody up here and nothing moving except him, passing through it all, a single point of bright modernity. He reached over and flicked off the radio, tuning out the constant sound of the engine, listening instead to the silence that lay beneath; the one that had been there for ever. And then there *was* a place to stop, a place where the verge widened, and he quickly pulled in. Instead of adjusting the uncomfortable seat, though, he found himself stepping out of the car. He stood there a moment, the cold breeze folding itself around him.

The moor wasn't formless after all. His gaze snagged on something set into the slope below. There was the flat shine of water, and next to it something else: stones, standing like old weathered gateposts, but in a little group, like – *like mourners at a funeral*, he thought, but it wasn't quite like that, and he saw they were arranged in a rough semicircle, the pattern broken only by one that had fallen to the ground. They seemed intimately familiar, as if he knew every whorl set into their surface, and at once completely new, as if he was seeing them for the first time. It was an odd feeling. He examined them again, lingering on one so weathered that time had bored a hole through its centre, and then he saw it: dark shapes on a white background, scrawled so hard that the pencil had nearly torn through the paper, one of the forms bearing a white circle that looked a little like an eye. He had thought his mother had intended the shapes to be doors, or holes in the world. Now he saw that she had not.

He took a step towards the stones and his thin shoes slipped on the grass. Just ahead of him the greenness was subsumed by heather, its thin wiry stems twisting and clawing, leaving no path that he could follow. He wasn't even sure why he'd thought of going down there, where there was nothing for him. The whole afternoon had been odd, and with a pang, he wished he were back in his bright, freshly painted flat. He should be far away, amidst the bustle – and yet peace – of the city. In a way, his mother had been right: this place *wasn't* good for him. Even though he stood in the clear cold air, he could still taste the taint of dust from the dead girl's apartment. He knew that taste would still be there when he saw the blocks of the city rising before him, when he was seated on his own sofa at home; it would be there while he slept.

There has to be a way back, Damon had said. But there hadn't been, had there? Not for Jessica.

That hadn't even been what Damon had meant. In his mind's eye, he saw the expression on his old friend's face when he'd stabbed at the laptop keys. What had he said?

There has to be a way back. So we can see what it was she found.

And Damon had no doubt assumed that Ben didn't have the first clue what he was talking about; that he had no idea, when he was leaning over Damon's shoulder, what it was he was even looking at.

The problem was, he *did* know.

I told you. I told you she finished it.

Ben couldn't help feeling curious himself about what Jessica had seen. *I think it might help.* He wondered again what Jessica had meant. But he would probably never know. It might have meant nothing at all. He hadn't seen her for a long time and her passing was sad, but now it was behind him. Things had already moved on, and really, Jessica – and her death – didn't have any real connection to him, not any more. He shook his head, trying to convince himself that something about the day hadn't taken root inside him.

He turned to get back into the car, to drive away, to forget whatever it was he'd seen. As soon as he turned away from the stones, he felt better. This was the border, he decided. Once he crossed it, everything would be behind him. He need never think of it again.

Before Ben left, however, he took one more look over his

shoulder at Darnshaw. From here, he couldn't see the mill. All of it appeared grey, a black spire standing sentinel over it all, and he realised it was another one of Cass' pictures. He wondered again why she had drawn it. Perhaps part of her had been here all along, stuck in the past, though not the one he'd imagined. He had always thought she clung too hard to their childhoods: Gaila's and Ben's. Now he realised there was another more distant past, one he had barely begun to glimpse.

But that had been a part of his own past too, hadn't it? It was strange that, prior to coming here, he'd never even thought of this place, let alone tried to remember it. He'd blanked that whole time from his mind. But then, he hadn't spent much time here. The memories it summoned weren't happy. The last thing he'd expected was that he would find anything here that connected him to Darnshaw, like an old song to which he half-remembered the words. He hadn't expected to find a place that felt like home; what came as a surprise to Ben now was that, somehow, it did.

THE SECOND CIRCLE

ONE

King's Cross Station. The grand new terminal rang with footsteps and announcements and the meeting and parting of friends. Ben dodged between wheelie bags, ankles and children, the walk from the platform more tiring than the rapid passage of the Intercity from Leeds. Darnshaw felt impossibly far away, not just in distance, but in time. Once on the train he had settled back into his seat, closed his eyes and entered a kind of no-man's-land in which he couldn't sleep and couldn't think.

He'd called Cass before getting on the train, but once again, as if one thing led to another, he hadn't told her where he was going.

Stepping out into London was like stepping into freedom. He had missed it. He liked its anonymity, the way a short Tube ride could change everything; palaces giving way to parks or museums or pubs or throngs of tourists oblivious to all around them except the next photo opportunity.

Then he glanced up and saw his sister's face and everything stopped. Of course, she wasn't actually there. Gaila hadn't come to meet him; that wasn't the kind of thing she did. There was the high arch of the airy concourse, spider-webbed with bars of clean white metal, and there, hanging behind a raised walkway, was Gaila's picture.

He stopped dead to take it in, ignoring the exasperated sounds as the crowd parted around him. The banner was double height and semi-transparent; his sister's face was huge. Behind it he could just make out the framework of the roof. He could still see her eyes though, quite clearly. Anybody could. Even if he hadn't been staring at the picture directly, he would have known it was his sister. Gaila's eyes were like that: dark, almost black, they pierced the beholder; saw every thought passing through their head.

In the photograph Gaila was lounging on her front, resting on her sharp elbows, her face to camera. A company's slogan was just visible on her simple black T-shirt. This time her hair was jet black and harshly cropped, spikes of fringe cut just short of those startling eyes. Her features were small and she was the kind of thin that made campaigners accuse the magazines of encouraging anorexia. Gaila did not have anorexia. Ben had seen the way she could eat. If she was told to put on weight or lose it, she'd give the kind of answer that would have other models blacklisted. Somehow, in her, it was just Gaila. Her name was a single word, already, in the business; her surname was forgotten, her family name cast off. It struck

Ben afresh that Gaila looked nothing like him, nothing like her mother. Of course, she looked nothing like Pete.

He didn't quite know how it had all happened for her so fast. She'd never even wanted to be a model. She'd been spotted one day, in town with her friends. Then she'd been told she was too short to be a model anyway and she'd just laughed in their faces and reeled in the jobs, one after the other.

She wasn't laughing in the picture. She wasn't even smiling. She was bold; she was defiant. Everything about her was gathered in those eyes. Ben could hardly look away from them, even though he knew it was just her, his little sister, the one who'd run to him, her eyes red from crying, when Cass had said some of the things she'd said.

Sometimes, their mother had said terrible things. Ben frowned. Gaila always roused this in him: an urge to think badly of his mother, and at the same time, feel guilt that he should. Cass was troubled, that was all. She'd had odd ideas but she had done her best, hadn't she? She would have given her life for either one of them.

He dragged himself back to the present, reminding himself of why he had come. Gaila may look as if she was surrounded by an aura of glamour, but she *was* just his little sister. She wasn't yet eighteen years old, not quite; she was barely an adult.

That made his lip twitch. *Yeah, right.*

He started moving, eliciting more spurts of irritation from

people who'd been in the process of walking around him. Then there was only the endless echoing of footsteps as he veered away and headed towards the taxi rank.

Ben had never before visited Gaila at her latest address, and the place wasn't at all as he'd expected. Cass had had to sign a release form for the agency so that his sister could live alone, but then, she hadn't been alone. They'd organised everything for her – a shared room in a shabby house, everything crowded and loud and always full of other girls who would borrow her clothes or steal them. The thought of it had prompted Ben to say he would stay in a nearby hotel, but his sister had insisted and now there was this: a tall silver arrow of a building. When Ben buzzed her number on the entry system, Gaila answered it herself. He listened for noises in the background, competing stereos or conversations, but there was nothing. He wondered, for the first time, just how much her job paid.

'Come up!' she said, sounding like the old Gaila, full of excitement and suppressed energy, and the door began to swing open on its own. Ben grabbed the handle so it couldn't close on him and stepped inside. A bank of lifts waited, their doors all clean, shining metal: no graffiti. He pressed the button for her floor and only had time to notice that it was the top level before the lift began to smoothly and swiftly carry him upward.

The door opened onto a white corridor with a single

framed print hanging on the wall – two black scrawled lines, one sharp-edged and one smudged – and he walked down it. Hers was the only door on this side of the building. Ben reached out to knock, his movements automatic, and the door opened without his touching it and his sister was there, her squeal spilling out before her.

She grasped him around the neck, half hanging from him, and dragged him inside. It was the way she'd always been, barely any weight but full of her own wiry strength, and Ben couldn't help but grin. He pulled away and held her by the shoulders. She hadn't changed her hair since the King's Cross picture, but her T-shirt was plain white and she had a new piercing, a silver stud through her lower lip.

'Is that allowed?' he laughed, pointing to it, and she snorted.

'Who cares? Come on.'

She took his bag from him, dropped it unceremoniously on the floor and pulled him further into the apartment. He tried to say something about her being the birthday girl and she just slapped at him, the look on her face telling him it didn't matter. He had seen that look before. She had shown it to Cass many times. But of course, it mattered. The gift he'd chosen for his sister was tucked away in the pocket of his jacket. Cass would have posted a card of course, probably bearing some treacly sentiment and, most likely, a cheque. Ben had wanted to do more than that, to *make* it more than that. Anyway, there was little need to send his sister money.

He could see that from his view of her apartment, most of which he could take in at a glance.

All of it was white, open plan and clean, save for where she'd dumped shoes or bags or clothes. It was also huge. On one side was a picture window as large as the banner at King's Cross. The glimpse of the view beyond made him nervous, but Gaila took his hand and dragged him towards it. He let out a brief laugh at his own reaction and went the rest of the way. She tapped his shoulder – *look* – and raised herself onto tiptoe, then let herself fall forward until her head met the glass with a dull sound.

She gazed out at the city. Ben didn't much want to do the same, but after a moment he let himself go, lights sweeping dizzily around him, and he saw it all; the smallness of everything. There were grey blocks, jutting towers, tiny streets and tinier people, and even, poking from a gap in the structures, the top of the London Eye looking back at him. Further away a soft haze blanked out the sky, hanging over the city. Ben swallowed. He'd never really minded heights, but somehow this made him intensely uncomfortable. He wanted to back away from it all – no, sink to the floor and *roll* away – but he forced himself to stay as he was. 'Fabulous view,' he told her, knowing it was what he was supposed to say, but then, it was fabulous; an *all-of-this-can-be-yours view*, he thought, and didn't know why.

She punched his arm – she knew he was putting on a front. They stepped away from the vista and he was glad to do so.

Then she spun around, waving a hand at it all: the apartment, the view, her life. He noticed that the hair at the back of her neck had been shaved and it wasn't even; he found himself wondering if she'd done it herself or if it was supposed to be that way, if a thousand-pound-a-day stylist had done it for her. With Gaila, it was impossible to tell.

She flashed him a smile, not a *for-the-camera* look, but an easy grin. When she smiled like that she was just Gaila again, his little sister. Anyway, she didn't often share her smile. It was her glare that had won her the admiration of thousands.

'So come on, sis,' he said, 'all this? Really? Spill.' It wasn't so long ago that he'd lived in London, but it hadn't been like this. He'd rented the basement flat of a converted Georgian terrace, and it had been cramped and dark. It was a fifteen-minute walk to the Tube. He'd stepped out every day at the crack of dawn in order to get to work. It hadn't been as central as this either; she probably couldn't even see it from her window. He suddenly felt glad she'd never visited him there, and yet there was regret too. It had been small, but at least he'd been in the capital, in London, at the heart of things.

She shrugged as if it was nothing. 'Oh, the agency sorted it. Do you like it?' Her grin was mischievous; it brought out the dimple in her cheek. Ben found himself looking for the scar he knew was there, on the other side, though it wasn't something he wanted to see. When he'd been younger – still a boy but old enough to know better – he'd thrown a stone at her. It wasn't something he ever would have planned to do; he still didn't think he really meant to hit her with it. If the stone hadn't just been *there*, a rough piece of pale rock lying in their garden, not something he'd ever even noticed before, he wouldn't have done it at all. His own smile faded at the memory and it was replaced, as always, by shame. Why had he done that? He could only ever remember a taste of the anger he'd felt. He thought it had probably been one of his mother's bad days, the ones where she would accuse Gaila, not of some childish naughtiness but of worse things, terrible things; not of something she'd done but what she *was*.

He didn't want to think about it. He wasn't sure Gaila even remembered how she'd come by that scar, though that made him feel more guilty than ever. He reached out and touched her cheek, just lightly. How could Cass ever have said those things about her? That she was born bad. That she was *evil*. Once upon a time, it had made Gaila cry. Later she became hardened to it and she would just listen, stony-faced. It was their mother who wept over her own words. Later she'd clutch Gaila to her, telling her that she was half *hers*, that she loved her in spite of everything – what she meant, Ben wasn't sure – and Gaila's eyes would darken and she'd never say a word.

Perhaps that was why Ben had thrown the stone. Had he actually listened to his mother's rants that day – had he maybe, for a moment, even believed her?

He reminded himself that it was a good thing that he

hadn't told their mother about his trip down to London. If he had, Cass would have narrowed her eyes. It would have been like her warnings about Darnshaw, all lectures and promises, but this time she would have told him it was Gaila who wouldn't do him any good.

'What's up, bro?' Gaila raised her eyebrows, but she had a knowing expression, almost as if she already knew.

'Nothing.' Ben forced a smile. At least, in Gaila's photographs, that scar was never there. He would look for it, sometimes not even consciously, knowing that there was something missing. He wondered how many times it had been airbrushed away, just as if it had never existed.

'So, metalface,' he said, changing the subject. 'They really don't mind the facial decor?'

She snorted again. 'No choice. Anyway, some of them like that stuff. They lap it up, in fact . . .' She paused. 'Everyone wants *different* now, didn't you know? Only none of them seems to know what that is. Lucky for me.' Her face straightened. 'You know, all of this could be gone tomorrow, or the day after that. As soon as they decide "different" isn't me, or I'm too old or at least not young, and not the in thing any longer.'

All of this could be gone, he thought. Yes, it could, but it was here now. It was odd, though, to hear Gaila say it, sounding like the older one, the wiser one. And she'd seen so much, was *doing* so much. 'Well, not quite yet, eh, sis?' he said. 'Farewell, London, next stop Japan.'

Tears rose to her eyes.

'Gaila? What is it, what's wrong?'

She shook her head. 'Nothing. Absolutely nothing, that's kind of the problem. Ah, Ben, you wouldn't understand.'

He frowned. Why on earth wouldn't he understand? Because he wasn't in the thick of the city any more – because he'd left? But he was being selfish; he put his hand on her shoulder. 'Tell me.'

She took a deep breath. 'It's the perfect job, Ben. Five-star treatment. It's for a big fashion house over there; massive profile, and I'll have all the free clothes I want. Bags of cash too. It's fucking brilliant.' She seemed more on the verge of tears than ever, but instead, she laughed. It wasn't a good laugh.

'I'll tell you all about it, but first I'll get you a drink and I'll show you where you're going to sleep. You should tell me that I haven't got any manners, you know. I'm a pig.' She reached out and pinched the shoulder of his sweater between her thumb and forefinger and started to pull him along. 'I'm glad you came, you know, even if you do wear cheap feckin' jumpers. And even if it was only just in time to see me off.'

TWO

It wasn't until later that Gaila mentioned the thing she'd so clearly wanted to talk about since Ben had walked in. He'd taken his bag into his room – small, white, the window covered by a single layer of sheer curtain – and when he'd emerged she'd passed him a beer and gestured towards the leather sofa. He sat while she slumped to the floor, cross-legged, and sipped delicately from a bottle of Bud. Ben could hear the sound of the city, the buzz of traffic distant but always there, like the undertow to his thoughts. Then Gaila had said, 'Does she ever talk about me?'

He looked up, startled. His first instinct was to lie, and he nodded; he saw at once that she hadn't been taken in for a second. It had always been that way with Gaila. He never could fool her, not even when she was little more than a toddler. He sighed and opened his mouth to tell the truth, but somehow he couldn't do that either.

She stared down at the pale carpet, a shade darker than white. 'I don't know what I ever did,' she said, and tossed her head as if evading the thought. She tried to force a grin. 'Golden Boy.'

'Gaila, don't.'

'Oh, you know I don't mean it. I just wish—'

Her gaze went far away. Ben knew she *wished*. He remembered all too well the battles Gaila had fought. She'd wanted to live with Pete right from the start of the break-up. Despite the times when the cracks had shown and Cass revealed her odd ideas, Ben had never accused his mother of being crazy; but Gaila had, many times. Pete would have done it too, would have happily taken his little girl away, except that he never did have any legal claim on Gaila because of the thing that was unspoken but was always there: he was not her father.

Golden Boy. Gaila had always called him that, but in a tone of tolerant affection. She'd never said it in resentment and it always amazed Ben that his mother's love hadn't made Gaila hate him. He had seen the anger though, hidden away beneath the smiles she had for him, and he had respected her then more than he could have said. Even then, she had always seen that blaming him would be unfair. Somehow, it made her seem old beyond her years; in her own way, she had always possessed maturity beyond any of them.

Now there was this apartment with its vertiginous view. *In her own way?* Look at her now, the success of the family.

He took another sip of beer, forcing himself to swallow the sour fizz.

'Are you going to get that?'

He started and realised there was a high-pitched sound, louder than the constant hum of traffic. His mobile phone was ringing. He dived for his jacket, which was thrown haphazardly over the back of a chair, and retrieved the phone from his pocket just as it died.

'Anyone important?' she sniggered.

He looked at the missed call and frowned. 'Nope. It'll wait.' He paused. 'Actually, it's someone I used to know. I met him at a funeral. I've no idea why he's calling me now.'

'A funeral?' The faintest trace of suspicion laced his sister's voice. It was never far away with Gaila, that sense that she was missing something, that there were parts of Ben and her mother's lives she had no part in.

He shook his head. 'It was no one you know. I can barely remember her myself. It was from a place we lived before you came along. Mum knew her better than me, I think.'

'Oh.'

'It's nothing she would have wanted to bother you with. You're so far away, and – you know she's proud of you, Gaila.'

She shrugged. 'So, who's your friend?'

'No one that matters.' Ben switched the phone onto silent and slipped it back into its pocket. 'See? Gone.'

She settled back and took another sip of beer. She wasn't looking at him any longer; her eyes had slipped out of focus.

'Sis?'

She sighed. 'Ben, did you ever do something – for a joke? But then something happens, and you begin to wonder. I mean, that it might all be real. Something that was never supposed to be serious in the first place. It was just a laugh, or – well, kind of—'

Ben frowned. He didn't know what on earth she was talking about, but he swallowed his big brother's instinct to tease her. Whatever it was, she was finding it difficult to say. What drifted through his mind, though, were someone else's words, perhaps summoned by the call he'd just missed:

It doesn't matter if you believe it. It doesn't matter if it's real. It's what she *believed that matters.*

'I'm not sure,' he said, 'but if you want to talk, you know you can tell me anything.'

She shot one of her looks at him, one of those piercing looks for which people had paid fortunes. Ben wasn't sure why; she couldn't doubt he was there to listen if she needed it. He always had been. His sister had come to him whenever she felt she couldn't go to Cass, which had been often. Even when Cass had simply been their mother, there with open arms and hugs and smiles, Gaila would always go to Ben. She used to sit leaning against him, not looking into his face, just talking while he listened.

But this was different.

'I did something,' she whispered.

'Sis, whatever it is, it's OK—'

'There's this game, see. You must have heard of it.'

He jerked his head in denial or rejection, a reflex he hadn't been able to stop, but she went on without looking. 'You ask it for things. It asks you for things. It's a bit of a lark. But if you asked it for something and you got it—'

'It would be a coincidence.' He hadn't meant to speak so sharply.

She sighed. 'Japan,' she said. 'I had a go-see for that job weeks ago. The casting guy flipped through my book and didn't even watch me walk. Then he said I was too short, like they hadn't known I was short in the first place.'

'Then he was stupid. And he realised he was stupid.'

'No – listen. I was playing this game: it's called *Acheron*. You have heard of it, haven't you? It's named after the river that forms the border into Hell in Greek myth. You have to cross it and find your way in. It's not one of *those* games, where you shoot stuff. It isn't really for people who even like games. It's different; it's more like a puzzle. You go into Hell and you find your guide, and you have to get out again. There are all sorts of stupid stories about it. Urban legends, really. Not just about what happens in it, but how it happens. People say it's impossible, that it shouldn't be able to work. It's daft, but it's a bit of fun, right?'

A flashback: Ben's fingers dancing over a games controller. On the screen, men's heads exploding into red spatter. Damon, sitting in the half-light, turning to him and grinning.

'And it asks you what you want,' Gaila went on. 'You don't

have to pick different options – choose this or that. You just – you get a text box and you type it in, anything, whatever you want. And then the game tells you what the price is.'

Ben didn't reply.

I just want a job, he thought.

He tried to shake the memory loose.

I WANT A JOB, I WANT SOM RESPECT
THERES THIS GIRL I LIKE HER I WANT HER TO LIKE ME
I NEED SOME MONEY NOT A LOT I JUST NEED IT THIS
GUY HE SAYS I OWE HIM

'Ben?'

'It's stupid,' he said. 'You know it's stupid. You shouldn't waste your time on it.'

'But I *did*. And it wasn't a waste of time. I told it I wanted to go to Japan. I said they should have some respect and realise I'd be great at it. And the next day the guy rang me and said he'd changed his mind.'

He stared at her. 'You can't think it was the game that did that. That's just life, Gaila. It's a coincidence. You can't read anything into it.'

'But – I'm worried, that's all. Because if *Japan* came true—'

Ben felt unaccountably angry. First there had been Damon and his trip to a dead girl's apartment, and now this. He didn't even play games any longer; he didn't even like them, not since his dad came back from the war and said he didn't want anything to do with them – *They're not like life, Ben, life is not a game* – and yet here it was, not just a game but *the* game, the one that had almost taken over, lifting him from everything he had ever known and promising something new.

He pushed himself up, unable to sit still any longer. That huge apartment was all around him, everything still and silent, as if it was waiting. He shook his head. If he'd carried on, he might have lived somewhere like this. Instead he'd allowed himself to be dragged back, pulled by the apron strings, ties he couldn't sever but that instead seemed to be strangling him.

'Ben—'

'What did you say you'd do – in the game? What was the price for the job in Japan?'

'It doesn't matter.'

'It does. What did you do, Gaila?'

She looked away from him. 'I asked you to come and stay.'

Ben stared at her, incredulous. Silence spread from the corners of the room, and he broke it. '*What?*'

She swallowed; her throat worked. 'It told me to get you down here. Not that I wouldn't have wanted to see you anyway, of course I did. And – and it told me to tell you something.' She paused. 'It didn't seem important. I didn't even know what it was on about, to be honest.'

'Tell me what?' Ben felt the blood draining from his cheeks.

'It said I had to tell you the meaning of my name.'

'Gaila, you're not making any sense.'

'I know! But – the man called me, Ben. He said he'd changed his mind, that I was perfect for the job, and when could I leave? He even offered me more money, and I thought it was a sweetener, to make up for it, but at the same time – it was like he could hardly remember the way he'd turned me down. And it was right after I'd emailed you and asked you to come.'

'That's ridiculous.'

'It means "my father is joy".'

He looked blank.

'My *name*, Ben. Abigail. The game said to tell you what it means. Well, that's what it means. And my middle name – Enid – means "soul". Or "life".'

'What the hell are you talking about?'

She shrugged. 'I'm just doing what it said. I thought it would mean something to you. But that's not even the weirdest part, Ben. The game – you have to put your name into it, right? At the beginning, you create a profile, give it certain information. They say it uses that to find out about you – that it looks you up online, you see? So it knows things. It'll check your Facebook page and see who your brother or your sister is. See what you like and dislike. It goes through your hard drive, your photos, everything. It uses that information to make it all seem real, to make you think it really knows stuff.' She frowned. 'But no one knows my middle name is Enid. *No one*. I mean, who the hell would I tell? *Enid*, for God's sake. It's my best-kept secret. Mum named me that after the wife of some friend she used to know, Bert or something like that, someone I never even met. I've tried to forget all about it. But the game knew.'

Ben raised his hands, let them fall. 'But it is just a game, Gaila.'

'It's *not* just a game. It's not even like a game, not really. Didn't you hear me, about Japan? Weren't you listening to a word I said?'

'Too many,' he murmured, and flinched when she leaned over and slapped his arm.

'You're just like her,' she spat. 'Like Mum. You don't listen to me because it's only Gaila and she's just mad anyway, didn't you know? Mad, and – and *bad*. That's what she thinks, isn't it? Well, something weird is happening here and you'd better bloody well listen, because it isn't just about me, is it? The game wanted you here. The question you should be asking is, why?'

'No. No, it's not.'

'You're an idiot, bro. You think I'm the crazy one of the family but really, you – you and *her* – you never listen.'

'I am listening, Gaila. But this – well, it may not be what you imagine. But I need to think about it. And before I do, I also need to find out why I had that call.' He paused. 'It looks like I have to speak to Damon after all. I think I'll call him now, Gaila.'

THREE

What do you want?
   *I WANT HIM TO LOVE ME AGAIN. HE HASN'T CARED FOR
A LONG TIME. I JUST WANT HIM BACK THE WAY HE USED
TO BE.*
   What do you want?
   ££££££££££££
   What do you want?
   I WANT HER GONE.

Ben closed his eyes. He hadn't liked seeing the things that
people asked for in the game. He could see them again now,
as if they were written on the inside of his eyelids. He remembered them pinging into existence on the screen in front of
him, all those insights into the lives of others: their hopes,
desires, fears, their little jealousies and hatreds, the heartfelt
and the tragic and the pitiful and petty all at once. He hadn't

liked looking at them, but some of the others did. They'd read out the worst ones and laugh over them, hooting with mirth or with scorn.

Some of the requests had made Ben despair. Some made him feel like calling the police; others made him want to take a shower.

He had never known that his sister was among them.

What do you want?

That was the question that every player of the game sought, the question that made them consider just what they would do to achieve their desires; what price they were prepared to pay. It was all nonsense, of course. The rumours that it was true were nothing but marketing stories put out there by the company to build the hype. But still . . . he couldn't help thinking of the answer to his own question.

What do you want?

Deep down, he wanted never to have left. That was the truth, wasn't it? The thing that ached at the core of him. He'd had a promising future, but he had wanted to help Cass, to make sure that she was all right, and so he'd done what was necessary. He'd given up London, his life, his job.

And yet he hadn't *quite* wanted to stay there either, had he? It had been a long time since he'd been into computer games, and anyway, there were those requests, day after day, the things hidden inside people being dragged into the open. He hadn't liked the way the game did that. The way he was sometimes forced to wonder whether it had planted the thoughts in the first place and helped them grow.

He had never told Cass or his sister where he was working. With Cass, it would have been impossible. The name of the company, its product, its logo, even its figurehead – they crossed boundaries that would have shocked her. He could imagine her turning up outside the company offices, waving a banner or a Bible, chanting about going to Hell. That had happened, fairly regularly; people would show up with placards, the slogans some variation on *The End is Nigh* or *Repent*. The managers had loved it. They thought it added to the mystique. They'd discussed taking photographs of the protesters, the anger or fear on their faces, and using them in their advertising.

Ben had only had a back office role, but it had been early days and sales had rocketed from the start. In a company that was going places, couldn't he have gone places too? He thought he could. He remembered the excitement when it became clear that *Acheron* was going to be huge. They'd issued a new release, *First Circle*, they'd called it, and people had camped outside computer stores to be first in line to buy it. It had made the national news, albeit a brief item, and they'd watched it in the office and punched the air. Then the camera had panned back to show the picket line, the one that guaranteed even more sales, and there was a man holding out one of their promotional T-shirts and setting it on fire. The fabric had billowed as the flames caught it, by turns revealing and hiding the slogan: *I sold my soul.*

And now his sister; practical, successful Gaila had been drawn in by – what? Greed? Curiosity? She'd never been one for stories, had never much liked the ones his mother used to tell, and he couldn't imagine her being so credulous. He didn't like the way it sounded – had she really started to wonder if the whole thing was real? He knew other people did that. But then, perhaps in a way, it *was.* The game had made itself real. *It told me to get you down here.* And here he was.

But as he stared down at the phone in his hand, it was Jessica he thought of: her suicide. The *reason* for her suicide. He had never asked what that was, had tried not to think about it. He'd been too worried that he'd let her down, and anyway, the news of what she'd done had been bad enough. He sighed. He still couldn't reconcile the idea with that picture of the smiling, happy girl.

I told you, Damon had said. *I told you she finished it.*

It doesn't matter *if you believed it. It doesn't matter if it's real. It's what* she *believed that matters.*

He shook his head. Damon had been trying to find his way into Jessica's game, and now Damon's name was at the top of his missed calls list. His thumb was poised over it. He had no idea what he was going to say to his old friend, but he lowered it anyway and touched the screen. At once the number began to flicker and a green phone symbol appeared.

He heard the faint sound of ringing and raised it to his ear. Damon answered straight away. He greeted Ben and fell silent, waiting; as if he hadn't been the one to call Ben first.

Ben took a deep breath. 'Damon, I need to ask you something about Jessica. I heard what you said, about how it didn't matter if Ashley believed in something that had happened, because Jessica did. Her suicide and the game she was playing, on her laptop – I need to know if those things are in some way connected.'

'I think they were.' Damon paused. 'It's really weird you should ask that. I had kind of a feeling you'd understand – I'm not sure why. I wanted to sound it out with you. Ashley isn't the quickest, and – well, never mind. Look, I don't suppose you could get down to London for a bit, could you?'

The question brought a rueful smile to Ben's lips. How neatly things were slotting into place. It was as if he'd been manoeuvred into position; and perhaps he had.

He replied softly, then listened. Across the room, Gaila was watching him. She'd looked at him oddly when he'd said he was going to call Damon, but she hadn't commented. The sky had darkened to an orange glow, as if some fire was raging on the horizon. It lit the points of her hair and limned her cheek. Ben wasn't sure what he was going to say to her. He hadn't told Cass that he'd worked for the company behind *Acheron*, but then, he'd never told Gaila either. He wasn't sure why. He supposed he'd thought she might lose her temper with Cass at some point and tell her exactly what her Golden Boy had been up to. In other words, he hadn't trusted her. She hadn't deserved that, but there was no way around it now.

Damon fell silent and Ben took a deep breath, still looking at his sister. 'There's something you need to know,' he said.

She watched him all the time he spoke. She did not appear angry or disappointed or even surprised at his words. When Ben finally ended the call, she simply waited for him to explain. He tried to do that as well as he could. She didn't even blink. She just half turned away and looked out across the city, as if she wished she could drift into it.

Ben allowed himself to drift too. What he saw before him was not the lights of the city, warding off the approaching dark, but the office at Acheron. It was a particular day he thought of, one when everyone had been smiling and laughing. They'd just had a consignment of promotional stock bearing a new slogan. Their advertising had always been direct and shocking and, in its way, brilliant. There had been the T-shirts with *I sold my soul* emblazoned across the chest like a badge of pride. There were other gifts too, apples of temptation bearing the web address, gifts designed to be passed on, word of mouth made concrete: *I sold my soul. Will you sell yours?* Now they'd gone beyond that. People recognised the words and the style without having to spell everything out. The new shirts had only the company logo, a decorated cross that, at its base, curled in the shape of a question mark: a cross of confusion. Below it were the words *Would you?*

And people had, in their thousands. They'd done it because

it was the thing to do, the cool thing, the latest thing. They didn't have to sign a parchment in blood or anything else. The option was right up front, in the game's log-in screen. No soul, no game. All they had to do was click the right box and it was all done. Anyone who chose to play had to agree, and people did; they boasted about it to their friends, laughed about it and they played the game. For a while it was the biggest joke going, the subject of yet more light-hearted items on the news, the kind that went out at the end of the programme to cheer people up after the tales of murder and war and death.

Gaila must have done it too. She had found it hard to describe what it was like to play. Of course she wasn't really into games, but *Acheron* was like that for everybody. The hype told them the game was confusing, that each foray into its world was unique to the player, and people believed that too, and so that was what they discovered within it. It was all part of the growing mythology around *Acheron*. People bought into it because they wanted to become part of the club. If they helped spread the idea of it as a big mystery, it made the thing they had that little bit more special. It was a simple strategy and it was effective; too effective. Now Gaila would expect him to explain the whole thing, to tell her, simply and clearly, how it worked, to prove to her that it wasn't real.

The problem was, he couldn't do that.

Ben had never quite been one of the team. There was always one thing that had stopped him being that. It was the thing that, when it came to letting go of his life in London, made it a little easier to part ways. And really, it had all been because of Cass; the image of her face, if she'd known what he was about to do. He'd worn the T-shirt and he'd worked for the company, but no matter how much he longed to be a part of it, Ben had never actually played the game.

Gaila opened her mouth to speak, but her words surprised him. 'This Damon,' she said. 'I think I know who he is. I think I've met him too.'

FOUR

In contrast with Gaila's gleaming tower, Damon's flat was hidden away down a narrow stairwell that smelled of damp stone and traffic fumes. The top of it was edged by black iron railings, tipped by blunt arrows that pointed at the sky. They'd walked past several similar railings, which passers-by had evidently seen as an invitation to dispose of their empty coffee cups or crisp packets, but there were none such here. The gate was unlatched, but the stairwell was empty. Daylight hadn't quite faded, but the afternoon in the street, with its tall terraces shutting out the sun, was heavy with shadows. Ben thought he felt Gaila's hand brush his arm, but when he turned she was hugging herself, her face pensive.

'Is this the place?' Ben grimaced.

She shrugged. 'No idea. If it's the same person, I only know him because he temped in my booking agency for a while. When I went in he said he knew my family and I thought he was just a nutter, chatting up the models, you know. But then he mentioned you and Cass.'

Ben murmured something neutral, but he was thinking: *temping?* That hadn't been the image he'd had of Damon. He half smiled, then Gaila said, 'I still don't see why we're here.'

'I'm really not sure,' he replied, and it was true. Damon had asked them to come, had told him it was something about the game Jessica had been playing, and after his sister had spoken of *Acheron* Ben hadn't been able to turn him down. Still, he couldn't work out why Damon had invited him. He wasn't even sure this was the right place. The stairwell didn't look as if it led anywhere in particular. It just went down, leading under a thick lintel that was covered in scab-like swellings. He half expected to see words carved into it: *Abandon all hope, ye who enter here.*

He smiled at his own fancifulness and went down, ducking under the lintel without pausing. What had appeared to be a deeper shadow beneath was in fact a door. It was painted black and the surface was scratched and peeling. There was no name-card next to the buzzer, but he pressed it anyway and at once heard something on the other side, rustling and shifting. The faintness of the sound didn't prepare him for the door swinging open almost immediately.

'You made it.' Damon didn't look surprised to see that Ben had brought Gaila with him. He was thinner than Ben remembered, his cheeks sunken and with an unhealthy shine. His hair was untidy, as if he'd been running his fingers through it repeatedly. Ben wondered where his fancy Audi was parked; surely it wasn't here. Maybe it wasn't even his.

When Damon stepped back, drawing them inside, Ben saw that the hall behind him was clean and white. It was blank except for a single painting, nothing like Ben would have expected; the hall would suit something like the one at Gaila's place, abstract lines he could connect with nothing, but it wasn't like that. Two figures stared up at a third, whose agonised body stretched over a shape a little like a cross.

Damon saw him looking and shrugged. 'Dali's *Crucifixion*,' he said, 'or one of them, anyway. *Corpus Hypercubus*. Death by hypercube, a shape that can't really exist. Odd, no?'

He turned sharply and led the way to a plain white door set into a plain white wall. He pushed it open. The room within was different again, various lamps turning it into a warmly glowing den, blurred and shadowed faces turning towards them. A memory came: Ben as a child walking into a circle and sitting there cross-legged, in a room as dim as this; the curtains had been drawn against the pale sun. There had been plates in the centre of the ring. *Ben's turn*, a woman's voice said. *We share, remember? Families always share.*

He swallowed the bitterness that flooded his throat. This room wasn't so dark after all. It had only seemed so, after the bright corridor. Now that his eyes were adjusting he could see four people, sitting on mismatched chairs. He thought one of them was a child.

'I'll introduce you all,' Damon said. 'This is Ben, a very

old friend of mine, and his sister. Glad you could make it, Gaila.'

There were brief nods; no one else appeared to recognise Gaila. She still had her arms wrapped around herself.

'Ashley you already know. This is his friend, Simon Lawrence.' A man with cropped brown hair and a striped business shirt tucked into his jeans grunted a hello. 'And Raffie – Rafaella Mauro.' A worried-looking woman with olive skin, maybe in her late thirties, but with curly hair gone entirely grey, nodded at him. She did not smile.

'And this is Milo Tate.' Ben saw that the child in the corner wasn't a child after all. He was maybe nineteen or twenty, and thin; little more than a boy in build. His skin was deathly pale and made Ben think of dark rooms. His eyes, though, were not those of a child. They were knowing, and narrowed to the point of suspicion. When he gave a brief wave, a chunky Rolex slid up and down his wrist.

'Drinks are over there,' Damon said. 'Why don't you help yourselves? Then we should get started.'

Ben poured lukewarm coffees from a cafetiere and turned to see Damon and Gaila sitting next to each other, leaning inward to talk. He swallowed down his misgivings at the sight and stepped across the circle, handing a drink to his sister before taking the last seat. It felt as if he was taking his place, like an alcoholic at a self-help group, ready for the confessional. He just had no idea what he wanted to confess, or why, or what it was supposed to achieve.

Damon had told him he'd contacted everyone he'd known who had paid their respects to Jessica Winthrop, or who he thought might be able to help. Ben had never met any of them, except Ashley, not that he'd really come to know him. He didn't even know how well Damon knew these people, which was a source of more apprehension. Ben hadn't even known Jessica all that well. He didn't know what it was she'd found in the depths of her computer screen. END, it had said, and that was where it *should* have ended, but the sight of Acheron's logo, that cross with its questioning curve, meant that he couldn't refuse the invitation to come here.

Damon looked around the circle. 'Perhaps I should go first,' he said, his words doing nothing to dispel Ben's impression of a self-help group. Now though, as Damon paused and leaned forward, he reminded him of something else: a storyteller preparing for his audience.

'Six months or so ago,' Damon said, 'I had a call from an old friend of mine. She was someone I used to know as a kid, though back then she wasn't even allowed to talk to me, not for a long time anyway. Her family didn't approve of mine. My mum had some odd ideas, got involved with some weird people, and I – well, I did run wild for a time.' His head twitched and Ben had the sudden feeling Damon was looking for him; why, he couldn't have said. But – run wild? Yes, he had some inkling that was true. He had the feeling that he had disapproved of the boy in some way, or perhaps his mother had.

'Jessica sounded odd on the phone. She was a little too bright, you know? Like that was how she thought she should sound, so she was doing her best, even though she didn't really feel like it. Anyway, she said she'd been playing this game, and that I should give it a try. She said I should try it for *her*, as if we'd been best mates or something and it was a personal favour. Then she said that if I did, I'd discover something to my benefit.' His Adam's apple bobbed as he swallowed. Slowly, he held up his left hand, turning it so that everyone had the chance to see. A thin, pale scar bisected his palm. Ben's throat was suddenly dry. He clenched his own hand into a fist. A memory: his mother, her mouth opening and closing in some rant he'd long since forgotten, and then the thing he could not forget; plunging her hand down onto the hob and holding it there. The hiss – worse, the *smell* – of burning skin.

'The sign-in screen didn't trouble me,' Damon said. 'According to my mother, I'd sold my soul long ago. She said I'd signed the contract in blood, hence the scar. She said that I was *dedicated*. I know that sounds crazy. I did say she was strange.'

He shrugged and stared down at his hand, rubbing his fingers against his palm as if he could erase the mark. 'She'd got mixed up in some sort of cult when I was just a kid. I never really had much of a choice about it all. But anyway, you can't sell something twice, right?' He smiled, though no one else did.

'Anyway, it all just sounded like a laugh. So I figured it didn't matter and I started to play *Acheron*. So far, so normal. The game began and I was in Hell, which is where most people end up when they sell their souls.' He let out a spurt of a laugh. 'I had to find my way out. That was the purpose of it. But then I met people in the game. One of them was Jessica, or something that looked very like her. Only – not quite like her.'

Gaila nodded. Ashley stirred uneasily.

'That was why I kept on playing, because of her. Up until then I'd found it pretty dull, to be honest. All that, *Which way do you turn?* or *Do you open the box?* stuff – I never liked that kind of game. I preferred shoot-'em-ups back when I was a kid, and I hadn't even been interested in those for a long time. But that was when I first heard the rumours, and I *was* interested in those. Perhaps they could be said to be more than rumours: urban legends, maybe.

'The first thing I saw of the game was on TV. Everyone was going mad over it. It looked like something new – I'd never seen anything like it before, anyway.'

Ben closed his eyes. He could remember the kind of piece Damon was talking about. They'd replayed them in the office, over and over, crowing over the free publicity. One in particular had stuck in his mind: a young blonde reporter – a newbie, probably – standing in front of a line of young lads wearing *I sold my soul* T-shirts. 'It's the latest craze in gaming,' she'd said, flashing her even white teeth. 'It promises fame, fortune and even love . . . whatever the heart desires. And the cost of playing? Your soul!' At this, the lads behind her cheered. One was waving a large wire cross that had been twisted into a question mark. She turned and pointed her microphone at him. 'So, what did you ask the game for?'

He laughed. 'I thought it was a joke,' he said, 'so I asked for a thousand quid. Next thing, I've scored on the scratch cards. That exact amount! I just wish I'd asked for more. But it shows it works, right?'

Ben had never known if the lad was a genuine bystander or a plant. He'd always assumed the latter. But then the lad had stared straight into the camera and there had been delight in his eyes, and laughter, but also the trace of something else. *He looked dead,* had been Ben's first thought. *Dead from the inside out.* But of course, the lad's heart wasn't in it. It was only an act, and not a particularly convincing one. Then he had patted his chest, indicating the words written there, and his odd expression had passed. After a moment, the camera did too.

The scene on the television had changed to something else: a man standing on top of a car. It was a black stretch limo, no logo or markings on it at all. He wore a cloak lined in crimson silk and both his arms were outstretched, taking in the crowds around him, the office buildings, the journalists, everything. In one hand he held a silver-topped cane and in the other what looked like a very old book. His face was thin, gaunt even, and he had a small goatee beard. All he needed was a puff of sulphur and a flash of flame and the look would have been complete: the Devil incarnate, standing in the streets of London, gathering in the souls.

Then there *was* a flash, a moment of brilliance that flooded the camera, blanking out everything else. Colour returned slowly as the voice-over said, 'The self-styled Mephistopheles Jones, inventor of *Acheron*, CEO of the company and devilishly handsome figurehead. So, is it all just a PR stunt or is it real?' She appeared on the screen again, still flanked by her laddish acolytes. 'These guys sold their souls.' They grinned, opening their mouths to shout in rehearsed unison: 'WOULD YOU?'

Would you? Ben curled his fingertips into his palm and squeezed.

Damon was still talking and Ben forced himself to concentrate. 'Later,' he was saying, 'Jessica called me again, only she was different. She sounded scared. This time, she begged me not to play. She said it was all a trick meant to drag people in and make them do things, and that some of those things were terrible.'

He took a deep breath. 'She said that she thought the game was real. And by then other people were saying it too, but it all just seemed like a laugh, something put about by the company to get people interested.'

Gaila's mouth twitched and she shifted into a cross-legged position, balancing on her narrow seat. Damon shot a glance at her and looked down at the floor. 'I'm sorry, Gaila,' he said. 'It was before that when I met you. Back when I thought none of it was serious. When I suggested you should play, I had no idea—'

Ben stiffened.

'The thing is,' Damon went on, 'I didn't find the game was like that. People were saying all this stuff about how it asked them to do things, real things. But it wasn't like that for me. I'd been on it for hours by then, and it didn't ask me for anything at all.' He shrugged. 'I decided it had to be all in her head—'

'It wasn't,' Gaila muttered, and Ben shot her a look.

'But then I realised it didn't so much matter if it was real or if it wasn't. The game was damaging people. It led them to have crazy ideas, just like—' for a moment, Damon hardly seemed to be looking into the room at all, and then his eyes focused. 'Whatever it is, it shouldn't be allowed,' he said. 'Jess didn't have to discover anything real. What mattered was that it made her believe, and after that she killed herself. I think it was something in the game that made her do that, something it said to her or made her think, and that's – it's just—' His voice faltered. 'I decided I had to do something. I had to make it stop. To make sure that it doesn't happen to anybody else.'

Ben found himself looking at Ashley. It was hard to recognise him as the same man he'd seen laughing in the photograph with Jessica, his eyes shining. His hair was too long and he hadn't shaved, and he stared down at the floor, even after Damon said his name. 'Your go, Ashley.'

His lip twitched. That was followed by a shrug. 'I don't really get it,' he said. 'I played it too. I were never that bothered about computers, me. But a mate said I should, so I tried it. Lot o' rubbish, far as I can see.'

'Well, that rubbish got Jessica killed.'

'So you keep sayin'. And mebbe she did get some funny ideas, I mean I know she *did*, at the end, but—'

'So you don't think there's a need to do something about it?' Damon's glare grew more intense, though his skin kept its candle-wax pallor. 'To stop the thing that did this to her? Don't you even care? That game changed her, Ash – don't you think that's true?'

Ashley shifted once more. He couldn't sit still. 'Well, aye. Prob'ly.' Ben hardly heard the words.

'They give people hope,' a new voice cut in. It was Raffie, leaning forward in her seat. 'That's what they do. They give them hope and then they don't deliver. Maybe that's what happened to your friend. It's – it's what they did to me. I did things, for that game, but it didn't work. It never worked.'

'Doesn't that prove it's not real?' Ben said, but she ignored him.

'Of course it's real. I knew that from day one. You find your way into Hell, right? Well, I didn't have to. I was in Hell from the beginning.' Her voice hitched, then she went on.

'I was in Hell and my guide appeared. You'll have heard about that, won't you? You go in and find someone there, and they're holding a candle. They come closer and closer until you can see their face. And then you realise it's *your* face. It's the player's face, only different. Some say it looks darker. Some say it's just like them only it looks evil, or it looks as if it knows everything. And then it speaks, and their voice is the player's voice, only that's somehow different too.

'The thing is, my guide, they didn't have a face. It looked like – oh, they wore a hood, but I knew there was nothing underneath it, you know? I don't know how, but I did. I knew it was empty. It was Death. And then they didn't guide me at all, they didn't show me anything. They just turned and walked away.

'You see, the game – it kept hinting that it would give me what I wanted, what I needed, if only I'd do this or that. It was different for me, don't you see? With other people, the game asks them first, doesn't it – it asks them what they want and then it tells them the price. Not me.' Her voice faltered. 'Me, it knew – somehow – that it didn't have to. It knew I would do whatever it wanted.'

She blinked back tears. 'My girl, my daughter, has leukaemia. I just wanted to find a way to help her, if I could. That's why I played. It sounds stupid when I say it like that, but so many people were talking about the game, saying it actually did things for them, that I – well, I was desperate. Clutching at straws, I suppose. And the game knew all about me, the things I could give; the things I *would* give. And I did, I gave them all, and the game just went on taking and taking, and it never – it never helped us.' She took a deep breath, then another.

'So that's how I know. The fact that it didn't work the

way it was supposed to – that was proof, for me. That's what makes me think the game *does* work. Because it knew.'

There was silence for a moment, then Simon broke it. 'It kind of worked for me,' he said tentatively. 'I mean, at first. Didn't it, Ash? I wasn't bothered about it, not really, but Ashley gave me a call. He asked me over one night for a few beers, and when I was there he asked if I wanted to give it a go. The weird thing is, the game knew I was there.'

'What do you mean?' asked Gaila.

'Well, there's a sign-in screen, isn't there? You put in your details and it starts your game from where you left off. But when I was there the screen came up and instead of asking for one name, it asked for two.'

'For both of you?'

'For both of us.'

'It must have used your webcam,' Ben said. 'It could have analysed a picture, seen two people sitting there . . .'

Simon looked at Ashley, who shook his head. 'It could,' he said, 'except I 'aven't got one.'

Simon nodded. 'It just *knew*. The weird thing is – I mean, nothing else worked. Not like you said, Raffie. Not like any of the stories. Knowing there were two of us there – well, maybe it was just something Ash had done.' He shrugged, dismissing it all, despite Ashley's rapid shake of the head.

'Well, it got me a job,' Gaila said. 'I asked it for something and did what it said and, hello, the next day this guy calls and says the gig's mine.'

'You should have asked it for more.' Milo's voice was oddly deep. He leaned forward, smirking, then threw himself back in his chair, like a chairman in his own private boardroom. 'There's obviously something strange about the game,' he said. 'I'm not familiar with the programming or the protocols, and if the stories are true there are parts of it that shouldn't work at all. Not being able to get a screenshot – that's just standard stuff. But I've tried filming the screen while I played, and everything just came out as a grey blur. How? It shouldn't do that. And the way it uses the player's own face, their voice – it could possibly use an amalgam of online photographs, snatches of recordings, though it would take a huge level of sophistication. It wouldn't even be commercially viable. The thing is, they've done it *somehow*. I just don't really believe in things that can't be possible. What I do believe in is the power of suggestion – particularly so when it's used on the vulnerable – and that's where the whole thing got out of hand.'

Raffie's face tightened. Milo didn't look at her. 'I also think, however, that part of what the company does is single people out – bloggers, journalists, opinion leaders who can spread the word. So they focus on those people through the game, find out about them and send them particular messages. So it's not just a computer program doing its thing; I think Acheron's staff get involved. Maybe they even pick people at random – anyway, what happens is, the player gets all excited about it and starts telling their friends. That's how it's become so popular so quickly. Word of mouth is better than any amount of advertising. I've been running a gaming blog for some time now—'

'And that makes you an opinion leader, does it?' Ben asked. 'You think you were singled out?'

'I do.' Another smirk. 'But that's beside the point. Singling out individuals and playing games with their heads proves nothing. But they've gone too far. When they do that to people who can't handle it, it needs to be stopped. And I intend to stop it.' He rose to his feet. Ben almost expected him to start punching the air. Instead he touched a hand to the Rolex he wore. 'I'm going to bring them down,' he said. 'I don't care what programming they use. Somewhere there is a server with a record of every log-in and every player they've ever had. I mean to erase it.'

'They'll have backups,' said Raffie.

'They will, but from what I hear – what their own glorious leader said, in fact, in an interview – is that nothing is held off-site. *Nothing*. This Mephistopheles character sat there and spouted on about how it's all about security, how no information can fall into the wrong hands, just as if he wasn't telling the world how very insecure it all is. If we can get inside and I have a little time at it, I think I can wipe everything. I'm not saying it'll finish them. He was probably lying; they probably *do* have backups somewhere, probably more than one, but it'll be a start.'

'And the souls?' Gaila said.

'There are no souls,' Ben said. 'Let's just get that straight, shall we? It's all just—'

'It's all just a nasty exploitation of people's minds,' said Milo. 'I know it. They're clever bastards who found a new way to sell us things, and that's all. But it's time someone hammered at least one nail in their coffin. And I for one am looking forward to it.' He rubbed his hands together, that too-large Rolex catching the light.

'You mean you're going to break in?' Ben's voice was incredulous.

'Of course we're going to break in. Are you with us or not?' Milo gave an unpleasant smile.

'I'm not a thief. I'm not a vandal either.'

'And yet you're here.'

Damon didn't speak. His eyes flicked from one of them to the other, as if greedy for what they would say next.

'I came here because I was invited,' said Ben. He couldn't give any credence to what Milo had said. Break in? The idea was madness. Anyway, he couldn't imagine Milo as some latter-day Robin Hood, stepping in to save everyone. 'I came here to listen to what people had to say. It was curiosity, nothing more.' And Ben thought of the thing that he had left unspoken: *and because of Gaila.*

'So you're not going to help us?' This time it was Raffie who spoke and her voice, though quiet, silenced everybody.

Ben shifted and slipped a hand into his pocket. 'Look, after what I said on the phone, I can see why you asked me here,' he said to Damon. 'I thought it was odd, but I get it.' He withdrew, holding a bunch of keys. He sorted through them and found the object he sought, started to work it free of the bunch. When it came loose he threw it towards Damon, who caught it. It wasn't silver or brass, like the rest. The thing was matte black, and light, and Damon stared down at it. Then he held it up so that everyone could see. It had a long barrel, a short crosspiece and a curve. He turned it upside down: a question mark.

'It's a key,' Ben said.

Damon frowned. 'It doesn't look like one. A key to what?'

Ben snorted. 'You know what. It's why you asked me here, isn't it? You knew. You must have known.'

Damon shook his head.

'It's a key to the offices of Acheron. It's electronic. You hold it near the reader by the door and it lets you in. You can keep it; just never say where you got it. I shouldn't even have it any longer. I should have handed it in when I gave them my notice. Now I wash my hands of it. And that's me done.' Ben stood, but Gaila remained in her seat.

'You can't just leave,' Damon said.

'Excuse me?'

'We're all in this together, aren't we?' said Raffie.

'We're not in anything. You're talking about breaking and entering.'

'Not with this,' Damon said, smiling, turning the key in front of his face. 'We won't need to break anything, will we? This is great, Ben. Good work. But you must see that we can't do it without you. I'm not planning on walking in at midday, but what if someone's there after hours? There's only you who'd be able to wing it, to make them think we belong there.'

'What? They *know* I don't belong. I left the place. Anyone there who knows me will be aware of that.' Even as Ben spoke the words, he knew them to be false. From what he'd heard the company had grown exponentially since he was there. It would be easy to say he'd come back or sub-contracted a project, been seconded maybe. There were hundreds of things he could say.

'You were inside, Ben. The rest of us weren't. You know where things are. If you have to talk us out of a tight spot, you can do it. I know you can.'

Ben looked at him sharply. 'You don't know anything.'

'Maybe. But, well – call it a hunch. And you know, it was a hunch that made me call you in the first place. Look how that panned out.' He gazed at the key, so perfectly shaped, softly shining in the dim light: the cross of confusion. Ben knew how it felt: smooth and dry and just a little cold. He knew why Damon couldn't look away from it. That was the reason he'd kept it, after all; it was a perfect thing, a beautiful thing. He had left it on his fob, partly because it would make a nice key ring, and partly so he could say he'd just forgotten it if they asked for it back; but mainly because he wanted to keep it somewhere close. Anyway, they hadn't asked. At the time he'd told himself that it was their own fault. Now he wasn't so sure.

'They might have changed the settings,' he said at last. 'The key might not even work.'

'Then it wouldn't work for any of us.' Damon gave a half-smile. 'You see, Ben, we need you. I know that's not enough reason why you should say yes. But think about it. Think about what they've done to Raffie, to Jessica. To your sister.'

Ben frowned. He tried to swallow down his indignation. Damon had asked Gaila to play; if it weren't for him, they wouldn't even be here. And now he was using her that way? But then, it was Ben who hadn't been honest with his sister about his involvement with the company. And how could Damon have known what he was doing? It was only fortunate that the game hadn't harmed Gaila, not really – had it? He cast his mind back, summoning an image of her face when she'd told him about *Acheron*. She hadn't seemed quite herself, not the confident, carefree Gaila he knew. But oddly, it was his mother's face that came to mind:

On your soul, Ben.

All his mother's talk of souls, and here he was, planning to break in to the offices of *Acheron*, the biggest soul-stealers of the lot if you believed the hype. But he *didn't* believe the hype. None of it could be real. At least Milo had said that too. He glanced at him and saw the lad was leaning back in his chair once more, a smile playing at his lips.

Ben straightened. 'We should leave, Gaila.'

'We're going fucking nowhere.' Her voice was tight with fury. 'I can't believe you, Ben. You knew about them all the time, that place. You *worked* for them. And you never said a fucking word to me.'

He stared at her. She knew this already, didn't she? She'd heard every word he'd said to Damon on the phone and she hadn't even reacted. Her expression hadn't changed. And now this, her eyes narrowed to slits, her cheeks reddened, as if uncontrollable anger was bubbling just beneath the surface.

He opened his mouth to remind her of why he'd come to London, that the game had asked her for him and she'd handed him over, doing whatever it wanted without even thinking; but he saw the fury in her eyes and found he could not. She stood, squaring up to him, and her hands curled into fists. A flashback: a bright summer's day, him running down the street, Gaila following at his heels. He had been furious with her. He couldn't remember why he'd been so angry, didn't even know what she'd done, except that it was something to do with their mother, and their lives, the whole sorry mess of it; the fact that Cass was *different*. He'd run in through the garden gate and slammed it behind him, but then he'd heard her opening it, following him like always, *there*, like always, and he saw the rough chunk of stone on the ground where there had never been one before, and before he'd known he was going to move he'd picked it up.

He blinked the image away. The anger was fading and he

was left with only sorrow. He had never meant to hurt his sister. He couldn't even remember *why*.

'Gaila, I'm sorry.' He was alarmed to find that he was close to tears. It was the memory, that was all; not this room, not these people. Now he just wanted for him and his sister to leave this place, to be alone once more. To tell her that everything was all right. Wasn't that what he did? Always, except for that one time.

'I can't *believe* you.' She was standing at Damon's side now. 'The game – I promised it things. And it conned me, just like everyone else. I told it things I never should have. I want them back, Ben. They were my words, my things, and I want them all back.' She turned to Damon. 'When are we going in?'

'I'm really not sure.' There was a question in his voice and he directed it at Ben.

'Gaila, we should leave here, now.' She wouldn't even meet his eye. 'Look, you can't do this. You could get into trouble and anyway, you won't be here. You're going to Japan.'

She tossed her head. 'No,' she said, 'I'm not.' She turned to Damon. 'I'm with you.'

'Gaila, no. You can't.'

'You don't tell me what to do, Ben. I'm not a kid, remember? You – you're not even really my brother.'

Saturday, thought Ben. *You're still a kid until Saturday.* But he knew he was only trying to delay the moment when her words would sink in, the words that cut: *You're not even really my brother.*

But he *was* her brother. They may only be half siblings by blood, but that had never stood between them. They had always stuck together. She had come to him when her own mother had no comfort to give her. And he had always been there; *except that once.*

'Gaila,' he breathed. When she didn't reply, only staring at him with those too-bright eyes, he said, 'All right. I'll come with you.'

There was a long pause. He was barely conscious of Raffie's long exhalation, of Damon's smile, his hand on his shoulder. He could only look at the girl he had always thought of as his sister, at the anger still burning beneath the surface.

'Friday,' said Damon. 'There's less chance of anyone working out of hours on a Friday evening. They'll all be headed for the pub, or home, or whatever. That's two days from now.'

There were murmurs of assent. Ben could barely bring himself to nod. Something would change before then. He'd talk his sister out of it. He'd take her to the airport and watch her step onto the plane and fly away. She'd leave; they both would.

'All right,' Gaila said. Her voice was eager. She was talking to Damon, but looking at Ben. Her eyes were darker than ever, but the fire in them was fading. And then she punched Ben at last, a blow on the arm that he barely felt. He was already numb.

'We go on Friday,' she said.

The meeting broke up soon after that. Ben and Gaila were

the first to ascend the dark stairs, returning to the cool of the night. The leaves of the grubby plane trees struggling to grow at the side of the road shivered and stirred. A fast-food carton skittered in the gutter and a black cab sped past, its 'for hire' lights firmly off. They started to walk in silence towards the Tube station. Their footsteps, almost in tandem, echoed along the empty street. Ben tried not to think about what they'd agreed to do. There were two days left; it must still be possible to change Gaila's mind. He glanced at her profile; her lips were pressed into a firm line. He pushed his hands into his pockets and found the thing that Damon must have returned to him as they left: the key.

As he wrapped his fingers around it, gripping tightly, he felt Gaila slip her hand into the crook of his arm. He looked at her again. He couldn't see the scar on her cheek, it was too dark for that, but he knew it was there. She turned to him and smiled. Her eyes were dark; he couldn't read the expression hidden in their depths.

FIVE

Ben knew, even as he dreamed, that the scene before him wasn't real. His hands didn't look right, for one thing. They were the hands of a child, the fingernails chewed, the knuckles chapped with cold and a smudge of ink staining his finger. The main difference, though, was something that was missing: his palm was whole and pink. The scar, so familiar to him, was gone. Without it, the skin was too fresh and new. That thin white line had been there as far back as he could remember.

He felt a hand tugging on his sleeve. It was Damon, his long fringe hanging in his eyes as usual. Ben couldn't make out his expression.

Ben knew he was supposed to follow and he did. The others were already gathered in the room. The curtains were drawn across the window, making everything dark, but he could still picture the wintry hills that encircled the village. His mother might be up there now, knee-deep in snow, trying to get out. He frowned. He didn't know why she wanted to get out – they belonged here, didn't they? His new friends kept telling him so.

He sat, taking his place in the circle. For a moment no one spoke and he wished he was up there too, braving the cold of the long walk, and then he felt something being pressed into his hand. It was a pencil.

'We're going to do some drawing, Ben.' The woman's face was bright and smiling. He didn't know why she smiled so much.

'I'll help you,' she said. 'Let's draw a picture of your daddy. Because we're all family now, aren't we?'

He looked around the circle. He recognised the boys from school, but he didn't recognise the look in their eyes. They gleamed in the half-light, expectant, waiting. He almost felt he didn't know them at all.

The woman – Damon's mother – patted him on the shoulder. Everyone was looking at him. The pencil shook in his hand. He didn't want to do any drawing. He didn't even want to play games. He wanted to be outside in the clean air, holding his mother's hand, going where she said they needed to go. But it was too late for that. Damon's mother's hand closed over his shoulder and squeezed, a little too tightly.

Ben opened his eyes. It was cold. The first thing he saw was whiteness shifting across his vision, translucent: powdered snow snaking across a hillside. It resolved into a sheer curtain across a plate-glass window, points of light gleaming through it from the city beyond. He could hear it too, the low murmur of traffic that never stilled.

He wiped a hand across his eyes. The dream stayed with him; the feeling of being pulled into a group he hadn't chosen and didn't belong to, and then he remembered what he'd agreed to do and he let out a long sigh.

He sat up and leaned over to his holdall, slipping his hand into the top. The key was there, on top of his clothes. He set it down on the sheet in front of him and regarded it. He'd always thought he had kept it because he appreciated the thing as an object, something beautifully and expensively made. He could still remember the day they had given it to him, the sense of optimism it engendered, the emblem of a new start, a new life. He could recall the exact way it had felt against his skin the first time he slipped it into his pocket. He had liked the faultlessness of the surface, the way it always remained slightly cool under his fingers, resisting the heat of his hand. Now he didn't want to touch it. He still couldn't believe that he'd said he'd go back to Acheron. Now that promise was more dreamlike than ever. There was no way he could break in to a building. He couldn't do it, not even with the key, not even if it didn't mean actually breaking anything. And the others in the group – he didn't really know them. Nor did his sister, despite her unfortunate prior contact with Damon. He had no idea what any of them might do in there. At best their actions might be considered trespassing, but Milo's plans to delete everything – that was criminal damage, wasn't it?

He tried to imagine what it might be like to be arrested, to have police grab him by the shoulders, spin him around and place cold metal around his wrists. What it might be like to be tried, to go to prison, for God's sake. He couldn't imagine any of it, not really.

He closed his eyes. He couldn't face not speaking to Gaila again, either. *You're not even my brother.* The way she had said that, it was easy to imagine it being for ever. It was easy to imagine it being true.

THE THIRD CIRCLE

ONE

Damon had wanted to go as soon as dusk fell, but Ben had made them wait. Most of the office workers would be out of the door at five, he knew that, but Damon hadn't thought about the cleaning staff who would arrive shortly afterwards. And so they had waited, Ben tight-lipped, no one saying much at all. Now it was full dark and the pavements were busy with Friday-night drinkers, heading out early or going home late. Earlier it had rained and tyres hissed on roads that shone blackly, reflecting the orange glare of street lamps.

Ben walked in front, leading the way, gripping the key tightly in his pocket. The sound of their footsteps followed, reminding him of another evening not so long ago when he'd been to see Cass. *On your soul, Ben.* He hadn't taken her notions seriously since he was a small boy, but then, weren't they in some way the real reason he'd stopped working for Acheron? Now here he was, about to enter its world again.

He shrugged the thought away. He was considerate of his mother's feelings, but that didn't make him a believer. The game was simply a game.

It doesn't matter *if you believe it,* he thought. *It doesn't matter if it's real. It's what* she *believed that matters.*

But this wasn't just about Jessica. What Gaila believed mattered too. She was out here on her own, a young girl in a big city with only Ben to help her.

He let his mind empty as he walked. He hadn't been paying attention to where they were going, but his feet knew the way. When he looked up he realised he was already in the streets west of Paternoster Square. Ahead of him was the corner leading onto Ave Maria Lane, the street name set above a sports shop whose windows screamed of THIS WEEK'S OFFER. He started, really thinking of the street plan for the first time. He walked along Ave Maria Lane and passed Amen Corner, its sign half hidden by a notice regarding a City Wi-Fi Zone. It was as if he was being drawn down some path he'd been meant to follow. For a moment he was back in Kirkstall, tracing the lines of a past long vanished. Somewhere behind him the shadow of Saint Paul's Cathedral loomed large across the surrounding streets. He knew the company's offices were close. He wondered if the choice of location had anything to do with the traces of history beneath his feet.

For a moment, the footsteps around him grew louder, echoing from everywhere at once. He turned another corner and the office was there. It was just the same as it had always been, a matte black facade with narrow red key-lines running around the door, a simple symbol written upon it. Now, though, the place had assumed an air of mockery. The street was empty and there was a chill to the night and everything looked absolutely ordinary except for that single black door.

Ben took the key from his pocket, wondering if the chill he felt was coming from the night air or something within him. It wasn't until Damon touched his arm that Ben realised he was standing by his shoulder, waiting.

'All set?'

Ben didn't reply. He was here, wasn't he? The key was in his hand. That must be answer enough. He stepped up to the door. The step was clean, not a single cigarette butt or crisp wrapper to be found. It had always been that way. No one might have been here in years, yet the flat panel mounted next to the door was polished and gleaming, even in the darkness.

The others pressed in close. He could smell something spicy and musty, like old books. He moved the key closer to the reader, that flat panel, wondering if it was dead after all, if they had changed the coding or cut off his access. Then he heard a single dull *beep* and, coming from the door itself, a distinct *click.*

Ben's voice, when he spoke, sounded hollow. 'It's open.'

Damon reached for the handle. The door swung inward, as smooth and silent as it had always been, and they all stood there, each waiting for someone else to move. Ben stepped ahead of them, through the doorway and into the dark. He paused and listened. He thought he could detect the faint hum of computers, but there was nothing more. He could barely see. The only lights were tiny red or green standby signals from electrical equipment, and he thought he could make out the faint green glow of an emergency exit. The darkness between was deep and thick. For a moment it seemed he was standing on the edge of a chasm, and then someone nudged his back and he pushed the idea away and stepped forward.

Everything was there after all. The floor was still covered with the same ubiquitous grey carpet tiles he remembered, and then he made out the first desk, and more resolved as his eyes adjusted; a row of them, each with a waiting empty chair. Everywhere were computer monitors, some of the desks bearing three or four. He remembered joking about the employees' relative importance being denoted by how many they had. They had grown in number since he'd left.

The others shuffled around him. Someone knocked into a desk and smothered a curse. Ben thought he could just make out the lighter patch of the white T-shirt Simon wore under his jacket. The others were a blur. 'Keep still a minute,' Ben said. 'The windows are blanked out anyway. They didn't want people peeking in, seeing how ordinary it all is. Not good for the mystique. I'll put on a couple of lights.' He edged around someone, feeling what he thought was leather – Damon's jacket perhaps – and he put his hand to the wall, running his fingers along it until he reached the smooth plastic of light switches. He found the one furthest to the right.

'Hold on,' Damon murmured. 'I'll close the door first.'

Ben jumped as it banged into place behind him. He flipped the switch and a single strip of fluorescents flickered on, making him blink. He had expected everything to have changed, but it was as he had said; everything looked perfectly ordinary, the desks, piles of paperwork, pen holders, staplers, in-trays. It was only them – the intruders – who were out of place. He suddenly felt he should have worn dark clothing, maybe a balaclava, something more suitable for their clandestine actions. He had to smother the laugh that rose to his lips.

'So, where do we go?' Damon hissed something to Milo and then said, 'Ben, where are the servers?'

Ben nodded towards the back of the room, where the humming sound was loudest. 'Through the next office. There's a server room at the back, but you should be able to access the files from any terminal. It's all networked.' He walked around Ashley and Simon once more. There was quite a crowd of them standing in the office's central passageway, and the thought struck him: why so many? He could see they each had their own reasons to get involved, but had they all really needed to come? Surely it only increased the risk of getting caught.

There was a cold feeling in the pit of his stomach. Ben led the way between the ranks of silent desks towards the back of the room. He passed the small kitchen fitted into the corner with its peeling notice – DO NOT FEED TECHNICAL SUPPORT – taped to a cupboard door, the empty mugs that had been left to dry on the draining board. The others followed, knocking and shuffling, far too loud in the quiet room, and he could feel their expectation building, all of it focused on him. Inwardly, he shrugged. He had brought them this far. After that, his work was done. He might even be able to leave them to it if Gaila could be persuaded to come with him.

He reached out and found once more that his body had remembered the way more accurately than his mind. The door handle was under his fingers and he pressed it and opened the door and entered the next office. This was where his desk had been. So many times he had walked in here, said 'Morning' and thrown his coat over the back of his chair. Everything was just as he remembered, right down to the troll toys lined up on the edge of the desk next to his. He could just see the multi-coloured hair on each of their ugly heads. The light was dimmer in here and he realised he'd walked past the panel of switches, but he could still make out the darker shapes of shelving and cupboards against the back wall, in the light spilling through from the last room. Shadows stretched and danced as everyone filed in, and as they settled Ben saw something that shouldn't be there, that *couldn't* be there, and his gaze fixed on it just as he realised exactly where it was and the coldness in his stomach turned to ice.

It was a figure, sitting in the dark. A figure sitting at *his* desk, the one Ben had used every day. *No.* It must be a coat hanging there, or something else, positioned behind his old seat and giving the impression of a figure. If someone was sitting there, they would have said something. They wouldn't be waiting in the dark, perfectly motionless, while everyone just walked in. And then someone behind him flipped a switch and the room flooded with light. Ben almost cried out. There *was* a person there, and he was looking straight at Ben. The man smiled as he sat back, folding his arms behind his head, just as if he'd been expecting them.

His face was so gaunt the shape of the skull shone through it. His skin was sallow and intensely black hair was slicked back against his head. He had a goatee, twisted tightly into a point and held in place by a carven metal ring. He was also wearing a cloak. A *cloak*, its high collar circling his neck, like some pantomime personification of evil. Part of Ben wanted to laugh, but a larger part of him did not. It wasn't just the shock of seeing him there – *caught you* – but the man's expression. It was his *eyes*.

He knew exactly who he was. The man was the figurehead of Acheron, the owner of the company, someone he'd only previously seen on television, never in person. It was the self-styled Mephistopheles Jones.

'Welcome,' the man said at last. His voice was deep and resonant. 'May I ask what it is you're doing here?'

For a moment, no one spoke. Silence spread between them, filling the empty space where some possible reason ought to be, and then someone said, 'I've come to put you right, you murdering bastard.'

Ben wasn't sure who had spoken, but Ashley shoved past him. 'Your fuckin' game killed a friend of mine, and I'm goin' to—'

Damon grabbed him by the arm and pulled him back. 'Ash,' he said, 'Calm down.' He turned to Mephistopheles. 'My colleague here has a point, Mr Jones. Your game – if it is a game – has had some rather nasty consequences. We're here to make sure that it never happens again. I'm afraid we must ask you to remain where you are until we've done what we came here to do.'

Ben's mouth dropped open. They were *caught*, for God's sake. This was already over – what were they going to do, hold the man hostage?

Jones' lip twitched. 'And what may that be, pray tell – a little industrial sabotage? Steal the hard drives? Wipe the servers, clear the boards, that sort of thing?'

Ben frowned. Jones had pinpointed their exact intentions. Had he already known? And the man looked amused rather than worried. Ben knew, from his expression, that there must be backups. Of course there were. What kind of company wouldn't have any? The whole idea had been ridiculous.

As if reading Ben's thoughts, Jones said: 'Please, help your-selves. I have no copies, no backups, no *cloud*, if that's how they're doing it these days. I am, truth be told, a little dark for clouds. I am, in fact, as you may be able to tell, no angel.

But I'm afraid it's all rather pointless. One game leads to another, don't you find? And people are so very, very careless with their souls. It isn't as if I'm simply going to stop.' He grinned. His teeth looked very white, expensively cared for. 'You see, the game is probably up anyway, so to speak. People are actually beginning to think it's real. Can you believe that? I must admit it rather defeats the object. This was all supposed to streamline the process. A quick click and it's all done: signed, sealed, delivered. No one gives it a thought. Now they're starting to do that. Though it does make it all the sweeter when they make their choice. When sacrifice is tempered with belief . . .' He breathed in, savouring the idea. Then he turned to Raffie. 'Doesn't it, my dear?'

She did not reply. Instead, Milo spoke, not to Jones, but to Damon. 'I'm going to get started,' he said. 'Just keep him out of my way.'

'Please, be my guest.' The man dressed as the Devil leaped to his feet. 'This terminal has all the access you require. I merely switched off the monitor – I do so like sitting in the dark. And I didn't want to spoil your entrance.' He winked, reached out and switched on the screen. It whirred into life, light playing across Jones' features as he licked his lips, catching the redness of his tongue.

Milo started to edge around the desk and Jones swivelled the monitor on its base so that it faced him. Milo looked at it, then started and raised his eyes to Jones. 'What the fuck is this?'

'Let me see.' Damon reached for the monitor, but Milo was faster. He grabbed it, fumbled for the switch, darkened it.

'Nothing,' he muttered.

'It can't be—'

'I said it's *nothing*.' Milo moved around to the back of the desk, twisting the monitor with him, switching it on again before pulling the keyboard within reach. He made a few keystrokes then peered into the screen. 'It looks like I'm in. Just' – he nodded towards where Jones stood, without meeting his eye – 'keep him away.' His expression was wary, almost fearful.

'What just happened?' Gaila demanded. 'We all need to know what—'

'*We* need to know nothing,' Milo said, 'unless you're going to help me with this.'

'But of course she won't,' Jones said. 'She's not here for that, are you Gaila?'

Ben heard his sister's gasp. 'Leave her alone,' he said.

Mephistopheles laughed, and there was silence. Only Milo moved, his fingers twitching above the keys. In a low voice, as if barely interested, he said, 'He's been watching us.'

'Ah, clever boy.'

'He must have been. Right from the start. You have cameras, right? You linked up to them on this computer. You saw us come in, ran some facial recognition software, looked us up—'

'You give me too much credit, dear boy. Really, I don't know a thing about computers. I just know rather a lot about people. Not all of it good, I'm afraid.' He flicked a glance towards Ashley and Simon, who stood a short distance away, shoulder to shoulder. 'Like you, for instance.' It wasn't clear to whom he was speaking, but both of them flinched.

'You all come in here like a team of crack criminals, is that right? But I have the feeling you aren't a team at all. Oh, no.' He peered into each of their faces, one by one. Ben felt his gaze pass over him, but he couldn't meet his eyes. He felt Gaila's hand reaching for his own and he grasped her damp fingers.

'You're not a team. You're not even friends. You come in here, each counting on the discretion of the next, on your – your *need*. Yes, that. Your need.' There was laughter in his voice as he turned his attention back to Raffie, then to Ashley and Simon. 'Some of you barely even know why you're here, do you? How can you, when you don't even trust each other?' He focused more sharply on Simon. 'You only ever made one request of the game, didn't you?'

Simon didn't answer, but Jones wasn't waiting. 'One request and one only, and it didn't come true – isn't that right? That is what you told your friend here, is it not?'

A patch of red slowly spread across the back of Simon's neck, where it lay exposed above his collar.

'Money, you asked for. Isn't that always the way?' Now Mephistopheles sounded bored. He laughed again; it wasn't a pleasant sound. Then, abruptly, he stopped. 'You even specified the amount. You made it quite specific, so that you'd know when it arrived. Six-hundred-and-sixty-six pounds. Most amusing, you no doubt thought. Most – original.' He stared at them. White points lit the centre of his eyes, like a badly taken photograph. Ben suddenly wanted to step backwards, to keep backing away until he was out of sight of those eyes. He didn't want to hear what came next, didn't want Jones' voice echoing inside his mind. But Mephistopheles went on.

'You asked for the money together, a silly little test to prove the game wasn't real. And then the money arrived, didn't it? But you told your friend here it hadn't. Now, what form did it take? A bequest from a parent's cousin, someone you barely remembered. Such a small step away in terms of family, and yet so easily forgotten. She didn't have much; perhaps that's why she mattered so little. Two-thousand pounds to be split equally among her remaining family, the rest to go to various children's charities – that was rather sweet, don't you think? And there it was, six-hundred-and-sixty-six pounds. The fact that they forgot to add on the sixty-seven pence . . . well, that was my little touch. I like to be exact. I keep my promises.' Here he leered, not at Simon, but at Ben.

After a moment, he turned back to Simon. Ashley was watching him too. They all were, but Ashley stared harder than anyone.

'And what was the price the game requested of you, Simon? You were both playing, but the game only had a price for you.' His voice went distant. 'It's as if it knew you wouldn't share the money with your friend here—'

Ashley choked. 'I knew it. I *knew*. I told Simon I knew, and 'e just looked at me and said I were wrong. If I'd known back then, if I'd been sure—'

'You'd have given up, would you, Ashley – *Ash*? Is that what you would have done? You'd have had your curiosity answered and stopped playing, just like that – not got into any more trouble, is that it?' Jones sounded teasing, like a taunting lover. And then he turned those eyes on Ben, knowing he was watching, spying on an intimate moment, and Ben felt his cheeks redden.

Jones' expression changed. Ben didn't like it, but he couldn't look away. It was accusing. It made him think, not of the way he'd broken in, but of how he used to work for the company. He'd been a good worker. He'd never missed a day, never taken too long on his lunch breaks or left a little early. And now here he was, not a loyal member of staff but something else. And Mephistopheles Jones had been waiting for him, sitting at the very desk Ben had used to call his own. That couldn't be a coincidence, could it?

But Jones said nothing. He didn't speak to anyone. He simply sat down on another chair, at another desk, and waited while Milo probed Ben's old computer. Light flickered across the lad's face as he found – what?

Ben had forgotten that Gaila was still holding his hand until she squirmed out of his grip. He realised he had been squeezing, crushing her fingers.

Simon muttered something under his breath about it being

his price and his money, about how it was no one else's business, and something else that Ben didn't catch. He thought that was the end of it, but then Ashley started to push through the group, not towards his friend, but away from him. There were clouds in his eyes, and they were dark. Ben caught his arm as he passed. 'What price was it?' he asked quietly. 'You were playing together. What did the game ask him to do?'

Ashley's face whipped around. 'It told 'im to stop playin'.' He sneered. 'To let me go on alone. And 'e did. Si stopped, just like that. I din't see him again, not for ages. Good thing too.' He spat out the words. 'I should 'ave known the damn money 'ad come. You know what t' worst thing was?'

Ben shook his head.

''E said 'e stopped because we'd tried it and proved it was all crap.'

'And so you decided you didn't believe in it?'

Ashley didn't answer. There was something in his eyes, and Ben peered into them, but Ashley shook him off and walked away. He took an empty seat, swivelling away from the others, and he sat there with his back hunched over, hands in his lap, picking at his nails. His unkempt hair hung across his face.

Ben turned to look at Mephistopheles Jones. The Devil of Acheron wasn't hiding his face, wasn't looking down, wasn't fidgeting. His back was ramrod straight, his head up, and he was watching them with those bright little eyes. He wasn't smiling and he didn't seem afraid. He simply looked amused – and curious as to what they were going to do next.

TWO

'Everything's here.' Milo's voice was bemused. 'All of it. There's no protection, nothing. It's *all* here: a list of people who signed up, everything that anybody ever said they wanted, linked to their account—'

Gaila pushed herself up from her chair then stopped, her eyes fixed on him as he scanned the screen. They were all sitting, chairs pulled haphazardly from various desks. Mephistopheles sat a short distance away from them, watching everything that passed with that same amusement. His smile broadened.

'You can read it all,' Milo said, his fingers flying across the keyboard. 'God, some of it—' He glanced up and Gaila flinched; she caught Ben's eye and sank back into her seat.

'Delete it,' she said. 'Delete it all.'

'God, if you took this stuff and looked up who the people

were—' Milo chuckled. 'You wouldn't need to earn rent for a while, that's for sure.'

I WANT HER GONE, thought Ben.
JUST ONE WIN ON THE HORSES THAT'S ALL I NEED
I WANT TO WYPE THAT SMUG EXSPRESION OF HIS FACE

Milo kept shaking his head over the computer, letting out spurts of air. No one else laughed until, low and mocking, Mephistopheles did. It came out as a parody of devilish glee, a pantomime sound. 'You could look each other up,' he said. 'Why don't you? Go on. Just a little look.' He sat back in his chair, watching Gaila. He shrugged. 'Really. It would be *fun*.'

Ben didn't like the way his sister looked. She'd been pale before they came in, but now her face was white. Damon had flicked off most of the lights and they were sitting in the half-dark, but he could see the tension in the line of her back, the way she picked at the seat of her chair. He didn't know how long this was going to take, but Milo wasn't doing anything at all; he was simply reading, his lips twitching over the things he'd found. Ben could feel the expectation building, the sense of everyone waiting, each of them wanting some kind of miracle. And if they got it – what then? It struck him that he didn't even know what they would do with Jones after they'd finished.

Milo's fingers were poised, unmoving, over the keys. He appeared fascinated, even bewitched. Ben closed his eyes.

What do you want?

THERE ARE SOME BOYS AT COLLEGE THEY DON'T LIKE ME YOU COULD GET RID OF THEM

What do you want?

I WANT TO PASS MY EXAMS, I WANT AN A, MAKE THAT HAPPEN AND I'LL DO ANYTHING

What do you want?

THE GIRL FROM THE CORNER SHOP, SHE'S A BITCH, SHE KNOWS SHE'S PRETTY – I WANT YOU TO CHANGE THAT

'Nice, isn't it?' Jones' voice broke into his reverie. 'The desires of sad, lonely hearts. Or just – hearts.' Ben realised the man had stood up and moved closer. He couldn't have planned his position to greater effect; a single light shone behind him, highlighting the edge of his gaunt cheek, the twisted goatee, the brilliant scarlet lining of his cloak. It made him think more than ever of a stage, and then Jones said, 'Ben knows all about it, don't you, Ben?'

Ben frowned. He'd never had any direct dealings with Mephistopheles Jones in the whole course of his work. He hadn't been important enough. It was odd to see him in person, this character he'd known only from the posters or a television screen, something that had been styled and invented right in these offices. And yet he had called Ben by name. He had been sitting at his desk.

Still, Ben didn't reply. Instead he spoke to Milo. 'Delete it,' he said. 'Delete everything. Let's move it, and then we can go.'

'Quite right,' Damon cut in. 'Get on with it, Milo. We have an agreement; do it.'

Milo twitched. He was leaning in close to the screen so that Ben could see the trace of lettering reflected in his eyes. He stirred. 'All right. This is going to take a while. Looks like I can access the whole network from here.' But he still didn't move. His hands remained poised over the keyboard, his ridiculous watch catching the light. For the first time, Ben wondered how he came by it.

Milo turned towards Jones. 'This will work, won't it?' His voice was little more than a whisper. 'If I delete my name, that means it's done. Our agreement – it's void. My soul is my own, and – what we said—'

Mephistopheles Jones smiled at him. He did not reply.

Ashley snorted impatiently. Raffie shuffled her feet, stopping when Jones spoke, suddenly all attention.

'There is something you should see,' Mephistopheles said loudly, 'before you make any attempt to wipe the slate clean.' He pushed back his sleeves, making a show of it, and flexed his fingers with a loud crack. 'Allow me, Master Milo.'

'What, and have you shut it all down – lock us out?' Damon said. 'No way.'

'Oh, please. I told you, I have no interest in computers, none at all. But as you wish. Milo, if you please, call up the user database. You will find a link to it right there on the desktop. Most of my employees have full access. We have no secrets here.' He winked at Ben.

Milo made a few keystrokes and waited.

'Now search for Jessica Winthrop.'

'What? You've no right,' Ashley said. His voice was distorted with fury.

Mephistopheles' head swivelled towards him. 'I think you'll find I have every right,' he said. 'Her soul belongs to me. You *all* belong to me.' As he spoke, he cast a quick glance at Ben. Ben straightened, reminding himself of what set him apart from the others: he had never played the game. He had never ticked the box that signed over his soul, had never agreed to anything. If Mephistopheles knew who he was, maybe he knew that too.

Damon crossed the room and stood behind Milo, reading over his shoulder. 'All right, Jessica's record is here. There's a photograph.'

'Of course there is.'

'And links.'

'Click on "Requests".'

Milo reached for the mouse.

'Wait.' Damon moved to stop him, but he was too late. Ben heard a distinct click and Milo's eyes narrowed as he stared at what had appeared on the screen. Then Ashley's chair scraped back and he blundered across the room towards Milo, knocking Raffie aside. He didn't stop; he moved around the desk and grasped the side of the screen as he read what was written there.

His eyes went wide, then narrowed in anger. 'I fucking

knew it,' he said. 'The last thing she said—' He turned to Mephistopheles Jones. 'It *was* you. You who did that to her. Damon was right all along.' He curled his hands into fists and stepped towards the cloaked man, but Damon put out a hand and stopped him.

'We 'ave to,' Ashley said. 'It's what she wanted.'

Ben stepped forward too, ready to help restrain Ashley. It was bad enough that they'd broken in here; he didn't want assault to be added to the list of charges. But Jones wasn't afraid, or even troubled in any way. He wore the same expression as before, half amusement, half curiosity.

Ben and Damon grabbed Ashley's shoulders and pulled him back. Jones stepped forward to the computer screen and turned it around once more, this time so that it faced the whole room, so that everyone could see. Ben couldn't help but look at it. A single word was written there, bright and shining against a black background.

'Behold,' Jones said. 'The last request of your dear friend, Jessica Winthrop. It's the last thing she asked for before she spilled her blood.'

The words remained there, steady and unblinking.

What do you want?

And the answer was writ large.

REVENGE.

THREE

It wasn't such a long time ago that Ben and Gaila had discussed what it meant to have a soul. It had been early in the morning and Ben's head had been foggy with sleep, the heavy sleep of someone who hadn't expected to be woken at such an hour. Still, he stirred when his door creaked, and he had rubbed at his eyes, not just to brighten them but to show his irritation. Didn't his mother know he was tired? After the things she'd told him the night before, she surely couldn't be surprised that he hadn't slept well.

But it wasn't Cass standing in the doorway.

There, tousle-haired and appearing so much like a child he could almost imagine her sucking her thumb, was Gaila. Ben sat up straighter. Gaila never came into his room. He'd heard the tales his friends used to tell of their annoying little sisters, sneaking into their rooms and messing with their things, but it had never been like that with her. Possibly it was because of the age difference between them, but mostly, Ben knew, it was because of the way Gaila was. She had always been a serious child.

She padded across the room and perched on the end of his bed. Then, oddly, she *did* slip her thumb into her mouth. She removed it, looked at it for a moment and then said, 'I heard you last night.'

Ben frowned. The conversation he'd had with Cass had been like so many others, so strange that it had taken on a dreamlike quality, like the silver-grey half-light of dawn he could see through the gap in his curtains.

It had been a few days after his mother had burned her hand on the hob. It still hadn't healed and it wouldn't for some time. She tiptoed around the house, her expression closed, trying to cook and clean with one hand strapped and too painful to be of any use. She hadn't been saying much and Ben hadn't pushed her and nor had Gaila, but Ben had felt the way the divisions were re-forming between the three of them: he and his mother on one side, Gaila on the other. But the night before, his mother *had* spoken to him. Cass had been tired and perhaps a little drunk – she'd opened a bottle of wine before bed, something she rarely did – and Ben could remember the sour tang of it on her breath when she put her face up close. He hadn't even known that Gaila had been listening.

'She said you gave your soul away,' Gaila had recounted then. 'But she said that you were too young to understand and so it didn't count. She said she had thought it was best to give everything over to the Devil, so we could all be together. But then she said that he hadn't come back and he *wasn't* coming back, and she wasn't going to wait any longer.'

Ben hadn't needed her to remind him of Cass' words. She'd spat them in his face. 'You're *mine*, Ben,' she'd said. 'He fooled me once. He won't fool me again. Don't let him fool you either. We're not his now, not any more.'

Gaila had screwed up her face. 'She's wrong.'

'What do you mean?'

Gaila had smiled, then let the expression broaden into a grin.

'You shouldn't listen to her, sis,' he'd said. 'It isn't – she was just confused.' *And his sister was so young,* he'd thought. It had been confusing enough for Ben, but his sister was eight years younger than him. No wonder she said odd things sometimes.

He'd had a sudden stab of fear that whatever sickness had taken root inside his mother would also take hold of his sister. He remembered how he'd talked Cass into going to see a doctor once. It hadn't done any good. Doctors couldn't cure whatever was wrong with their mother.

But Gaila's smile had faded and she'd said something that was so simple, so obvious, it had come as a revelation that Ben had never seen it before. She had also looked as if she was about to cry. 'She never talks to me like that.'

Ben had known that it was true. It wasn't that Cass had never acted like Gaila's mother. She'd always made a point of doing things with her daughter; taking her to the ballet or the zoo. There were days when they'd make biscuits, or heavy, sticky cakes that Ben forced himself to eat. They'd laugh together, Cass' face pressed against Gaila's elfin features that were so unlike her own, their smiles different and yet the same.

But Gaila was right. Cass had said things *about* Gaila sometimes, odd things about her real father and what could be done when someone was half bad already, but she never spoke *to* his sister the way she spoke to Ben; as if she could save him. As if she had to make sure he stayed on the right side.

It wasn't the words Gaila had spoken that had sunk into him, though, so much as the expression on her face when she said them. The way they had made her feel – the way their mother made her feel. Why hadn't he seen it before?

He had stared at his sister and after a moment she had raised her head and looked back at him, as if daring him to look away first. Eventually, he did. He had to, because he knew exactly why Cass never spoke to her daughter like that, and so did Gaila, but it wasn't knowledge that he could voice.

Gaila had started to cry then. She sat there on the end of his bed, the curtains failing to keep out the growing light, and she hadn't tried to hold back the tears, and she hadn't said anything else. She simply cried. Her eyes shone, dark and soft and somehow far-seeing, and he'd known that she'd understood every thought that had just passed through his head, and suddenly he'd felt like crying too.

He'd reached out to touch her arm and she'd jerked away. 'Don't,' she'd said, and stood. She'd glared at him with those eyes that saw everything before sweeping out of the room, leaving a space behind her, one that seemed somehow emptier and colder than the rest of the room; a space that could never be filled.

Ben thought of that as Gaila stepped forward and approached Mephistopheles Jones. She moved in close and stared into his face. Her eyes were unblinking, but the old pain was in them, and Ben could see it, quite plainly; surely everybody could.

'You destroy people,' she said. 'You take a part of them and you twist it and you break it. You take things that are good and you – you *sour* them.' She jabbed a finger towards him. 'Well, you're going to make it stop. It doesn't matter what he deletes or what anyone does. *You* are going to make it stop, because it's real, isn't it? It is real. I knew it was the minute I clicked that button and started to play. I could feel it leave me.'

Jones didn't speak. He tilted his head to one side, as if he was looking at some museum exhibit too strange to name. Ben clenched his fists. He stepped forward and put his hand on Gaila's shoulder. He felt the tension thrumming through her. *I could feel it leave me.* He shouldn't have been able to understand what she meant, but of course he did; she meant her soul. And suddenly he knew why she'd decided to play the game, to sign up to whatever it asked of her. That morning she'd sat on the end of his bed and cried was with him again, as if it had only just happened. He could see the expression in her eyes and hear the pain in her voice. And he knew why she'd held her soul in such light regard.

She never talks to me like that.

So many times in his life he'd felt angry with Gaila, for her recklessness, her blindness, her selfishness. Now he didn't. He only felt angry with Cass.

Mephistopheles Jones was not surprised by Gaila's confrontation. He didn't seem disturbed or harried. He was more like a man who was about to sit down and enjoy a perfect dinner; someone who was savouring the aroma before he started to eat.

He mouthed something at Gaila, the ghost of words that Ben couldn't catch. An instant later she pulled free of Ben's grasp and flew at the man, her hands curled into claws and flailing. Ben tried to grab her and felt her sleeve slip through his fingers. She raked at Jones' cheek.

Ben strode forward, but somehow Damon caught her first. He grabbed her shoulders and got between her and Jones, putting his face up close to Gaila's.

'Sit *down*,' he hissed.

Jones didn't react. He stood there, only a small trace of blood on his cheek. He looked at them with curiosity. But it was too late. When Gaila had flown at him, Ben had seen something else. For a brief moment, the mask had slipped; for a moment, Jones had been startled. Now, though, he smiled and watched, and stroked that twisted little goatee.

FOUR

'She wanted revenge,' Damon said. 'Jessica wanted revenge against *you*. What was it that you did to her?'

Mephistopheles Jones simply smiled at the question. 'Do you think she did, my friend?'

Damon glowered. 'I'm not your friend.'

'I'm afraid I'm not going to do your work for you. We all have our crosses to bear, so to speak. Mine is – well, never mind what mine is. Jessica Winthrop is yours.'

'Bullshit. Your game did something to her, or asked her to do something. She couldn't live with it. What happened to her is your fault.'

'I aim to please.'

'You're going to undo it. All of it.'

Mephistopheles' smile grew wider. 'I'm afraid that really isn't possible. I can't bring back the dead. Life is not a game, my friend. You can't simply hit control and 'Z' whenever there is something you wish to undo. It doesn't work that way. Soon the six of you will realise that.'

'Seven,' Gaila muttered. 'There are seven of us.'

Mephistopheles bowed.

Damon turned to Milo. 'Delete everything. Now.'

'It's about time,' Mephistopheles said.

Milo rose to his feet. 'I'm sorry, but I don't think so.' He reached around his body with his thin arms, his watch snagging on the fabric. He tugged his shirt free of his jeans. Then something came loose and when his hand reappeared, he was holding a gun.

Ben stared at it. It was silver and heavy and he knew at once that it was real. It had *weight*. There was something fascinating in the way the light gleamed off its sides, in the tiny black void in the muzzle.

Ben's insides felt light, as if he was floating free, leaving the solidity of everything he had known. *Now this*, he thought. *Of course*. The world, somehow, had swung out of kilter. He wondered how he hadn't known when the time had come to turn away from all of this; when the time had come to say no, he wasn't going to take part in any of it.

'What the hell?' Damon said. He didn't sound afraid.

Ben waited for Milo to turn the gun on Damon. It seemed inevitable, as if, in some parallel universe, it had already happened. Maybe the bullet had already left the gun, driven forward by the rapid expansion of air until it reached Damon's skin with its waxy sheen, his high, pale forehead.

It didn't happen. Instead, Milo swivelled to face Mephistopheles Jones. He pointed the gun at him. He said, 'I'm not deleting anything.'

No one spoke. Ben didn't think that any of them could move. Even Gaila remained where she was. He couldn't hear anyone breathing.

Milo said, 'I want to know how it works. It isn't *right*. The game does things it can't possibly do. It knows things it can't possibly know. It shouldn't be able to do that. I've been programming all my life, and I've never managed the half of it. I want to know how you did it.'

'Oh my goodness, dear boy, I couldn't possibly explain. Not in words you could understand.'

Milo stepped closer, jerking the gun, gesturing for more.

When Jones spoke again, his voice had changed. It was lower, more resonant. Gentler. 'Look at the screen.'

Ben could feel the pull of that voice, as if Mephistopheles was a mesmerist who almost, but not quite, had him under his spell. He didn't know if Milo felt the same effect or if it was simply what the lad wanted to do, but he backed away, still waving that gun with his thin arm, like a stem that couldn't possibly support the fabulous bloom it had grown. Milo edged around the desk and examined the screen. He frowned, looking up at Mephistopheles once more. 'How did you do that?'

Jones gestured towards it; an invitation.

Ben heard the air escaping from Gaila's throat, as if his

sister had just begun to breathe again. He wanted to go to her side, but he couldn't move. None of them could, except Milo. He leaned over the keyboard, darting looks at Jones as he tapped something into the computer. He finished with one last hard stab: *Return*, thought Ben. And he watched the blood suffuse Milo's cheeks as he sank into a chair before the screen. He seemed to have forgotten all about Mephistopheles Jones. Light and darkness played across his face. His eyes were unfocused, as if he were falling under some dark spell.

Jones folded his arms across his chest. 'Have you solved it yet?'

Milo's lips started to move, but for a moment, he didn't speak; he appeared entirely unconscious of anyone else. Then he said, 'That's not right.' He glanced at Jones again. 'Is it? That can't be right. It *isn't* possible.'

Mephistopheles started to laugh. It was quiet at first and then it grew louder, and then he bent under the force of it. He rested his hands on his knees as tears of mirth sprang to his eyes. He laughed so hard that Ben could see his teeth, small and white and wet. Eventually there was nothing but a high wheezing.

Jones straightened and looked at Milo. 'It *isn't*, is it? I always said those things were miracles.' He pointed towards the computer. 'Or black magic, of course. Now, my young disciple, I must bid you to remember the price.' He winked and dissolved again into spurts of laughter. His face had turned red. He didn't look so much like the Devil, Ben thought, as a schoolyard bully, and then he saw something else that was odd about Mephistopheles and he frowned before pushing it out of his mind.

Milo slowly shifted his grip on the gun. He returned it to the waistband of his jeans. He didn't trouble to conceal it. His face was no longer full of wonder; he just looked weary and a little jaded. 'I'll never do that,' he whispered, and Mephistopheles merely nodded, as if he wasn't talking about Milo meeting his price at all; as if he knew exactly what he meant, and he understood, and he sympathised.

FIVE

'I'll do it myself,' Damon said. 'It's not difficult. We can all delete stuff. If you're not going to do it, Milo . . .' He said the words and then sat there without moving. He didn't need to say anything else for Ben to know that he was thinking about the gun, tucked into the back of Milo's jeans. He imagined they all were. Simon and Ashley were standing at opposite sides of the group, not looking at each other and not speaking. Ben sat by his sister, their chairs drawn up to the same desk. Damon was staring at Milo. Raffie was a little further away and turned aside, trying to distance herself from the others, and Mephistopheles Jones stood before them all, wearing an easy grin.

Ben chewed at the skin around his thumbnail, an old habit he thought he'd lost. *Funny how things come back,* he thought, but it was Cass' face in his mind: all of her mixed-up ideas about God and the Devil and souls.

Mephistopheles wasn't the kind of Devil he'd imagined. He had all the accoutrements, the arty little goatee, the cloak, the gleeful laughter. But somehow there was something missing. Ben still didn't believe. He found himself wondering if this was what became of devils when the majority of people stopped believing in them; if that was what became of all gods.

And yet the others *did* seem to believe. Even Gaila; worldly, earthy Gaila, with her easy laugh and carefree ways, had fallen victim to this game they'd been playing.

'A penny for them,' Jones said, and Ben looked up to see that he was watching him. Jones' eyes were narrowed and they shone, whitely, in the dim light. *He couldn't have positioned himself better*, Ben thought. *Not even if he'd rehearsed it.*

Jones smiled at him. It reminded Ben of his father's smile, open and honest and guileless. Its sincerity, the similarity of it unnerved him, but then Jones looked away and the feeling passed.

'You're right. Perhaps now isn't the time.' Jones leaned against a desk, all casual insouciance. His gaze snapped to Raffie. 'My dear, why don't you tell me what's troubling *you*?' His voice had grown warmer, loving.

Raffie looked startled. Even in the dim light Ben could see the tautness of her skin, the lines etched deeply into her forehead and around her eyes. She carried care in her face; it was there for anyone to see. Now Mephistopheles Jones was calling on it, just as a cheap clairvoyant would pick out a woman in a black veil from a theatre audience. *What do you want?*

He realised Mephistopheles had actually used those words, whispering them as a man whispers to a lover in the night. And Raffie responded, just as he'd no doubt meant her to do. Tears sprung to her eyes, drawn from her by that honeyed tone. Ben opened his mouth to protest, but she spoke first.

'She's dying.'

No one moved.

'My little girl. My Laura. She's dying. She's getting worse and she doesn't have long left and you still haven't shown me how to help her.' Raffie's voice broke.

'What makes you think I can help you?' There was no sly smile, no glint in Jones' eyes. He looked like he genuinely wanted to hear the answer.

'Because you *knew*,' she said. 'The game's supposed to put you in Hell, isn't it? You're in Hell and you have to find your way out. Well, my game *did* put me in Hell. It put me in a hospital.' Her face had turned red, though she wasn't crying. 'It was just like hospitals are. I was in this room full of chairs, plastic ones, and the walls were painted green, that shade they always are. I could *smell* the place. And I could move around, but there were trolleys everywhere, in the corridors, in my way, and there were shapes on them covered in sheets. I could have lifted them if I'd chosen to and seen what was beneath. And there were all these rooms, wards with numbers, and I had to get through them to find where

Laura was. And that was when the game started asking me to do things.'

She drew an unsteady breath. 'I did them,' she said, and her voice was changed. 'I did them all. I'd do them again. But then I got to ward seventeen and I found her bed, but instead of a bed there was a coffin, a fucking *coffin*—'

'Ah – there, there,' Jones said. The slyness was back in his voice, colouring his words. 'There, there.'

'Then the game said – it said, "You have nothing to trade."' She looked at Jones. 'I knew I could lift the lid of that coffin if I chose, and it would show me what was inside. It would show me *her*. But it was never going to ask me what I *wanted*, not like everybody else, because I'd already done it, hadn't I? I'd done everything it asked of me. I had nothing to trade, like it said. It *knew*. It bled me dry. It – it was feeding on me.' She sniffed. 'That's what it did. It fed, and I gave and I went on giving, and it was never going to help my girl. It never even meant to.'

Jones nodded, considering. Raffie started crying again. A chair scraped – Ben jumped at the sound – and he realised it was Gaila. She leaped to her feet and went to the older woman, and she wrapped her arms around her shoulders.

Raffie shook her off. 'I did things,' she said. 'Don't touch me.'

No one asked what it was she'd done. The only sound was Jones, as he let out a long sigh. 'You gave it away,' he said, 'like a cheap whore. Why should anyone pay for it?' He looked around the room, giving an incredulous smile, as if waiting for everyone to agree with him. When his gaze reached Milo, though, he paused, and he repeated the question he'd asked earlier: 'Have you solved it yet?'

The only sound came from Raffie. Through her crying, she said, 'You aren't going to help me, are you?'

He tilted his head. 'You know, names are interesting. Rafaella means "God heals", did you know that? But did He?' He shook his head. 'Did He even listen? What a shame. What a terrible shame it all is.' A tear glinted in the corner of his eye.

'Don't you say that. Don't you say that to me.' Raffie leaned towards him, as if she would attack him; as if she wasn't broken.

'Ah! That's what I like. A bit of fight, like this man here.' Mephistopheles gestured towards Milo, who didn't respond. 'Soon you'll understand. You all will.' He turned to Gaila. 'It will be your turn soon,' he said. 'Yes, we're going to talk, you and I.'

She flinched. Her dark eyes widened.

'Don't you speak to my sister,' Ben said.

'Ah – your sister, is it? If you say so.'

Mephistopheles looked around the room, focusing on each of their faces one by one. 'All of you,' he breathed. 'How splendid it all is.'

Ben frowned. 'What did you say?'

'Splendid. How very *splendid*.' Jones' expression had

changed; even his face had narrowed, and Ben realised the light in the room was fading. The windows were blanked out, but the darkness was growing anyway. For a moment, there were only the two of them in the room. 'Why did you come here, Ben?' Jones whispered.

Ben couldn't answer. He found himself leaning in, as if to share some confidence, but he had no words to give. He had no answer. There was nothing he'd come for; nothing he wanted. Then the words came to him: *I shall not want.* He pushed them away, didn't even know why they were there. He didn't even believe in any of them. He looked away and saw Damon. His old friend, the one he scarcely knew, was also leaning inward, as if he wanted to hear what Ben had to say. As if he was *hungry.*

Jones spoke brightly. 'Of course, the game is real,' he said. 'You're here because you know that, each and every one of you. You're here because you have faith.'

Not me, thought Ben. At the same time he remembered his mother, pushing him down onto his knees, the cold stone of a church floor beneath him. It suddenly *felt* real. He could smell the church, its dustiness, its shut-in, timeless smell, and he could feel his mother's hand gripping his shoulder.

But it wasn't his mother's hand. It was Jones, reaching out to him, though he hadn't actually made contact. For a moment Ben felt the urge to reach out and take his hand; instead, he drew away from it.

'So resistant,' Jones said. His voice was intimate, and for a moment Ben imagined he could feel the man's breath on his ear. 'But you're asking yourself the wrong question, my boy.'

'Which is?'

He gave a low laugh. 'You're the only one here who doesn't believe. So why is it that you're the only one who refused to play the game?'

Jones drew back and spoke louder, like an actor declaiming. 'For those who are a little slow,' he said, 'the game is real. I own your souls. I own *you*.

'The only one close to understanding it is Milo here. I say it again: *I own you*. So, how do you become free? How do you take back that little shining part of yourselves, that part you gave away so easily, that left you feeling empty inside – willing to give more, to *do* more than you ever thought possible, if it would only give you the smallest chance to win it back?'

He smiled. 'What is more important – your soul or your life? It's time to decide.'

He swept his cloak back with a flourish, baring his chest. 'You could kill me and own yourselves again, couldn't you? Be master of your souls once more, and lose your lives; go to prison, and know that you are *free*.'

His words were met with a shocked silence. Ben looked around at their whitened faces. He wanted them to laugh at Jones, to *hear* them laugh, but nobody did. It was bad enough that Milo had brought a gun to what should have been a simple task; now they were taking Jones seriously. He could see it in their faces. Gaila couldn't take her eyes from the man. Raffie too stared at Jones, her eyes bright with tears she hadn't wiped away. Simon was frowning, deep in thought. Ashley looked eager. Even Milo had shifted his focus from the computer screen and had tilted his head, echoing Jones' posture. Only Damon was unblinking, expressionless.

'You're insane,' Ben said. 'Look, everyone, we need to shut this down now and get out. He's playing with us.' But nobody seemed inclined to stop; no one was inclined to leave.

'You don't get it, do you?' Ben said. 'He says killing him will give you back your souls. All it would do is turn you into murderers. If you really want to think of your souls, if there even is such a thing, you can't win them back that way. You'd be killers. You'd be damned by your own hands. You'd lose your soul anyway.'

An odd noise began in Ben's ears, a slow rhythm that soon quickened, and he realised that Jones was clapping. 'Bravo,' he said. 'Bravo, dear boy. You see the conundrum, everyone? It's hard to dance with the Devil on your back, isn't it?'

The light had faded further, but Ben thought he saw Mephistopheles wink. 'It's a riddle. As you are beginning to see, it is a game you cannot possibly win.'

SIX

Ben wasn't sure who moved first or what they'd meant to do. Everyone was suddenly on their feet, all shouting at once, and scuffling; trying to get near Jones, as though he was some hero and they his followers. Someone behind Ben threw a wild punch, their arm knocking into his head, and then he was barged aside by someone staggering into him. He turned to see Simon and Ashley grappling with each other, and then Ashley pulled free, his face red, and he hit out. The blow made barely any sound, but Simon cried out, clamping his hand to his nose. He put out his arms to protect himself and his hand left a smear of blood across his cheek.

Ben twisted free and waded in, trying to separate them, but his leg gave, the back of his knee burning where he'd been kicked, and he nearly went down. He gathered himself and dragged Ashley with him. The fight went out of the man all at once and he shrugged Ben away, the same expression he always had back in his eyes, his shoulders hunched against the world, his face a blank.

Ben turned to the others. Milo stood away to the side, holding the gun high, but it wavered in his grip; he wasn't pointing it at anyone and he didn't seem to know what to do, let alone want to shoot. Damon was in the middle of the melee. His arm was wrapped around Gaila's neck.

Ben didn't think; he charged in. Gaila struggled against Damon's grip, but it didn't loosen. Next to Damon she was tiny, twig-thin, no weight to her, and Ben couldn't swallow his fury. It was Damon's fault she was there. He had done this to her. He didn't even look at Milo again; he didn't care about the gun.

The thought briefly entered his mind that Damon might only be trying to hold his sister back, to save her from something worse, but it didn't stop him. He grabbed Damon's hand and twisted it, wrenching him away from his sister, and then they were all standing apart, glaring, breathing heavily. Ben wanted to laugh. It wasn't like fighting in films. It wasn't all neat fists and *thwocking* sounds. An image rose before him of children scuffling in the snow, heavy in their thick coats, unable to stand firm in the whiteness that choked and drowned everything; their slow, cold hands numb and clumsy. And he thought of a girl falling to the ground, the soft sound it made, the shock as he realised she'd hit something solid after all; a stone or ice or some other buried thing. He saw the brightness of blood on her cheek, remembered the shock of it. The girl had long brown hair. *Jessica*, he thought, and then he shook the vision away and looked around to see Jones half lying, half leaning against a desk, his face paler and thinner than ever, his eyes wide open in disbelief.

Everyone shuffled back from him. Someone swore under their breath. Ben didn't know who it was and he couldn't see what was wrong, but then he did: Jones' hand was at his chest and it gripped something tight: a small black object. It was a handle.

Something cold happened inside Ben. He made a choked sound in the back of his throat. *It can't be*, he thought, but it was like this whole night; the world was out of kilter. Nothing was as it was supposed to be; things that couldn't possibly happen had come to find them all.

He realised someone – Raffie – was muttering under her breath. 'I didn't – I didn't—'

Jones let out an odd sound, a spurt of air that sounded a little, not quite, like a laugh. He was finding it difficult to breathe. His cheeks swelled and hollowed, swelled and hollowed. Now there was no sound at all. It had been drained from the world. It was silent and nothing moved except Jones as he slipped bonelessly to the floor, landing half propped against the desk. He tried to rock himself, and then he stopped.

Sound flooded back as Jones' eyes scanned the group, focusing at last on Ben. 'That wasn't—' he said, quiet but perfectly clearly, and then he moaned, a protracted, animal sound.

Ben swayed, suddenly dizzy. He thought he might fall. *Any moment*, he thought. *Any moment, I'll wake up. I wonder where I'll be.*

Damon threw himself down next to Jones. The crack of his knees on the thin grey carpet tiles, such ordinary, everyday things, was loud, but he didn't flinch. He put his hands on Jones' chest, ignoring the blood darkening the man's shirt. He pressed down, applying pressure, and Jones cried out in pain. Blood spilled faster between Damon's fingers and Ben gulped in air and realised he could smell it. No. It wasn't the muskiness of blood. It was the sharp stink of urine.

Jones gasped for breath. Each attempt was quick and painful, cut short and interrupted by the next. Ben saw what Damon was about to do and said, 'Don't.'

Damon's hands were on that short black handle. He didn't listen; he pulled. The thing slid out of Mephistopheles, the glint of silver shining through the red that suddenly spurted in a dark gush and the man jerked forward, his eyes bulging. His face flushed crimson and then drained to white, all in a second. He clutched at the wound but the blood kept coming, his insides bright and shocking, and Damon dropped the knife and pressed both hands to Jones' chest, spreading them as if he could keep it all inside.

Ben strode to a desk and grabbed for the nearest phone. Someone knocked into him, hard, and the handset skittered across the desk, trailing a corkscrew wire. He leaped for it, thinking it had only been some accident, but this time someone grabbed his arm and pulled him back, twisting him around and then pushing. Ben found himself on the floor, his shoulders pressed against the edge of the desk, and then Ashley's face was up close to his. His eyes weren't expressionless, not now. They were narrowed and sharp and bright, as if the man had come alive.

'Too late,' Ashley said.

Ben saw that he was right. Mephistopheles' face had greyed. He wasn't gasping for breath any longer. He lay like a broken puppet, his legs splayed, urine darkening the floor between them. There had been no flash of sulphur or spark of flame. His cloak was dishevelled, like a worn-out Halloween costume. There was no doubt in Ben's mind that the man was dead.

Damon stood over him. His hands were scarlet. His head was bowed.

'We're free,' a voice said, low and shaking.

Something inside Ben shrank.

He turned, slowly, and saw Raffie. She was standing at the back, moving away from all of it, and her eyes were too bright. She twisted her hands in front of her and Ben saw that there was blood on them. She rubbed her fingers together, spreading it across her skin.

Ben wanted to reach out and make her stop, but he couldn't move. And then someone else did.

Gaila went to Raffie's side and once more wrapped her arms around the woman's shoulders. This time Raffie let her.

Gaila started to make soothing noises. She started to say, *It's all right.*

Ben wanted to laugh. It wasn't all right. It would never be all right again. The little voice in his ear, the one that had told him not to come here, whispered to him again, but it was too quiet and too late. And the word came to him: *murderers.*

It didn't matter if he hadn't wanted to come, if he'd only been persuaded by the others. He *had* come here. He'd walked right in through the door, along with everybody else.

No: not like everyone else. He had led the way. It had been Ben who'd let them in.

SEVEN

What do you want?
REVENGE.

Damon was the first to stir. He stepped forward, being careful where he put his feet, and leaned over the body. Jones was lying quite still, and thankfully his eyes were closed. Ben thought of crime dramas on television where someone had to press down on the corpse's eyelids to close them, maybe even weigh them down with pennies, and he shivered. Damon reached out and lifted Jones' eyelid, revealing a slit of white like an undercooked egg.

Ben closed his own eyes, concentrating on letting his stomach settle.

'He's definitely dead,' said Damon, and Ben bit back the urge to laugh again. Of course Jones was dead. He only had to look at the dark slick across those dull grey office tiles to see that. His insides were outside, had escaped into the air, and there was no putting them back again.

He took a deep breath and caught a scent, like a butcher's shop but sharper, fresher, and he grimaced. 'We have to call an ambulance.'

Damon held up a hand. 'Wait.' He reached out once more and touched the body, the thing that had once been a man; that had, perhaps, been a devil. Doing so did not seem to trouble him. He caught hold of Jones' arm and pulled it away from the body, the arm limp like a marionette's, and Damon felt for a pulse so that everyone could see. Ben felt laughter rising once more inside his throat, threatening to choke him.

'Dead.' Damon nodded.

Some of that sound escaped Ben's lips, turning into a cough, and heads swivelled towards him.

Damon let Jones' arm fall and felt instead for his neck. Ben was suddenly reminded of a man leaning over a car, the bonnet open, peering inside as if he had the first clue how to fix it, and then Damon said, 'What the—'

Yes, Ben thought, *he's dead. We know.* And he thought of sirens, blue flares lighting up the night, of police officers taking handcuffs from wherever they kept them. Perhaps, soon, he would find out.

'He's got something round his neck,' Damon said. He started to pull it loose and it snagged on that ridiculous cloak's high collar. The thing was twisted like a telephone cord, but it was made of transparent plastic, and for a moment it clung there, then Damon worked it free. As he did, Jones' head lolled. One of his eyes opened a crack, this time revealing a thin black line between the lids.

Damon stayed where he was, but he held out the object for the others to see. Ben peered at it. He wasn't sure what he was looking at. He knew what the object was, he'd seen things like them on more of those crime dramas, but still, it didn't make any sense.

'An earpiece,' Damon said. 'He was wearing an earpiece. It was hidden under his collar.' He pushed himself upright, still holding the thing, and stared down at it. 'I don't understand.'

Milo stepped forward. He reached out and took it from him. He examined the part shaped to fit the man's ear and said, 'I do. Someone was talking to him.'

'But why?' Ben said.

Milo squatted next to the body and Damon shifted to let him get close. One of Milo's shoes just touched the liquid darkness that had spread across the carpet and it clung to his sole, the surface of the blood already growing tacky. Milo didn't notice. He just started pulling at Jones' clothing, rummaging without fear or respect, searching out his pockets.

Wait, Ben wanted to say, but the sound didn't come. Milo was going through the man's things as if it was nothing, just like – *like a man without a soul.*

But Milo had stopped. He withdrew his hand holding a small, folded wallet. A cross of confusion was etched into the leather. *Would you?*

He passed it to Damon, as if he'd know what to do with it. Damon opened it and began to flip through the compartments. Ben caught sight of the ruffled edges of banknotes, just the possessions of an ordinary person who went to the shops and bought coffee in cardboard cups or pints of milk to take home. It suddenly occurred to him that the man might have a wife; he might have children. He closed his eyes.

When he opened them, Damon still had the wallet but Milo was leaning over the body once more. The scene had been rewound and for a moment, Ben felt he would be living it for ever; then Milo cried out and pulled something else free of Jones' pockets. Ben blinked. He appeared to be holding *light*, and then he saw it was a miniature tablet computer, its screen bright in the dim room. Milo ran his fingertips across its screen, tapping here, stroking there. *Fingerprints*, Ben thought, and didn't know why. They hadn't come here wearing gloves. They couldn't simply walk away.

'Oh, Jesus,' Milo said. He flicked through a few more screens. 'Look.'

At first, Ben wasn't sure what he was seeing. The screen was a mottled grey, covered by pale streaks that resembled nothing more than a cobweb. As he watched, the cobweb shivered in some breeze, and then he made out what lay behind it and he started. It was a door that he recognised. A plain black door set into a plain brick wall.

It was the entrance to the building.

'He really was watching us,' Milo said. 'It's a CCTV feed.

Just like I fucking said.' He took a deep breath. 'There was nothing clever about all this. He was watching us from the beginning. He'll have used facial recognition software to find out who we were. Then he looked up our profiles, all before we even walked in. That was how he *knew*. Who we were, what we were about.'

Damon flipped the man's wallet closed with a snap. He held out something else, his hand shaking, not really wanting to touch it. When he spoke, his voice shook too. The thing clutched between his fingers was nothing but a business card, a little worn around the edges, a perfectly ordinary thing. 'Some sort of agency,' he said, and cleared his throat. 'An *acting* agency.' He turned it towards him, reading from it. 'Models, presenters, actors, talent.'

'No,' Raffie said. '*No*.'

For a moment nobody spoke. Ben couldn't straighten his thoughts.

'That's not right,' Raffie said. 'He was real. All of it was. He just wouldn't – he wouldn't help me. And I had the knife in my hand, but I don't know how it happened. I really don't.'

'He was no one,' Damon said softly. 'He was nothing but a front. Just – just *marketing*. None of it was real. It never was.'

Of course it wasn't, Ben wanted to say.

'At least she had her revenge,' Ashley cut in, and everybody turned to stare at him. 'Jessica, I mean. She asked for revenge and now she's got it.'

'We know who you mean,' Damon said. 'No one's had their

revenge here, idiot. Someone is dead. He wasn't even a part of the company. He was just a *face*.'

'No,' Milo said, as if something was dawning on him. 'You're right. You – you should see this.' He strode towards the desk he'd been using: Ben's desk. He leaned across it and shuffled the mouse, clearing whatever screensaver had appeared. 'He had the game open and ready for me. Not just any game, but my own – right at the place I'd left it. I'd made it through the eighth circle of Hell. It seemed like I was almost out, like I'd reached the end. There was a door in front of me.' He stared intently at the screen. 'The thing is, I'd never been able to open it. But it looked just like the entrance to this building, which was why I knew I was on the right track, doing this, coming here. Once we were inside the office the door was still there, but this time it opened. So I went through, and this is what I saw.'

He spun the screen around. It had writing on it, glowing against the black.

FARTHER OUT AND FARTHER IN. YOU HAVE NOT YET REACHED THE INNER SANCTUM.

Ben's mouth went dry.

'That means something to you.' Damon's voice was sharp, and Ben realised he was watching him.

'I – no, it's nothing.'

'I think we all should decide that together.'

'It's just – that's what we used to call the private offices. The inner sanctum – it was a joke, that's all, an office joke. No one went in there except the management. It's a common enough term though, and it matched the theme of the game, the way they sold it. It doesn't have to mean anything.'

'But it could.'

Ben conceded the point with a shrug.

'We go on,' Damon said.

'What?' Ben exploded. 'We've done enough, don't you think? We have to get help. For him.'

Damon stared at the dead man. 'I think it's a little too late for that. I say we go on. Are we agreed?'

Raffie was the first to answer. 'Of course we go on. I knew it – I knew the game was real.'

Ben said, 'Raffie, you don't know anything. It's us who are being played. That doesn't change the fact that this has all gone completely wrong, right from the beginning. You want to think it's real because that would – that would make it all right, what you did. You're just clinging to false hope.'

Gaila stepped closer to Raffie, put a hand on the woman's shoulder and squeezed. She glared at her brother.

'Well,' Damon said, 'we may as well try.'

Ben knew that he was right. The picture he'd seen in his mind's eye was more real than ever: blue lights flickering off the walls, sirens blaring into the night, someone pushing his head down as he got into the back of a police car. The dead man would stay dead. There was nothing they could do for him. If they did as Damon suggested at least it would put it all off for a little longer. He gave another shrug, this time of resignation.

'You can't just follow, Ben,' Damon said. 'We need you to show us the way.'

Ben paused. *Farther in*, he thought. Always farther in, when it was the last thing he wanted. He looked at Gaila. She was holding Raffie's hand; she hadn't let go. He knew she would never let go.

He turned and walked across the office. He felt weightless, his steps unsteady. This couldn't be real. He didn't want it to be. He tried to tell himself he was just playing a game: *There are three doors in front of you. Which do you choose?*

He selected the door in the middle of the wall. He half expected it to be locked, but the handle turned easily and he pulled it open.

The corridor on the other side was long and narrow and dark. Ben had been down it before, several times, but not into the office beyond; he'd only left various items of paperwork in the pigeonholes at the end of the passage. It struck him that those pigeonholes didn't even bear names. It wasn't like the offices he worked in now, with 'Bobs' and 'Henrys' and 'Sarahs'. These had been identified only by titles: *Upper Management* or *Head of Games* or *CEO*.

The corridor wasn't entirely dark. A single door was set into the far end, and Ben knew that it bore a small grey sign with the word PRIVATE on it in small black letters. He had never been through that door. He had never even seen it open. It was open now. It stood ajar, and the gloom was leavened by the bright white light shining through it.

THE FOURTH CIRCLE

ONE

The man sitting behind the desk was in his late forties or early fifties; it was difficult to tell. He was too thin. His hair was cut short, a mingling of steel grey and white. His cheeks were hollowed and he had a slight hook to his nose that accented his aquiline appearance. He wore a grey shirt, quite ordinary. It looked like one that Ben and Gaila had once bought Pete for his birthday from Marks & Spencer. Everything about the man was colourless, except his eyes. They were blue and piercing and bright. His expression was one of amiable affability; only the hardness in those eyes made him look as if he might be the head of Acheron.

There were only two chairs on the other side of the desk and he gestured towards them, as if he'd called them in for a meeting. He did not speak.

Raffie sank into one chair and Gaila took the other. Milo

edged to the side and Ben saw him put his hand behind his back, making sure his gun was covered by his shirt.

'You're him,' Raffie said. 'Aren't you? The real Mephistopheles.'

The man smiled. He had perfectly even, bright white teeth. 'Oh no,' he said. His voice was dry, the sound of drifting sand. 'I am not Mephistopheles. I'm the fucking Devil.' He threw back his head and laughed. 'If you wish, however, I could show you who *might* have been Mephistopheles. Should I do that? Are you ready?'

Ben swallowed. He had never seen this man before. Did he know that Ben had once worked for him? Was that what he meant, about someone who might have been Mephistopheles – was that the future Ben could have had with the company? But he'd never even imagined it going that way. He would never have agreed to it; he wasn't even sure he could.

'You're quite right,' the man said, though he wasn't looking at Ben. 'Another time, perhaps. For now, why don't you make yourselves comfortable? We have a journey to make together, you six and I.'

'Seven,' Milo said. 'So it was you, talking to him – Mephistopheles. You were talking to him through that earpiece, giving him instructions, telling him what to say and do. You saw us come in, but somehow you only counted six on the CCTV, and that's what you told him: six. That's why he got it wrong, even though we were right there in front of him.'

The man didn't say anything. He merely gave a slight bow.

Ben realised he hadn't mentioned the death of the man in the office outside. If he'd seen them come in he must surely have seen that too, but he didn't seem affected by it in any way. He simply turned to Raffie and said, 'What was the first thing you did for me, my dear?'

She started. Her hands were resting on the very edge of the desk and she snatched them back. They still bore traces of blood; Ben thought he could see flakes of it on the polished surface.

'It gives me so much pleasure to think about it.' The man half-closed his eyes. 'I can tell you what it was, of course. But I'd rather hear you say it in your own way. Come: you will, you know. You may as well do it quickly.'

Raffie drew a long, shuddering breath. She looked down at her hands on her lap and then she spoke. Ben stood slightly to the side and behind her, and he couldn't see her face, but he could tell from the flatness in her voice that she wasn't crying. It was more like her emotions had *flatlined*. That was the word that came into his mind. Whatever was left of this woman after seeing her child's illness and putting a knife into a man's chest, it wasn't complete; she possibly never would be again.

'I stole something from a friend of mine. The game said I had to go into her bag when she came round and take something personal. I took a cigarette lighter. She didn't smoke. I knew she kept it because it had been her dad's.'

Jones smiled indulgently. 'And now that's out of the way,

you can tell me the next thing, can't you? It's easy now. It *does* get easier, doesn't it?'

Raffie shot him a glance with her red-rimmed eyes, but she did not pause; her next words came out in a rush. 'My dog. I killed my dog. The game said I should do it if I wanted to find what I sought, and I did, I took him down into the cellar because I knew he'd cry and I didn't want anyone to hear that.'

'Ah. Except you.'

'I deserved to hear it.'

'Indeed. How long had you had that dog, Raffie?'

She hesitated. 'Since he was a pup. Seven years, three months. I'd had him since he was so small he could sleep curled up in one of my arms while I held a book with the other.'

The man closed his eyes and nodded, as if that was what he had expected. He lifted one hand into the air and whirled the fingers: *go on.*

'I took him into the cellar. I knew I wouldn't have trouble getting him down there because it was somewhere he wasn't supposed to go. He knew that. He was – mischievous. I'd already dosed him with a bit of one of my pills, because I wanted him calm. I thought it would make him sleep. That would have been easier, but he didn't sleep. Though he was quiet.' She glanced up, looked away again.

'I could hear my daughter calling. She wasn't calling for me or for a drink, or anything else. She was calling for the dog. *Her* dog. It almost broke my heart.'

'And did he answer?' The man's voice was eager. 'Did he cry?'

She stared at him and nodded. 'He didn't die all at once,' she said. 'You'd think it would be easy, something like that. Animals die all the time, don't they? When you don't want them to, they die. I'd looked up where the veins were. I wanted to make it as easy as I could for him. I cut his throat, like the game said. He made this noise.' She caught her breath. 'The blood was awful. And he made that noise and it was bad, but most of all because she might hear – Laura. I didn't want that to happen. I couldn't let it; that was why I'd gone down there. But it was so loud. And he lunged at me and I thought he was going to bite me, but he didn't, I think he just wanted my hand – I think he wanted to know it wasn't true.'

'And then?'

'He just bled. He kept on bleeding. I wanted to stroke him, but he – he kept looking at me like that. Even after he was gone.'

'Did you love him?'

'Yes. I loved him.' Her voice broke.

'Ah. So sweet. So – *sweet*. Tell me, Rafaella: *Angel*. What was the worst thing about killing the dog you loved?'

'I would have done anything for her. My child is *dying*. I'd still do anything for her.'

'I know you would. That's not what I asked.'

'The worst thing? I knew how much she'd miss him. I mean he was my dog, for years. I knew how much I'd miss him too; he was always there. He used to follow me around the house. Even if he was sleeping in the corner – if I got up, he'd know. He'd wake up. He had the sense of it. He had to go where I went.'

'That's not the answer.'

'Stop it,' Ben said.

The man lifted a single finger in the air: *wait*.

'The worst thing was, the very worst thing – was that he trusted me.'

'Ah.' He let out a long sigh. A beatific smile spread itself across his face. 'Yes. Yes, that's it.'

'He trusted me for everything.' Raffie was crying. 'I fed him. I walked him and I cleaned him and I loved him. If he was hurt, he'd come to me. If he was hungry, he'd rest his head on my knee. And he trusted me, absolutely, right up until I stuck a knife in his neck.'

'Yes.'

'What the fuck is this?' Simon demanded. 'What kind of a game would do that – *who* would do that? Asking someone to kill a dog – holding out false hope, using it that way . . .' His voice tailed off.

Their host sat back in his chair and folded his arms behind his head. 'What kind of people break into an office and kill a man?'

Ashley jerked back, knocking into Ben, who steadied him.

'We're done here,' Ben said. 'I don't know what this is supposed to be, but we're not doing it any longer. We're not – we're not playing your games.'

'Oh, but you are,' the man sneered. 'Ashley here more than most, I imagine. After all, you're in the deepest, aren't you, Ash? You promised me a price. Don't forget that I haven't yet come to claim it from you.'

He turned back to Raffie and snapped his fingers. 'What do you want?'

She looked up. 'I want my daughter cured.'

'You have nothing to trade.'

He snapped his fingers towards Damon. 'What do you want?'

'I – I want my soul back.'

'So you say. You?' He jabbed a finger towards Ashley, who shook his head.

'Never mind; we'll get to that. Now, Gaila.' He smiled once more and his teeth looked sharp and slick with saliva. 'Happy birthday, my dear,' he said. 'You are standing on the edge. The key to the door is in your hand. You've come of age at last.'

Ben, confused, glanced at his watch. He saw that it was midnight. Whoever he was, this man was right: his sister had just turned eighteen.

'Six plus six plus six,' he said. 'Such a terribly pretty age, don't you think?'

TWO

'First,' the man said, 'my name. You may call me Jones. Theodore Jones, but I prefer to go by Jones. You may notice I had Mephistopheles adopt my surname. I rather like it. So plain, so ordinary, so very anonymous.

'The man you shamelessly killed was nothing more than my employee. All that fire and brimstone – I can't be troubled with it, truth be told. I am merely the humble ruler of all that you survey.' He smirked. 'A back office man.'

'That's not all you are.' Raffie glared.

'My dear, are you so sure? Words on a screen, my dear, words on a screen. I like to meddle, but there's a reason they call it a game, isn't there? A most definite reason. It's nothing special. Nothing clever. Nothing magical.' As he spoke, his voice became soothing. It didn't have the resonance that Mephistopheles had possessed, but somehow that made him all the more convincing.

Ben glanced towards Milo, at the place his shirt bulked around the gun. If this Jones had been watching them on camera, as he had said, there had been no use concealing it; Jones already knew it was there. The knowledge didn't seem to trouble him in the slightest.

Jones opened the top drawer set into one side of his desk and rummaged through it. Papers rustled, pens rolled. It was a perfectly ordinary sound. He tutted, like an office worker who couldn't find his stapler. Then he withdrew his hand from the drawer, holding a file. It was thin. There was no writing, or any other markings on its simple buff cover to suggest what its contents might be.

He held it out towards Ben.

Ben hesitated and then he took it. He thought it should feel odd under his fingers, warm perhaps, but it did not; the cardboard was dry. He still felt an urge to drop it or cast it away from him.

Jones' face was neutral. 'Who knows?' he said. 'You might even like it.'

Ben was being stupid, wasn't he? It couldn't be anything that could hurt him. He slipped his thumb under the edge of the cover and Jones added: 'Of course, once seen, such things can never be unseen.'

'More games,' Ben said, and he opened the folder and saw his sister looking back at him.

Her face was almost lost amid streaks of light and shadow, but he knew at once that it was Gaila. It was her eyes he saw first, their bright points shining from dark hollows created by the harsh lighting. She was wearing her trademark glare. It took him a little longer to notice the T-shirt she wore, the words WOULD YOU? picked out by a spotlight; it took him longer still to notice the fake red horns she wore on her head.

He frowned. He didn't know what he was looking at, or why. Gaila twisted in her seat, trying to see the contents of the file, and he half closed the cover so that only he could see; he wasn't sure why. He leafed through it. There were more pictures. In the last one, Gaila was smiling. It appeared to have been taken before she was ready, or after she thought she'd finished a job. It was a look he recognised from childhood, an *I know something you don't* smile, but with the words on that T-shirt strident beneath her face, it made her look evil.

He could hear his mother's words, low and urgent, running through his mind. *Don't listen to your sister, Ben. There's something bad in her . . .*

He didn't know what he was supposed to think. And he realised there was one more picture after all, a smaller one tucked away at the bottom. This one was a close-up of his sister's face. Gaila was pointing into the camera, like Lord Kitchener in the famous army recruitment poster. In her other outstretched palm, though, she held a bright-red apple. Juice welled on her purple lip, after she'd taken a bite. It hung there like a drop of poison.

'Eve,' Jones said softly. 'It suits her, don't you think? And it is rather fitting. But who is Adam, and who the snake?'

Gaila gave a little cry and half pushed herself out of her chair. Ben closed the folder. It didn't make a sound. *It should*, he found himself thinking; *it should sound like an iron door swinging shut.* Except the door wasn't closed, it stood wide open, and all kinds of possibilities were flooding through it. The oddest thing about the pictures, he realised, was not that his sister was wearing a T-shirt emblazoned with the company's slogan, or the fact that they were in Jones' possession. The oddest thing was what he could see, quite clearly, on her cheek: her scar. He had never seen one of her modelling pictures that showed her scar. It had always been erased, the past made as if it had never been. If anything, here, it was accentuated by the harshness of the light.

The file was snatched from his hands. Gaila pulled it open, ripping the cardboard, and she riffled through the pictures, letting them spill across the desk and onto the floor. 'You bastard,' she said. 'We agreed – you said – when I didn't get the job—'

'We agreed not to use them commercially,' Jones said. 'And I honour my promises, no matter what anyone might say. We did not use them. You auditioned and you failed, my dear. We chose our Mephistopheles over you, and he did do a good job, don't you think? Right up until you killed him.' He paused. 'It's rather lucky for you that you did not pass muster, isn't it? Would she have stabbed *you*, do you think? Anyway, you wanted the role for a somewhat selfish reason, didn't you?'

Gaila flung herself across the desk, her hands reaching out. Ben grabbed her again and pulled her back.

'Ah, how – emblematic. The fiery sister acts without thinking. The ever-steadfast brother tries to save her from herself. Come now, you don't need saving, do you, Abigail? Why *was* it that you wanted the role?'

'Because it paid.' She spoke through clenched teeth.

'Oh, I think not. I think there was another reason, one much closer to your heart.' He reached down without looking and pulled open his desk drawer. There was a dull click and then a voice, small and tinny but unmistakeably Gaila, came from a place they could not see:

'It'll kill the daft bitch when she sees me.'

Ben froze. He knew at once who his sister had been speaking of: he could see it all.

He heard women's voices, laughing in the background. 'She's a complete nut. She'll never see it coming – me, the face of the game.' And then she said, 'My smart-arse brother'll probably shit himself.'

'Oh dear,' Jones said. 'If you wish to use the facilities, Benjamin, please do feel free.'

'You had no right to tape me. It was a job, that's all, just another job—'

'It really wasn't, though, was it?'

Ben had kept hold of his sister's shoulder. He wrapped his fingers more firmly around it, feeling the small roundness of her bones under his hand. 'Gaila, don't.' His voice was quieter than he would have liked. He felt her tension through his fingers; every muscle and tendon strung with wire and pulled taut, like a puppet. 'He's playing you,' he said. 'He's playing us all. We can't let him do that.'

Gaila sagged in her chair and began to shake. She twisted around to look at her brother and for a moment, her tears shone back the fluorescent light. 'You – you don't—'

Even more softly, Ben said, 'You should have told me.'

She slumped back, all the fight draining out of her. 'I didn't mean what I—'

'No, but you said it all the same. And you were right, Gaila, it *would* have killed her.'

Suddenly she was full of fire again. 'Except it wouldn't, would it? It wouldn't have killed her at all, because you were the only thing she cared about. She wouldn't even have thought I *had* a soul, would she? Not after that day she burned her hand, and – and she *changed*. After that it was like I was some sort of evil burden she had to carry, and you – you were her Golden Boy. She wouldn't have given a shit if she'd seen those pictures, Ben, because she didn't bloody care.'

'Of course she cared.' Ben spoke automatically, but even as he said the words he could hear his own lack of conviction. The truth was that Cass might *not* have cared. Worse, she might have seen it as the vindication of all her odd ideas about her daughter. She might have triumphed in seeing those pictures, her black sheep of a child revelling in the symbols of evil: proof that Cass had been right all along.

Ben closed his eyes. Suddenly, he could feel the heft of the rock in his hand, the one he'd found just lying there in the otherwise smoothly paved surface of their garden. He felt the anger burning in him. He could hear Gaila coming, her feet patting along the street, sounding so normal, so everyday.

Jones' voice tugged him from his reverie. 'Goodness,' he said, 'families! Oh, their depths and wonders. The cogs and wheels that none outside can see or even guess at – aren't they glorious?'

He banged the drawer closed with the sweep of a hand and leaned back in his chair, spreading his fingers across the surface of the table. 'Now, whatever next? Ooh – I know!' He sounded like an excited child. Ben half expected him to start clapping.

'I think it's time for your present, Gaila.' He raised an eyebrow, as if surprised by their lack of reaction. 'Well, birthdays are for presents, aren't they? Ben, didn't you get her anything?'

Ben's hand snaked towards the pocket of his jacket. He hadn't meant to move, not with Jones' greedy eyes watching everything he did, but his hand had betrayed him. He touched the small black box hidden there. It wasn't something he'd intended to share with anyone else. He'd planned to press it into Gaila's hand when he saw her off at the airport. He wouldn't even have seen her face when she opened it. When she'd decided not to go, he'd put it out of his mind; he would have presented her with it when this was all over and they could put it behind them.

That was then. It was different now.

'I knew!' Jones said, and now he *did* clap his hands. You are such a *good* brother, after all. What is it? What is it?'

'It's none of your business,' muttered Gaila. This time she hadn't turned around. She probably didn't expect anything at all. Ben wasn't good at presents, and their mother's cheque wouldn't raise much of a response. He felt a stab of guilt. Only Jones looked excited. But he suddenly wanted her to have it, to see that he'd thought about her. He'd trailed around the shops for hours to find something she might like. Of course, he'd probably failed. He had very little idea of what his sister liked. She mingled with photographers and designers and other models all the time and anything he could choose would pale in comparison to that; how could he possibly match up to it? And yet it was – something. Before thinking about it further, he leaned forward and placed it on the desk in front of her.

'How delightful!' squealed Jones, and yet Ben saw that it wasn't. He'd asked the sales assistant to wrap it for him so that it would at least be neatly done, but he realised he'd torn the corner of the shiny pink paper when he'd pulled it from his pocket, and the bow was crushed, a limp, sorry thing. He felt like taking it back and stuffing it into his pocket again. He already wanted to apologise for it.

Gaila reached out and picked it up between thumb and

finger, as if she didn't really want to touch it. 'You know what this is?' She wasn't speaking to Ben.

'Not at all! What's a birthday without surprises? Go on – open it! Do!'

She reached out with her other hand, pulled the bow apart then ripped the paper away. She stared at the box for a moment before prising off the lid. Inside, nestled amid purple velvet, was a pendant. It was silver and in the shape of a star. Ben had had it engraved: on one side was her name and birth date. On the other was a single word: SISTER.

He had taken such a long time choosing it. Now it looked pitiful. Gaila didn't say anything. She took it from the box, holding the pendant in her hand, letting the chain dangle from her fingers.

Ben saw that it was too fine a chain for the weight it had to carry. Then he realised his sister had started to cry. She folded in on herself, making herself smaller. He reached out, squeezing her shoulder once more, but she didn't seem to feel it.

'I don't know,' Jones said. 'Women! Can't live with them, can't stick a knife in their ribs. Unless—' he looked at Raffie, cocked an eyebrow. 'No? Really? No, I suppose not.' And then he drew a long sigh. 'Right! Whatever shall we do next?'

THREE

'Before we go any further,' Ben said, 'perhaps you could explain to us how the hell you knew we were coming?'

Jones gave a mock gasp. 'Me?'

'It's not just the CCTV cameras. You were ready for us. You knew our names. You had the pictures of Gaila ready, and the recording, set to the exact point you wanted me to hear. The game even had Gaila ask me to come down to London, just at the right time. It all looked odd from the beginning – you're not *still* telling us that you didn't know?' He paused. 'Except, something's off, isn't it? Because you really only expected six.' He glanced at the others. 'So, which one of us isn't supposed to be here?'

Simon stirred. 'I wasn't meant to play. Maybe it's me. The game could have warned me off on purpose.'

'And yet Mephistopheles, or whatever his real name was,

knew about your request for money. And he knew you hadn't told Ashley,' said Ben.

Ashley grunted. 'That might have been because I kept playin'. One o' the requests in the game – well, I said it 'ad to prove something to me.'

'And it did, didn't it?' Jones smirked.

'We're reading too much into this,' Damon said. 'He watched us come in. He had plenty of time to look us up. He must have been watching us all the time Mephistopheles was stalling.'

'But he was *here*, wasn't he?' said Ben. 'And Mephistopheles – he wasn't a part of the company. But they were both here, on a Friday night, when everyone else had gone home. Why were they here? It's not as if they were taking pictures or doing a PR stunt or filming an ad – so what was it? Mephistopheles was only an employee, someone hired for the occasion. He wouldn't have been here for no reason.'

'Oh, he was more than that,' Jones said. 'We met often, you know. Strategy, my dear friend. He and I often put our horned little heads together to have a good chat. Where to go next, whose mind to mess with . . .' He winked.

'And you just happened to be here late on a Friday, the same night we decided to come along?'

'Astonishing, isn't it?' Jones beamed.

'And you happened to know it's Gaila's birthday.'

'Dear fellow, you can't give me credit for that. Apart from, of course, the fact is clearly written on the profile we received from the modelling agency. It was after all you, not I, who chose not only your means of ingress, but which night it should take place.'

Ben shifted uneasily. 'It's beside the point. You say you want to mess with people's heads – well, that much is clear. You messed with Jessica's until she couldn't face whatever it was you did to her. You made her kill herself. Well, I'm not playing your game any longer; I never was. And you don't seem to care about what happened to your colleague out there, but I do. It's time we called the police.'

Jones' eyes misted over. 'How very touching.' He looked at Damon, then at Ashley, and at Raffie. Finally, he winked at Milo, who jerked away. 'What about the rest of you? Majority rules, doesn't it – don't you want to play? Gaila did, didn't you – the day he did that to your face, this man who calls himself your brother?'

Ben caught his breath. He met Jones' eyes and found he couldn't look away. He had thought Mephistopheles' eyes piercing in a dark, theatrical way, but this man's were different; there was something in them. They had clarity and an ease that spoke of power, of an intention that wouldn't be turned aside. As he watched, Jones' lips moved. There was no sound, but Ben knew exactly what he said, and he knew the word was meant for him: *remember*.

And suddenly he did. He saw exactly why he'd been running away from Gaila that day. He could remember everything; why he'd reached for the stone, why he had been so angry that he couldn't even think. He knew why he had thrown it, even though he hadn't meant to, had meant for it to fall short and frighten her into going away – anywhere, as long as she left him alone.

It had all been about Pete. Gaila was always the one who started on the subject, even when Ben didn't want to talk about it, or perhaps especially then. Ben was the one who went with the flow, putting up with things, but Gaila would never let it alone. Back then, Ben would bend before Cass' moods like a sapling, straightening again after they had passed. This time he hadn't bent.

He heard Gaila's voice again: *I don't want to be here any more, Ben, why don't we go and live with Dad, Ben?* And there had been so many things that he wanted to say to her, the words coming so thickly they had choked him, and he'd bitten them down and instead, he'd run.

It had been Gaila's fault that she followed him.

She wouldn't let it go; she never had. It was no secret that she and Cass didn't get along. When Cass treated her like the black sheep of the family, Gaila responded by acting like one. She broke Cass' things on purpose. She'd promise to come in for tea then sneak off and hide until it grew dark. Cass never said anything out loud, not in front of Ben, and she never called the police when Gaila failed to come home. It might have been better if she had. It was always Ben who went after his sister, trailing the streets, Eden Mount, Abbey Walk, shouting her name and listening for her answer.

The thing is, he *had* wanted to go with Pete.

He hadn't fought with Gaila that day because he disagreed with her. His sister, so much younger than him, always saw everything so clearly. She saw the contents of people's hearts, and Ben had known that she was right.

He remembered Cass' words when she'd called him, alone, into her room earlier that day. She'd already been crying before she'd even heard his answer, but she still asked him the question he'd unconsciously been waiting to hear. 'Do you want to stay with me, or do you want to go and live with your dad? Well, Ben – *what do you want?*'

And he'd looked into her face, seen the lines already etched into her skin, and he had lied. 'I want to stay with you, Mum.'

He had seen the tears in her eyes, the despair hiding under their blankness, but that hadn't been the reason he'd turned his back on Pete and chosen to stay.

And later, he'd fought with his sister and he'd run. All he'd wanted was for her to leave him alone. He hadn't wanted to talk about it, or even think about it any longer. He'd shouted over his shoulder for her to go; he'd tried to tell her. He'd sworn at her, all the worst words he could think of. He never swore at his sister. He remembered the shock on her face as he ran, leaving her behind him. *She* was the bad one, wasn't she? Not Ben. She'd been taught that every day, by the things Cass had said to her; by all the things she never said.

And Ben had run. He remembered the momentary revulsion at the sight of Gaila's pale face staring after him, the face that was so different to his own. He ran, tasting salt, shocked to find that he was crying. Part of it was sorrow at the whole mess, but there was guilt in it too; all the times Cass had railed at Gaila, treating Ben like her little angel, and his sister had never once blamed him.

He could hear her footsteps, coming after him like an echo. Still, she was younger than him, and Ben was fast. He was a good way ahead when he reached the gate and slammed it behind him.

But she wouldn't stop. She was always there, his younger sister, so much smaller and stranger and *different* to him.

And he'd suddenly felt so tired. So he'd said it, the words that had always remained unsaid. 'You can't go, Gaila. Because Pete isn't your dad.'

She stopped as if he'd slapped her. She knew that the words were true; of course she did. She always had. Cass had never made it a secret that Gaila had bad blood in her, that she didn't belong.

Ben's eyes blurred as the tears came in a rush. He couldn't stop himself as he said, 'But *I* could. I could go with him if it wasn't for *you*.'

Ben looked at his sister now. She was sitting with her head bowed. Her hands were on the desk, the fine silver chain looped between her fingers, and she turned the pendant in her hands so that the words appeared and disappeared: *GAILA. SISTER. GAILA.*

They were mocking him.

Ben shook his head, pushing away the memory. That day, he had wished Gaila gone. He had wished that he didn't have a little sister, one he needed to look out for, to take care of, to be there for.

What do you want?

He had wanted, in that moment, to go. He had wanted so badly to leave her behind, leave her to Cass and all her strange fancies and obsessions. His life could have been different. It could have been *normal*.

And Gaila had gone on and on about leaving, just as if she wasn't dark-haired and pale where Pete was sandy-haired and stocky and tanned. as if it was possible. Why hadn't she just shut up?

And yet, even after he'd hit her with the stone that was suddenly there in the garden, when he wiped the blood from her face – *I'm sorry, Gaila, I never meant . . .* – she had never once blamed him. She'd never hated him for having their mother's love. But he had hated her, hadn't he? Just for that moment, on that day. He had hated her.

He reached for her shoulder before letting his hand drop to his side. He did not touch her and she did not move.

'So painful,' Jones said, 'To be parted from family. I feel it. I feel it, you know. I'm not a monster.'

'You couldn't have known about those things.'

'No.' Jones steepled his fingers.

'Gaila, did you tell him about that day? When you did the photo-shoot for them, did you tell him about what I did to your cheek?' He felt Damon's eyes boring into him at that, but he didn't care. 'Gaila?'

She stirred, looking down at the pendant as if she'd forgotten it was there. Then she stuffed it into her pocket. 'Of course I didn't. He knows, because he's – he just *knows*. Ben, you have to see it, sooner or later. There's something impossible about all of this.'

'Because it's all *real*? So you said.' Ben couldn't stop his exasperation showing. When Gaila didn't reply, he said more softly, 'I'm sorry, sis. But let's deal in the realms of the possible, shall we?'

'That's all right for you to say.' She hunched her shoulders. She still didn't look up. 'You never played. Isn't that right? Golden Boy never let himself be – *corrupted*. You wouldn't be sold, not like me.' Her voice was small.

'Gaila.' Ben leaned forward and this time he did touch her, drawing her to him. 'You're not corrupted. You're you. You're my sister, right? Gaila?'

He jumped when a peal of laughter rang out across the room. 'Bless you,' Jones said. 'Really? Your *sister*.' Laughter burst from him, louder this time. 'Oh – bless you, my son.'

FOUR

Jones stood, pacing the floor behind his desk, a musing expression on his face. 'We are all called to account,' he said. 'Forgive me for sounding like a priest, Ben, but in a way, I do feel fatherly towards you. Or like a teacher, perhaps. A guide. A friend, if you will.' He spread his hands wide. 'All you need do is believe. Come to me and drink.'

Ben grimaced. 'That's not what you said before.' The similarity suddenly struck him: Jones' posturing, his mother's vacillations. And how far awry had that gone? For a moment he could hear the sound of her skin sizzling on the hob. He could almost smell it. He sighed. 'You know, you can try to play these games all you want. It's gone too far already. I don't know how you got that man out there to take part in it, but now he's dead. And you can blame her all you want' – he nodded towards Raffie, who barely acknowledged his look – 'but it was you who set this up. Mephistopheles told us to kill him. He said it was the only way we'd be free. You've messed with people's heads and this is the result. Is that what you wanted, really? Is it what *he* wanted?'

Jones threw back his head and laughed. 'Of course not! But he had taken a role, and a good one. He thought it was all a stunt, you see. He was the mouthpiece, I the mind. When I told him you'd be bringing a weapon, he thought it was all play; he never imagined the gun would be loaded. *Is* it loaded, my friend?' He raised an eyebrow at Milo, who did not reply.

'Why, I believe it actually might be. Of course, he never suspected a knife. Which is now – where, exactly?'

Ben remembered the blade as it slid from Mephistopheles' body, the splash of crimson that followed it. He glanced at Damon. He'd pulled it free – he could still hear the sound it had made. But what happened after that? He'd put the thing down, hadn't he?

'So Jessica never had her revenge after all,' Damon said in a soft voice.

'No.' Ashley stepped forward, spreading his hands across the desk, leaning into Jones' face. 'She din't.'

'Careful, Ashley.' Jones' voice was genial.

'It's about time she did.'

'Ah – perhaps.' Jones winked. For a moment, they stared at each other. Then Ashley subsided. 'I thought not.'

'I don't know what you've got over him,' Ben said, 'but it's time we did what we came to do. Milo, delete everything. Then we call the police. And we face whatever's coming to us.'

'Perhaps you should face whatever's coming to you, and *then* call the police,' Jones said. 'After all, it's been coming for you all your life, Ben, hasn't it?' He opened the desk drawer and this time removed a slim silver laptop. He held it out towards Milo. 'Please, be my guest.'

Milo took it. He held it steady with one hand, opening the lid with the other. Light flickered across his face as it woke, and a look of greed passed across his features.

Ben leaned over and took it from him. The screen didn't show a list of files, ready for deletion. It showed a simple room with a desk in its centre. A man was sitting behind it, his face in shadow. A single word beneath it said WAIT.

'What the hell is this?' Ben said. 'You're doing whatever he tells you, is that it?'

Milo shook his head. Then he shrugged. After a moment, Ben pushed the laptop back into his hands. 'You know what? I don't care. I don't even know who you are. For all I know—' He caught his breath.

'Enough.' There was authority in Jones' voice. Ben didn't have time to object before he realised that everyone had already turned to the man, their faces rapt.

Jones rubbed his hands together. 'It's time to offer you all a little deal,' he said. 'And the beauty of it is, I shall not ask for anything you haven't offered already. You can leave here, scot-free. There won't be any police. There won't be any murder charges. No one is going to come knocking on your door in the middle of the night. No fingerprints, no forensics, no trace will ever bring them to you. You don't have to live in fear. All of you can be free – at least, of Mephistopheles' death.'

There was silence.

'For most of you, that part is a gift, a sweetener. Do you wish it?'

Everyone glanced around, waiting for someone else to be first to reply.

'We're calling the police ourselves,' Ben said. 'We have to.' He felt pressure on his arm and looked down to see Gaila gripping it tightly.

'Yes,' Raffie cut in, 'that's what we want.' She looked around the group. 'For God's sake, this isn't on you. It's on *me*. My daughter needs me. It was – it was an accident.' She looked at the floor.

'No,' Ben said.

'Of course,' said Ashley.

Jones turned to him with new interest in his eyes. 'Really? Because this is actually all on you, Ashley. The game asked you for something, didn't it – when you made your very *special* request? The price was just one *small* thing.' He smiled, and for a second the light reflected back from his eyes, making him appear feral.

Ashley let out a spurt of a laugh. 'You've got to be joking.'

'I rarely joke, my friend. Did you think it a joke at the time?'

'I – course I did. A price like that – it couldn't be serious. It were just a game, that's all.'

'I take games very seriously, as well you know.' Jones smiled broadly, revealing his teeth. 'You didn't think it a joke when you gained your reward, did you? Now it's up to you, Ashley. Give me what you promised and you and your friends go free – of this at least. The other thing – well, there's still that, isn't there? Don't forget, I know exactly what you did. If you refuse me this – well, there's no shame in telling, is there? Not if the game was *real*. Not if poor Ashley didn't have any choice.' He sneered. 'So what's it to be?'

Ashley looked around the room as if searching for a way out. 'This is stupid. It never – it never meant owt. It was a joke, that's all. Words. Words on a screen. That can't be real, can it?'

Jones laughed. 'And if so – the reward you gained – that wasn't real either, was it? It was just something you took, all by yourself.'

'I – no. That *was* real. It 'ad to be. It 'appened, din't it? Just like the game said it would. It *knew*. Of course it were real.'

'Why, then, you have to pay.' Jones grinned and turned his back. There was a cupboard set against the wall behind him, its doors plain grey. He pulled it open. Ben had expected it to be like similar cupboards in the main office – stuffed full of files, stationery maybe: boxes of cheap ballpoint pens, blocks of photocopy paper, slippery plastic wallets, paperclips no one ever used. There was none of that. The top shelf was empty save for a single object, which Jones removed and cradled in his arms. It was something that didn't belong in an office. It didn't even look as if it belonged in a city.

He placed it on the desk in front of him. 'The left, wasn't it?' he said.

The thing was a blade, long and curved and dull. The handle was short and black, made out of thin strips of leather or some other porous material wrapped around and around it. It was darkened, perhaps with sweat from the palm of a hand, possibly with something darker still.

'I don't care how you cut it off, incidentally,' Jones said. 'You can have someone else do it for you, if you wish; that might be easier. Though it might be less painful, at least on the inside, if you take care of it yourself.'

'What the fuck is he talking about?' said Simon.

Ashley didn't reply. He stared down at the object on the table, the thing that was a little like a machete but not quite, and his face paled.

'We're talking about a choice,' Jones whispered. 'So, Ashley. What do you want?'

'He's not doing anything of the kind,' Simon said. 'You're fucking crazy.'

'And you, dear fellow, are party to murder. Which one of us is crazy now, do you think?'

Ben looked at Damon. He didn't know why he expected him to step in, and anyway, Damon didn't move; he too was staring down at the table. As Ben watched, Damon licked the edge of his lip.

'You can't,' Gaila cut in. She leaned forward to snatch the weapon, but Jones was quicker. He snapped his hand down onto the blade. It made a hollow chink against the smooth surface of the desk. Ben somehow knew, from that sound, that the blade wasn't sharp. He couldn't process what he was seeing. It was all wrong. It surely couldn't be happening – he couldn't be here, and Jones couldn't possibly be serious. Anyway, Milo had a gun. He could still see the shape of it bulking out the back of his shirt. He could stop all this any time he chose. But Milo didn't move. He was watching the exchange, his expression one of mild interest.

Ashley moved to the side of the desk and reached out towards the knife. His fingers shook; his whole arm did. He stayed there, perfectly balanced between going on and going back.

'It's all about belief,' Jones said. 'Do you, or don't you? If you do, take up that weapon and give me what you promised. If you don't . . . well, we'll call me a liar then, shall we? I am no one and nothing and our bargain doesn't matter. Everything that you've done was of your own volition and you can blame no one if—'

Ashley reached out and grabbed the blade.

Ben laughed. He heard that laugh afterwards, echoing through his mind. 'He's not going to do anything,' he said. 'No one would do that. That's stu—'

Ashley let out a low moan. Ben couldn't see his face because his head was bowed into his chest. His hair hung across it. Then he fell, except he didn't fall, not really; he lurched forward, spreading the fingers of his left hand across the desk, at once gripping the blade with his right hand. Gaila snatched for it again; again, she was too slow.

Ashley brought the weapon down in one swift movement. Gaila shrieked. So did Raffie next to her. Ben told himself that nothing had happened, it was just a game, and then he saw that his sister's face was spattered with blood. 'You didn't,' he said. His throat was dry, his voice a rasp.

Ashley let out another moan, this one higher, out of control. As Ben stared, waiting for Ashley to speak, to deny that he'd done anything, blood began to spill from under his arm and spread across the desk.

Gaila made a high-pitched noise and jumped to her feet, moving behind her chair. She still had blood on her face and Ben wanted to tell her to wipe it clean, as if she were a little girl, and suddenly that manic laughter had returned; he forced himself to swallow it down.

Ashley was hunched over the table, his arms shielding whatever it was he had done, his face almost in contact with the surface of the desk. A shudder ran through him; his spine writhed beneath his jacket. Ashley moaned again, but this time the sound rose to a wail. It wasn't the kind of sound a man should make.

Ashley began to straighten up. With his right hand, he tried to shift the blade. Ben heard it grinding against wood, saw splinters around it; then everything was subsumed with red.

Ashley shifted, half falling across the edge of the desk, and

as he moved his hand Ben saw that his little finger remained
where it was. Then it *did* move. It hadn't been entirely severed
after all. It clung to the stub of his left hand by a thin, wet
thread.

Raffie stumbled away from the desk, covering her mouth.
Someone was whispering 'Oh God, oh God', over and over,
under their breath. It was Milo. Suddenly, Ben wanted to hit
him. He wanted to hit *somebody*. His insides had turned to ice
and yet there was heat too, threading his veins.

Ashley swayed, about to faint. Ben caught his breath – he
could smell the blood – and he moved, not away from Ashley
but towards him. He steadied his shoulders, trying to guide
him towards a chair.

Ashley didn't move. He was a dead weight, swaying, his
head down. His eyes were closed.

'Not finished,' Jones said. 'The price isn't paid. Remember,
Ashley, the freedom of your friends depends on it. As to our
other little matter – well, perhaps we can settle that too.'

'What the hell?' Gaila's voice shook. 'Who does that? What
the hell would make him do that?'

Ben tried to pull Ashley away. It was like trying to move a
rock. Then Ashley's shoulder shifted under his hand and he
realised that he was reaching, once more, for the weapon.
Ben grabbed his arm, pulling his hand away.

'He won't thank you,' Jones said. 'You're only making this
harder for him. You and your bleeding heart—'

'Fuck you,' Ben said, and pulled harder, but then Ashley

bucked in his grip, slipping from his grasp, and he seized the blade. He pulled back and it wouldn't come free of the desk, but then it did, spattering fresh drops. Ben reached for it. He was too late. Ashley brought it down once more and this time, he screamed. He fell forward into the blood, into the thing he'd done.

'How dramatic.' Jones was holding a large white handkerchief. He leaned over, picked something up and wrapped the fabric over it. Slowly, a spot appeared on the whiteness. It began to spread. Jones make a 'tsk' sound, opened the cupboard behind him, placed the object inside and closed the door. When he turned, he was smiling. 'You may wish to bandage that,' he said, nodding towards Ashley.

It wasn't clear to whom he spoke, but it was Ben who responded. He took hold of Ashley's arm, careful not to touch his hand, and in response, Ashley moved easily. Ben led him to a chair and helped him into it. He tried not to think about the blood. It seemed to be everywhere; he could feel it on Ashley's sleeve. He didn't look at the wound, but he realised no one else had offered to help. He held on to Ashley's arm. His fingers were the colour of putty. Blood kept spurting from the stump of his little finger. Ben had to force himself not to pull away.

'Here.' Someone else responded at last. Damon pushed something towards him and Ben took it without turning. It was a plain white T-shirt, smelling faintly of aftershave. He wrapped it around Ashley's hand, pulling it tighter to try and staunch the blood. Blood soaked into it. Ben swallowed down nausea, wrapping it over once more, pulling it tighter, and Ashley let out a breath, an empty sound that was somehow worse than his moans.

Then it was done. Ashley slumped in his chair, cradling his injured hand. Ben glanced around to see Simon pulling on his jacket, his chest bared beneath it; it had been his T-shirt.

'We all pay,' Jones said. 'Eventually, all of us pay.' His eyes shone brightly. He smiled and looked towards the door through which they had come. 'The rest of you should thank him.'

Damon was the first to turn to face the door. Slowly, the others did too. Only Ashley stayed where he was, unmoving.

Simon stepped forward, but Ben was ahead of him. He strode to the door and pulled it open. The corridor was oddly quiet, as if all sound in the world had ceased, but Ben didn't hesitate; he strode along it towards the door that led into the office. When he reached it, he stopped. He had seen Mephistopheles dead. He did not want to see it again. But the others were at his back; someone jostled him and a hand grasped at his where it rested on the door handle. Ben had no choice. He had to go on. He opened the door and someone pushed him and they spilled into the room.

There was the place where they had grappled, the chairs pushed awry. There was the place where Ben had held onto Damon, pulling him away from his sister. There was the place where the man they'd called Mephistopheles had fallen, a knife between his ribs; the place the floor tiles had been soaked by his blood. Now there was nothing.

Ben moved closer, bending to the floor. There was no blood. There was no body. He could not see the faintest trace of where it had once been.

THE FIFTH CIRCLE

ONE

'In Dante's Inferno,' Jones said, clasping his hands behind his back, 'the punishment fits the crime. Everything has a price. There is a reason why they refer to it as the *wages* of sin.

'Take traitors, for example.' They were back in his office. He turned to face them, then turned another ninety degrees and began to pace back the other way. 'He shows us how one traitor is eaten, constantly, for all eternity. Actually, not all of him is eaten, but only his head, perhaps to symbolise the cerebral nature of the crime, betrayal being an emotional wound, regardless of the physical consequences. No: his head is consumed, over and over, by the person he betrayed.

'Now, here is the difficulty, is it not? For one can see why the betrayer is there, but' – he rapped his knuckles on the desk – 'why do you think the one betrayed is trapped in the icy lake of Hell?'

He looked at Ben. 'You see me as evil. Perhaps I am evil.

But in comparison to what? Your own goodness?' He smiled. 'You fail to see how the sinner is shackled to the saint. It's a false dichotomy, albeit one that is commonly held. And each is doomed to consume the other, for ever and ever.

'Of course, it is possible that Dante simply hadn't thought it through. He had so many punishments to invent – he enjoyed that part, don't you think? Yes, one can sense that he did. Possibly, one might say, a little too much.

'Ah – the united heavens we invent for ourselves, and the endlessly diverting creations of Hell! Would the game have so many players, do you imagine, if it set about exploring the heavens? Why, they'd be stupefied!' He rubbed his hands together. 'No, we *want* Hell. We *need* it. If it didn't exist, we'd jolly well have to invent it!' He let out a delighted laugh.

Ben blinked. He wondered if he were going mad. Possibly he had already done so. He might have imagined the whole thing. Jones couldn't possibly be real. Dead bodies didn't just vanish without a trace. Men in offices wearing crisp shirts didn't hand a man a blade and talk them into cutting off their own finger. If he was to open that cupboard, would the severed finger still be there? He looked down at Ashley. He was sitting as he had before, though he was rocking himself, a motion that made Ben think of a child in a cradle.

He realised no one had said anything else about calling an ambulance. *He* hadn't said anything. He didn't say anything now.

What on earth had happened to him? He had broken into

the place he used to work. His companions had included a man with a gun and a woman with a knife. He didn't know either of them, but still, he had come. The only one he knew was his own sister. Gaila stood in a characteristic stance, her arms wrapped around her body. He found himself wondering if he really knew *her*, if he could even predict what she would do, and she turned, feeling his gaze. She gave him a wan smile. Her eyes were dark against her pale skin; too dark.

Ben looked away, reminding himself that none of this was real. It was a *game*. They had been manipulated. Someone had crept into the first office while Jones had kept them occupied in this. They must have taken away the body, wiped the mess from the desks, taken up those grey floor tiles and replaced them with new ones.

And they had done everything that was required of them, following where they were led. With that thought, he looked at Damon. He had brought them here. Shouldn't he do something now? But Damon wasn't reacting to anything around him. He just stood there with his eyes half closed, as if it wasn't anything to do with him; as if he'd expected it to happen.

Ben's eyes narrowed. 'Jesus,' he said, before he could stop himself.

'I think you'll find not.' Jones sounded amused.

'Six. You said *six*.'

Jones raised his eyebrows, irritated by the interruption.

'We thought it was because you missed someone on the

CCTV, that you'd miscounted. And then I thought it was because you'd set us all up through the game, only someone had come along that you weren't expecting. But you're cleverer than that, aren't you? You expected all of us. You expected us because you'd picked us out. But there are still only six, because one of us *isn't* one of us. He's a—'

'A traitor?' Jones smiled. It was the smile a father might give upon seeing his child's first steps.

'You.' Ben turned to Damon. 'It was you who got Gaila to play the game. It was you who called me. You said it was because of Jessica, because I went to the funeral. I always thought that was a stupid reason, since I never really knew her at all, and you knew that I didn't. But that wasn't it, was it?' He looked around at the others. 'Don't you see? He set us up. And Jones, calling us six, to our faces – it's his way of laughing at us.'

'That's crap.' Damon looked from one of them to the next, his expression incredulous. 'That's rubbish. I'm not with him. I'm not with anyone.'

'You said that the game never asked you for anything,' Ben pressed. 'And that's why, isn't it? It didn't need to. You were a part of this, right from the very beginning.'

'Bullshit. I didn't even get myself into this, remember? If anything it was Jessica who set *me* up. I told you. She called me and she said I should play.'

'Ah – Eve with the apple.' Jones smiled. 'And what did she offer in return?'

'Nothing! Why should she? She was my friend.'

Jones bowed.

Damon spoke rapidly. 'This is ridiculous. I'm here because of her – and that's why I brought you in, because I thought you might be prepared to help. She's dead. Doesn't that mean anything to you? She's dead because of this man's games.'

'*Mephistopheles* is dead. Did that mean nothing to *you*?' Jones sneered.

'I asked you to stop this.' Damon turned to Milo. 'Why aren't you doing it? If you'd just deleted everything in the first place this wouldn't be happening. Ashley would be fine. Mephistopheles would have been fine. If we'd just got in and out, like we'd planned, like *I* planned . . . This is your fault. Yours, not mine.' Two hectic red marks had appeared on his cheeks. 'For God's sake. I've been running from this sort of stuff my whole life. My whole *life*. If it wasn't enough having a crazy mother – do you really think I'd throw in my lot with this maniac?'

A sudden image: Ben on his knees, his mother's hand on the back of his head, forcing him lower, words falling on him like blows. *My whole life*. He felt a pang of sympathy. Damon looked close to tears. He was still looking from face to face, searching for – what? Validation? Acceptance? Whatever it was, he did not find it. Even Gaila took a step away from him. It had struck Ben before that he didn't know these people; now he saw that Damon didn't really know them either.

Damon suddenly moved. He strode across the room to

where Milo stood, gripping the laptop in both hands. He grabbed for him. No one expected it. No one had the chance to move. Damon pulled the back of Milo's shirt free and, with his other hand, he grabbed the gun. He fumbled, nearly dropped it, then found his grip. Milo whirled, but Damon pointed it at him, motioning him to keep off. Damon backed away and when he was clear, he turned and pointed it at Jones. 'I can show you,' he said, choking back tears. 'I don't even care any more. I just want to be free of this shit. It's followed me all my life. *With* this guy? You think I'd plan all this with him? No. I'm not with him. Say the word and I'll fucking shoot. I'll take his damned head off, and there will be an end to it.'

There was a shocked silence.

'Dear fellow,' Jones said. 'There's really no need.' His words were casual, but his voice betrayed him. He was nervous.

'You say you're the fucking Devil. Well, I don't know about that. I think you're a pathetic little man who likes to play games. You're clever, I'll give you that. You had us all exactly where you wanted, right from the beginning.'

Jones held out his hands, the picture of innocence. 'Some people just want to believe. You believed in Mephistopheles, didn't you? How real was he, do you suppose?'

'Well, even if you're only a man, you played us. You manipulated us just as if you *were* the Devil. So what's the difference? It doesn't matter. I don't even care any longer. But this is where it ends. I hold true to the reason I came here, even if no one believes me. You are not going to do this to anybody else.'

'This is your time,' Jones said, his voice steady. 'Rafaella.' He smiled at her. 'For so very, very long,' he said. 'Terrible times. Dark times. You stole from your friend. You killed your precious dog. You slipped a knife between a man's ribs. All that, when you had nothing to trade, when I offered you nothing.' He paused. 'Now you do.'

She shook her head. 'I don't know what you mean.'

'I'm asking you, Raffie. We don't need a computer screen between us, you and I. I *am* the game, don't you see that?' He lowered his voice. 'What do you want?'

'You know what I want.'

'Tell me.'

'I want my daughter to live.' Raffie cast a glance at Damon. There was a note of eagerness in her voice when she spoke again. 'I want her cured.'

'And you already gave everything that mattered, even your very soul. You worshipped at the feet of a false idol. You knelt at the shrine of the great god Medicine. Did he answer, do you think? He gave you nothing. You know about principles, do you not – how brittle they are, how fragile in the face of need, real, physical need, do-anything-to-make-it-stop *need*. You offered me your soul and your heart, Raffie. Now I need your hands. Kill him.'

Damon started as Raffie said, 'What?'

'The reward: your child, healthy as the day she was born.

The price: this man's life. He is nothing to you anyway, Raffie.
Now he stands in the way of everything you ever wanted.
I'll give you your daughter back. I'll give you your *life* back.'
Slowly, he smiled. 'You can have it all. Her blooming cheeks.
Her skin so clear and soft the sun practically shines through
it. Her laughter. You remember that, don't you, her laughter?
You haven't heard it in such a long time.' His voice went high
and thin. 'It hurts, Mummy. It hurts—'

'Stop it!'

'One simple thing, Raffie. So, will you do it? It is before you
at last, the thing you sought so eagerly. Reach out. Take it.'

There were sounds of protest. Ben didn't know who spoke.
'No one's killing anyone,' he cut in. 'Damon, put the gun
down. Raffie, stay where you are. Gaila—'

His sister saw what he meant, stepped forward and put
her hands on Raffie's arm. She had touched her before, to
offer comfort. Now she flexed her hands and her knuckles
gleamed white.

'Well, somebody do something,' Jones said. 'Damon, you
have a gun. Do you really have the balls? Raffie here does.
She's shown that already. She proved herself. Can you?'

Damon straightened his arm. The gun was heavy, Ben
could tell that from the way it shook in his hand. The barrel
shone back the fluorescent lights; and then they went out.

Someone screamed. It came from Raffie's direction, but it
didn't sound like her. It took Ben a moment to realise that it
must have been Gaila, that his sister must be hurt, and the

light flooded back and he saw a flash of Raffie's face, her eyes wide, the gleam of the blade Ashley had used on his hand held in front of her. Then the darkness rushed back.

'Gaila!' he shouted.

'I'm all right. She pushed me, took me by surprise—'

The lights came back on. Raffie was standing right behind Damon, and she still held the blade. Damon didn't know she was there. Something in him had gone dead. He barely seemed conscious that he had a gun in his hand, that he was pointing it at a man. He showed no sign of knowing where he was.

'Raffie, sit down. Damon, drop the gun.' Ben snapped out the words, but he wasn't sure either of them had heard. Raffie was intent on Damon; Damon stared into space; and Jones looked at them both, his head tilted.

Ben stepped forward. Something inside him clenched when he reached out and touched the gun's cold barrel, just lightly. He didn't want Damon to react, to panic or pull away. If he did that, Ben wasn't sure what would happen. The gun was still unsteady in Damon's hand. The bullets could go anywhere; they could maim or kill. He wrapped his fingers around the barrel. He half expected it to explode in his hand, for heat to blossom under his fingertips. 'Let it go,' he whispered. 'You can't win, Damon, you know you can't. Not with this guy. The only way out of this is to walk away.'

'I'm not with him. I'm not.'

'All right. We see that now.'

Damon woke at last. His eyes focused and he looked at Ben, nodding before he passed him the weapon.

Ben took it. He had never held a gun before. It felt odd in his hands, heavy, but not as heavy as he'd expected. He didn't know what to do with it; he knew he could never use it. After a moment he bent and dropped it between his feet. If someone tried to snatch it, he'd just have to stop them, but he didn't want its cold touch on his skin any longer. He turned so that he could see Raffie's face. Her eyes were full of tears, but her expression was full of hatred. She hadn't relaxed her grip on the blade.

'Raffie, you don't need that. *No.*'

A tear spilled from her eye and rolled down her cheek. She shook her head, a barely perceptible movement.

'*Raffie.*'

She didn't spare any words; she just raised the weapon higher, a snake preparing to strike, and Ben didn't think. He stepped in, pushing Damon out of the way and blocking her path. 'I said *no.* Are you crazy? You think stabbing this man will make your little girl better – that it'll make anything better?'

She heaved a ragged breath.

'Trust me, Raffie, it won't.'

'I – I have to,' she said. 'I have to believe, Ben. If I don't—' Her eyes went empty. 'What does that mean?'

'It doesn't matter what you believe. All that matters is what's real. If you do this, you'll be taken away and they'll throw away the key. You'll never see your daughter again. Whatever she has to go through, she'll go through it alone. Do you want that, really? Is it what *she* would want?' He paused. He expected Jones to cut in, to goad her along, but he didn't. 'I know you're desperate to believe, but that doesn't make this man's words real. You can't trust him.'

. 'You're taking away my chance.' She whispered the words. The blade wasn't pointing towards Damon any longer; it wavered, somewhere between him and Ben.

'No, I'm not. You—' *You never had a chance* were the words that came to mind, but Ben couldn't say them. Still, by the look in Raffie's eyes, he knew that she had heard them anyway.

She crumpled. The hand holding the blade dropped to her side and she almost let it slip from her fingers. Then she threw it and it clattered across the table, smearing a swath through Ashley's blood.

A sharper noise rang out. It was Jones. He was clapping his hands, slowly. 'Oh, what a show,' he said. 'What a hero! You splendid boy!' His face twisted. 'You weren't so brave when she burned, were you?'

Ben closed his eyes, slowly.

Jones mimicked his voice. '*What did you say?* You heard what I said, Ben. Don't pretend. When your mother burned her hand, you didn't stop her, did you? You watched. You breathed it all in. And then you ran to your room and closed the door behind you, just like a little boy, and you didn't come out until you'd had a good long cry, did you?'

Ben couldn't speak.

'And then, and then, and then . . . you play the good guy if you wish it, boy. *Golden Boy*. One day, you'll have to be honest with yourself. Maybe that day will be today.' Jones whipped his head around. 'Maybe it's time to talk about you, Gaila.'

She looked startled.

'*You* wouldn't have let her burn, would you? Your own mother?'

'Shut up,' Ben said. 'You've said enough. Look, we came here for a reason. If no one else is going to do it, I'll do it myself.' He reached out and grabbed the laptop Milo was holding. Milo hadn't fought when Damon took the gun and he didn't fight now; Ben felt his grip tighten, just for an instant, and then he let go. The computer was in Ben's hands. It was thin and cool and it made him think of the key – that perfectly formed cross of confusion.

The screen still showed the office in which they stood. The man who had been sitting at the desk was no longer doing so. He stood off to one side, his face in shadow, as if his identity was somehow hidden. Where it had said 'WAIT', there were no words at all.

Ben hit *Escape* and the image shrank back at once. A picture Ben had seen a thousand times before took its place: an arid landscape topped by a mighty dune, the sun beating down on it all. It was a standard background, the same one he'd always used at work. A single row of folders was arranged down the left side of the screen. He ignored them. Working one-handed he moved the cursor to the bottom corner, then hit the right-click button. Two options appeared and he selected *Explorer*.

'You're missing the best part,' Jones said.

Ben glanced up. He had no idea how Jones knew what he was doing. Probably the man didn't. He was just making a pronouncement and hoping everyone *assumed* he knew.

He viewed the available computer drives. When he'd worked for the company they'd had two servers to store all their data. Now there were three. He knew the servers themselves sat in a small room off the main office. Fans cooled them day and night.

'You really should check out the player database first,' Jones said. 'We have all the time in the world, don't we? It is rather fun.'

Ben scanned the list of folders kept on Server 1. None had names he could recognise; the logical filenames had been scrambled, replaced by random letters and numbers. He began to highlight them anyway. He didn't have to choose; he could simply delete everything. Maybe it would achieve nothing, but he could only try. He'd never had any real confidence in their plan anyway. The company would restore everything tomorrow, and everyone would play on regardless, sending in those awful requests. But at least they'd have done *something*. It was some kind of protest. And if it was done, Ben could get the others to leave. They could all turn their back on this whole affair, and see if they could live with whatever remained.

'You can look up all their requests, you know.'

Ben twitched. He knew he could. He didn't need reminding.

What do you want?
GIVE ME TEN MINUTES WITH HIM ALONE NO ONE THERE.
What do you want?
I JUST WANT TO BE ABLE TO KEEP MY HOUSE
What do you want?

Ben shook his head. He didn't need to know what people wanted. He'd seen it all already, their innermost desires, their hopes and fears and desperation.

'You can see anybody's game. Just go to the player database and search for their name. It's quite simple. Even I could do it. Your sister's, for example.'

Ben heard someone catch their breath. He knew that it was Gaila.

'That's it,' Jones said, a greedy look on his face. 'Go on.'

'No – Ben, don't!' she said.

Ben frowned. He hadn't accessed the database. He hadn't typed in her name. It was as he had thought; Jones was trying to convince her of what he was doing, even though he couldn't have any idea. He was manipulating them after all. But why would Gaila be worried? She'd asked the game for the job in Japan, and in return she'd given it – *him*. He knew that.

He paused, stopped moving the cursor down the list of files. What was it that she'd said, when they gathered at Damon's house?

I told it things I never should have . . . They were my words, my – things . . . I want them all back.

He'd thought she was talking about the way she'd got him down to London. No: the way she'd *betrayed* him. He shook his head again. That wasn't a word he would have thought of on his own – betrayed. It was Jones talking, in his mind – Jones' words, Jones' way of thinking. He didn't have to let it infect him.

He reminded himself that he'd once picked up a rock and thrown it at her, his sister. Perhaps she had betrayed him, in some small way, but he'd betrayed her first.

He opened his mouth and spoke at last. 'Gaila, I'm not looking.'

'Do you know what the cross of confusion means?' Jones cut in. He held something up before their faces. It was a key, the same as the one Ben had used to get them inside, a simple black cross ending in a curve.

No one replied.

'It means: question everything.' Jones sounded like a teacher. 'It was first used by the Romans who questioned the truth of Christianity. Of course, some say that Satan is the deceiver, the biggest there ever has been or ever will be, that he is the source of all confusion.' He smiled. 'But now it is taken to mean rather more than that. Question religion.

Question authority. Question *everything*. Question yourself.'
He flipped the key in his hand so that the curve was upper-most, the cross inverted.

'You surely cannot be content to let the mystery lie there, Ben. The questions are all in your mind already, are they not? The only thing left to do is answer them.'

Ben pressed his lips together. He couldn't stop himself from shooting a glance towards Gaila. What he saw shocked him. Her face was drawn, her eyes wide and panicked; she saw him looking and mouthed one word, 'Don't'.

And she had given him up so easily. The game asked for him and she'd lured him to London, just like that, at once and without thinking.

But she hadn't known what it would lead to. Anyway, Ben had played his part in that too, hadn't he? It was he who'd taken her to the meeting, who had agreed to this madness. He was the one who had brought them here, the one who'd opened the door. He looked again at the object in Jones' hand. He'd let them in. For all of them, it was Ben who'd been the key.

He didn't want to think about what that might mean. He had to get them out, extricate them all as quickly and cleanly as he could. For that, he needed to finish what he was doing. He looked down at the screen and blinked. It didn't show the list of files any longer. Now it had boxes all over it, plain text boxes on a grey background. He read the label on the first of them.

SURNAME

Letters began to appear in the box next to it. C ... A ... S ...

Ben shifted his grip, moving his fingers clear of the letter keys. He was sure he hadn't touched any of them. He didn't know how it was happening.

S ... I ... D ... Y

The screen vanished, replaced by a list of search results. There weren't many, only eight or so, and he could see Gaila, her full name: Abigail Enid Cassidy. It stood out, longer than all the other names.

He remembered what she'd told him. *No one knows my middle name is Enid. No one. I mean, who the hell would I tell?* And he remembered the expression on her face when she'd said, *It knows things.*

Now it was doing things. Her name flashed, as if he'd clicked on it.

'Ben, what are you—'

'I'm not doing anything.'

Gaila subsided, as if satisfied by his answer, but the screen changed again. This time it was all about her, starting with her address at the top of that silver tower. There was her date of birth: today. And beneath that, in larger letters, it said: REQUESTS.

What do you want?

THERE'S A JOB IN JAPAN. I DIDN'T GET IT. THEY'RE ARSEHOLES. I WANT THAT FUCKING JOB.

Seen like that, in plain black text on a pale grey background, the words lost something of the spirit of Gaila, his sparky, reckless sister, who shocked him and delighted him and made him laugh. They seemed stark. Even a little unhinged. *Selfish.* He imagined sitting in the office with the rest of the staff, shouting out some of the worst of the requests that strangers had put into the game. Would they have singled this one out? He thought perhaps they might. He didn't want to think of Gaila like that, as one of *them.*

He couldn't help but run his eyes down the screen anyway.

THE PRICE: Ask your brother to come to London. Tell him to come as soon as he can, because you're going to need to book a flight.

He knew that part of it already, but there was more text below that. Even without looking at it directly, he thought he could make out his name. He read down, hating himself.

I WANT HER GONE

He closed his eyes, opened them again.

I WANT HER GONE SHE NEVER CARED ABOUT ME ONLY ABOUT BEN, AND I'VE HAD IT SHE ISN'T EVEN PROUD OF ME I WISH SHE WAS DEAD

Gaila, he thought.

'Ben, no.' Gaila knew. She had seen the look on his face and she knew. Ben wished he could unsee the words, to forget he'd grasped the meaning behind them. She could never have meant them. She'd only written something in haste, perhaps even when she was drunk. Of course, he'd always known that she and Cass didn't get along. It wasn't a secret. But this? And she'd *believed* in the game. She'd believed it would work, and she'd wished it anyway. But she *couldn't* have meant it. Of course she couldn't, because this is what she'd wanted to undo, wasn't it? These were the words she'd wanted to erase, the thing she'd wanted to take back. This was the reason she was here.

He took a shallow breath. The words on the screen shifted and swam before his eyes. He blinked and read down. Below his sister's crazed request, it said:

THE PRICE: Tell him the meaning of your name.

That couldn't be right. That was part of the *other* price, wasn't it? It was what she'd done in exchange for the job in Japan, the one she hadn't even taken. She'd had to bring him to London and tell him the meaning of her name. That was what she'd told him.

But the words on the screen told him something else. There had been *two* requests. And the price for the second, the one that would, in her mind anyway, secure the death of their mother – *she had done it already.*

Not only that, but she hadn't even done it at once. She'd had to wait until Ben had come down to London. She hadn't been playing the game when he'd arrived at her apartment; she'd been packing her things, ready to fly halfway around the world. So she'd typed these words before that, submitted her request, and then, even after she'd had time to think about it, to reconsider, she'd done what she had been asked.

He looked up and met her eyes. Hers were wide, horrified, and he was glad. He could barely see her as his sister any longer. He saw instead a young, foolish girl, who cared about no one but herself: her looks, her money, her clothes, her career. Those were the things she cared about and there was nothing beyond them, not the past or family or anything; not even him.

'Ben, I didn't mean it.'

'I know you did.'

Her eyes filled with tears. 'I may have done, once. But not now. I changed my mind.'

'Changed your mind? What if she had died, Gaila? What if some stupid coincidence had taken her from us – would you have changed your mind then? What if you really had some kind of control over her life – what would you have done?' Ben shook his head. He knew what she'd have done, could see it all already.

'Ben, please.'

He couldn't speak. He didn't know if it was rage or sorrow that stopped his words; probably it was both.

'Fucking hell, Ben. Always the Golden Boy, right to the last, aren't you? You always were. You're always so ready to judge me.'

Now he was astonished. '*Judge* you? Gaila, you wanted her dead. Do I really have to judge that? Does anyone?'

She sniffed back tears.

'Oh dear, dear. Families. Such hotbeds of pain and simmering resentment.'

'Shut the fuck up, Jones. This is nothing to do with you.'

'Ben, you know I didn't mean it, not really,' Gaila said. 'You have to know that. You're – you're all I've got, and if you're honest about it, you'll know you always were.'

To that, Ben had no answer.

After a moment, it was Jones who spoke. His voice was so low that Ben wasn't sure, at first, that he'd really heard it. He said his sister's name: '*Gaila.*' There was tenderness in the word. There was love. 'Gaila, come to me.' He held out his hands towards her, ready to fold her within them. 'You'll never be alone, my child,' he said. 'Him – all you've got? No. What a pity that would be. But it isn't true, my dear. You came here fearing for your immortal soul. Of all of you, don't you see, you are the one who has the least to fear? You gave it to me, as should have been. I will keep it for you. I'll always care for you. You'll never be hungry, Gaila. You will never be alone.'

He drew a heavy sigh, closing his eyes, savouring it. 'My father is joy,' he said. 'Did you think that was an accident, Abigail?'

'But how—'

'I knew your name before you were even born. I have always known it.' There was a light in his eyes, a smile playing at his lips.

'Gaila, don't listen to him,' said Ben. 'He'll use you. He doesn't care about you.'

'So says the young man who gave you that scar.' Jones gestured towards it and Gaila's hand went to her cheek.

'That was—'

'What? An accident? Or something you did, only deciding afterwards that it was a mistake? You really are most tolerant of your own misdeeds, young man. We must see if we can't do something about that.

'Now, Gaila. We should have a chat about family, now that you are of age and alone in the world.'

'I don't know what he's trying to do,' Ben said. 'But don't listen. He'll try and rip us apart, Gaila. This whole thing, that's all he's ever tried to do. We should just go.'

She shot him a look of hatred so pure it took his breath away.

'Of course she wants to hear,' Jones said. 'It's something different from what you've always known, isn't it Gaila? From what you've been told. *The black sheep of the family. There's bad blood in you, Gaila. You've got an evil streak, Gaila. There's no curing it, Gaila.*' He said it all with love, crooning to her. 'You don't need to be afraid of such things any longer. I know it hurt you to be alone. I know it hurt when the man you saw as your father left you behind. He couldn't take you with him, could he? He held you in his arms as an infant and he cried. He used to watch you sleep, Gaila, did you know that? He saw the delicacy of your bones, the fragility of your breath, and he used to fear you would die before the morning came. And yet he still left you. He saw you and he loved you and knew you were never his.

'Cass never watched you sleep, did she, Gaila? She was grateful to turn her back on you. To forget you ever existed, to forget someone put his seed in her and left it to grow. She wanted to forget all the questions you made her ask herself, every time she looked at you.

'You're my daughter, Gaila. Now you know why you're here; because I called to you, and you heard. You answered. This is where you belong.'

Ben gawped. The words were insane, but Jones didn't look insane; he looked overwhelmed with love. He looked like a father, declaring himself to his child. And there was something else. Ben reached for it, the idea forming in his mind, and instead he remembered standing in Gaila's apartment, his sister next to him, grinning down into that wide, terrible view. He remembered the way she'd responded to it, grinning while he'd shrunk away. The words in his mind, when he had: *All of this can be yours.*

'Gaila,' Ben said, his voice breaking over her name. 'You can't listen. It doesn't even make sense. Mum always said that your father died. She said he died before you were born.'

'And now he is risen,' Jones said. 'My dear, I *am* your father. We are all one, if not in flesh, then in another – *iteration*.'

'Remick,' she whispered. 'My real dad – Cass said his name was Remick—'

'And a charming name it was. I was very fond of it at the time. For my current purposes, it amused me to take something a little plainer. Jones: it is an *everyman* sort of a name, don't you think?'

'So it wasn't you.'

He brought his hands together in front of his chest, his fingers steepled. 'Of course it was me. Now, Gaila, I cannot pretend to offer you cheap jewellery with cheaper sentiments. What I can offer you is – ah, but I've given you so much already, haven't I? A face that people worship. A body for sin.' He gave a wolfish grin. 'But I think you'll find that I *can* be your father. And you are of an age to choose. You did choose, didn't you, after all? You decided to play.'

She was crying again, this time silently.

'Leave her alone,' Ben said.

Ashley cut in. 'If 'e can find out your name and get your picture, 'e can find out you din't 'ave a dad. It wouldn't be that hard.' He grunted the words; it clearly pained him to speak.

'Oh, Ashley, Ashley. I would ask you not to interfere with me and mine. There's still so much between the two of *us*, don't you think? Don't forget, you got away fucking lightly when I took your finger.'

He turned to Ben. 'And you. Golden Boy, who never puts a foot wrong. I'm afraid that you're not my son. There's nothing of me in you. No, you were hers: all hers and the man who left you. Once to go to war, and again – well, that was a matter of choice, wasn't it?' He sneered.

'Fuck you, Jones.'

'Ah, a little spirit. You have that at least. There's hope for you yet.' Jones held out his hand towards Gaila. 'Come, my dear.'

She wrapped her arms tightly around herself. She stayed where she was.

'Don't.' The voice was quiet but they all heard it anyway. It was Raffie. 'You can't, Gaila. You can't go with him. He – he'll lead you on and fool you and lie to you.'

'I do not lie!' Jones suddenly yelled. His cheeks flushed. Those standing closest – Ben and Simon – flinched.

'Woman, you call yourself a mother? You stood by and watched your daughter suffer. At least Gaila's mother had some balls. You know the difference between her and you? If Cass had been standing here, a knife in her hand and the chance to save her child, she'd have used it. She wouldn't even have thought twice.'

He licked his lips. 'You know what Cass did? She gave herself to me. She signed her soul away, not just to play some stupid game, but because she wanted to save him.' He gestured towards Ben. 'I played her, though, just as I played you. It was always a game, don't you see? All of it's a game. Show them your hand, Ben.' He waited. 'Don't be coy! You know exactly what I mean. Show them my mark on your skin.'

Slowly, Ben reached out his hand, palm upward. He didn't look at it, but he knew what they could see; he'd been seeing it all his life. A thin white scar snaked across his palm where he had once been cut. He never had quite been able to remember why or when it had happened.

'You signed your name in my book, Benjamin. You wrote it in blood. A melodramatic occasion, but that was how we did things back then. You were just a child; you barely even remember. But your mother does.' Jones' eyes glinted. 'She tried to burn her own mark away, did she not?' He waved a hand and suddenly Ben could smell it, the charring of his mother's skin. He could hear her shriek echoing in his ears.

'And a part of you hated her for it, didn't you – her strangeness? You never imagined that you were the root of it all. She was lost in confusion, always trying to find the best way out, the best thing to do for *you*, and all you did was hate her for it as much as you loved her. After she gave all that she had for you! She traded her soul, the most precious thing she possessed, so carefully kept, so carefully guarded, in return for yours. Of course, you were still too young to give it away, but she wasn't to know that, was she? She thought you'd done it already, and she did what she had to do to save you. It was a fine joke. I laughed. Oh, I laughed until I cried!

'And now I'm back for you, Ben. I always collect, once I've had a taste. Will you stand beside your sister?' His voice became low, resonant, and suddenly there was silence: an intense, waiting silence.

A low chuckle broke it. 'But of course you won't. You would throw a rock in her face, wouldn't you, Ben, rather than do that. You turned away. You were right here, under my roof, taking my money, working for me, and – what? *You wouldn't even play the game.*'

'I—'

'No, I realise you knew none of this. You're ignorant, Ben. You stand there before us as a fine young man – isn't that how he appears, everyone? And inside, he knows nothing; what he wants to do with his life, who he wants to be; who he *is*. Now he cannot even hold his sister's hand while she cries.'

'Stop it.' Gaila spoke softly, but they all heard.

'Oh, my dear.' Jones sounded as if his heart was breaking. 'I feel your fear. I feel your pain. I do. I can take it all away. Will you let me do that, Gaila? You can have everything you ever wanted. My daughter: there are certain privileges that go with that. But most of all, you'll have a father again.'

'And be your toy? I'm not that. I'm not anyone's toy.'

'Ah. You are – magnificent.'

Anger gathered in her features, creasing her forehead, narrowing her eyes.

'My dear, please don't. You look quite ugly when you do that.'

'Where were you? If you were really my father, where were you?'

'Ah – the "my father is the one who changed my nappies" argument, is that it? Well, that didn't mean much to him when he left, did it?'

'Stop it.'

'You're free now. You're of age. All that was a long time ago. You can go wherever and to whomever you like. Just don't take too long about it, Abigail, because the choice will not remain open to you for ever.'

She pressed her lips into a thin line. Her eyes narrowed and they looked blacker than ever. In that moment, Ben thought that she *could* be Jones' daughter. But there was something new in Gaila's face too, a knowledge, and it made him want to shrink from her. It passed through his mind that their mother had been right. His sister did have an evil streak. There was badness in her, something that could never be destroyed, because it was a part of who she was.

His sister's focus changed and he realised that she was staring at him. Her eyes had always pierced him. She had a way of looking that made him think she knew every thought that passed through his mind and he found, now, that he couldn't meet her eye. He could still feel her gaze on him as he turned away, and it was like the touch of a cold hand.

TWO

'It's time we were a little more open with each other,' said Theodore Jones. He had taken his seat once more at his desk, had clasped his hands behind his head. 'It is time that some things were brought out into the light. Dragged out, if you like. Kicking and screaming.' He looked at Ashley, who was the only other one of the party now seated.

'Honesty,' Jones said. 'I'm a great believer in it. They call me the Father of Lies, can you believe that?' He raised his eyebrows. 'In some sense they may be right, though I may be more fairly called their midwife. I myself do not lie. It is distasteful to me. Sometimes, of course, I am so honest I am not believed. Click here and sign away your soul for all eternity! And they do! Why? Of course they don't believe.'

'And you six – sorry, *seven* – little liars, all in a row. You none of you are honest, not even with yourselves. You lie to yourselves about your motives. You lie about how you feel.

You lie by your secrecy and your – why, by your lies!' He grinned more broadly than ever.

'You say that I am the Devil.' He held up his hand. 'All right: *I* say I am the Devil. Do you believe that? Think of an answer. Perhaps you're lying about that too. Perhaps you would never whisper to a soul what you really believe, in your innermost heart.

'And yet when faced with a computer screen, people do tell the truth, don't they? They told *me* the truth, when they played my game. *Acheron* isn't just the River of Woe, or even another name for Hell itself; it can also mean a place of healing. And there should be more truth in the world, don't you think?' He stared at Ashley. 'Really, don't you?'

No one replied, but Jones wasn't waiting for an answer. 'Ben here thinks that I chose you, picked you all out in some way. But I barely needed to, did I? No one forced you to come here. No one made you break into my offices in the dead of night, like common thieves. You chose yourselves. Aside from my daughter, none of you is very special. You know what you are? Ordinary. You're ordinary people, and all of you are more than happy to be twisted. I never did anything to any of you. Think about that. You put your own desires into the game. You told it what you wanted and I merely replied. You created your own temptation and you wallowed in it. You know what the real beauty is? You *need* me.

'If there is no Devil, where did the evil come from? Who nurtured it? Who called to it?

'You're here, each of you – save this coward,' he looked at Ben before continuing, 'because you chose to walk into the dark. And what did you see? According to Nietzsche, if you gaze long enough into the abyss, the abyss will also gaze back into you. But what if it didn't? What if there was only silence? A long, cold silence, and nothing more, for ever and ever. Is that what you want – is that what anyone wants?

'No. I tell you the truth. You created this situation without me; you created it with your own avarice and envy and pride. You aren't here because I manipulated you, because I knew things you don't. You're here because of your own guilt.' He paused. 'If there was no Devil, if there was never a Devil, you would have to invent him. And perhaps you would create the Devil you deserve.'

He looked into each of their faces. 'Perhaps you did. Perhaps you called to me, and I came. And now there is no going back from this night. So be careful how you act. Be careful what you say. Lies are poison, and poison must be drawn. There is a reason the name Lucifer means light-bringer. Are you with me? Do we walk together, deeper into the dark? Do we finish what you began?'

Abandon all hope, Ben thought. He saw in his mind a dark stairway, leading down. A chipped and mouldering lintel. *Abandon all hope, ye who enter here.* According to Dante, they were the words written over the entrance to Hell. And at the same time he remembered a glossy image on a silver screen, a group of laughing kids wearing T-shirts emblazoned with a slogan: *Would you?*

'Well, Ben? You feel the dark waiting for you, don't you? I know you do. The cold dark. The endless night. The silence. The thing you stare into that doesn't answer.'

Ben looked away from him and realised that Ashley had started to cry. He was not making a sound, but Ben could see it in the way his shoulders heaved. Ashley didn't try to quell it and he didn't look up.

Jones reached out across the desk and put his hand on the man's head. He rested it there, not moving, a parody of some priestly benediction. 'Let it out,' he said. 'If thine hand offends thee, cut it off! I see how the serpent twists inside you, Ashley. I see how it squeezes your heart.

'But first! We must go back to the beginning, must we not, to the thing that started you all on this path. This night of chronicles and revelations and lamentations.' He winked. 'Or have you forgotten her? Ah, you who pretend to care.'

'Jessica?' said Damon.

'Jessica! Exactly. Well done, that man. A lovely girl, was she not? Did you enjoy the funeral?' He raised his eyebrows at Ben.

Ashley had stopped moving. He raised his head, watchful, and then remained motionless.

'Lovely, lovely. You knew her when you were young, Ben, though you probably don't remember much. She said things to you about your father – certain things I suggested she should ask. She didn't really understand what she was saying, but it made you rather angry. She was so much smaller than you were at the time, but still, you pushed her down in the snow. She cut her cheek, as I recall. Some people simply don't change, do they, Gaila? What an angel. What a little Golden Boy he was.'

'Jus' fucking do it,' Ashley said. His words were distorted.

Jones placed a hand behind his ear. 'What's that? Ah, you're ready now, is that it? I hear and I hasten, young man. But all in good time. You, Ben, come first; of course you do. Take a look at the wealth of information you hold in your hands. You already know Jessica's final request, but do you know all? It's quite poignant, actually.'

Ben hesitated. He didn't want Jones driving his actions any longer. The man had been in control of this from the start; that was enough, without allowing his claws to sink in deeper. Gaila's face was tear-stained. She was hardly paying attention to Jones; there were too many thoughts passing across her features.

'Do it, Ben,' Damon said. 'Let's end this thing. Do as he says and then we can all walk away.'

'If he's really telling the truth about Mephistopheles,' Raffie said. 'If the body's really gone.'

'Heavens, don't you listen? He's long gone! Believe me when I say he hardly matters at all.'

'Go on, Ben.' The voice was Gaila's. She was listening after all. 'We came here because of her, didn't we? Just take a look.'

Ben only hesitated for a moment before he typed in Jessica's name. There was only one name in the search results and he clicked on it. '"Request",' he read from the screen. '"I want you to prove to me that this is real." There's no price listed.'

'I gave her that one for free,' Jones said. 'I felt I owed her that at least, didn't I? She was of certain use to me, when she was young.'

'How did you prove it?'

'How did I prove it? I think I'll rename you Thomas, Benjamin. The one who doubts. You do still doubt, don't you? Why, I sent her a guide. Not an on-screen guide, such as many of you have seen, but a real one.' He tilted his head. 'Didn't I, Ashley?'

Ashley looked away. Then he covered his face.

'A simple nod will do. No? Never mind. I'll just tell them. Ashley here knocked on her door the moment she'd finished typing her request. After all, a delay wouldn't be quite the part, would it? I had something to prove, after all. And why did you do that, Ashley?'

'The game told me to.'

'The game told you to. Very good. So, there you were. And what did you say to her?'

Ashley looked up. 'The words you put in my mouth. I said I'd come to show 'er what was real. I remember she looked at me and she sort o' laughed, like it were a joke. Then she din't laugh.'

'And why not, Ashley?'

'Because – because she believed it, I s'pose.'

'And so she asked you in.'

He nodded.

'And you became friends of a sort, didn't you? Friends, because both of you were alone. And neither of you were people who liked to be alone. Particularly not her, because things started happening around her, didn't they? What do you know about that, Ashley – perhaps you could tell us?'

Ashley closed his eyes. His face paled. He looked like a man in despair.

'You will tell, Ashley. Do I need to do it? My telling will be worse, I fear.'

Ashley winced. 'I started to do things. It was what the game made me do. I wanted 'er – to be my friend. I asked it if I could see 'er again. And the game told me the price.' He drew a shuddering breath. 'I went into the mill at night. The game told me when and it gave me the entry code. So I'd go in an' tramp along the corridor above 'er place. I knocked on the walls. I scratched along 'em with my nails. Childish things. It were stupid, just stupid stuff, it din't mean anything.'

'So neat, wasn't it? Poor Jessica. Imagine it from her point of view. She'd moved out of her aunt's home the year before; she wanted to be independent. Funny, isn't it, how you people take that step? You desire to be alone, and then your alone-ness drives you mad.

'*She* thought she was going mad, didn't she, Ashley?' Jones smirked. 'Poor, poor girl. There she was, all alone, all – *independent*, and she found she couldn't sleep at night because of the sounds, those odd sounds that she *must* have been imagining, that simply must have been phantasms of her troubled mind. Because she was troubled, wasn't she, Ashley? Some little disturbance when she was young, I believe. Her beloved mother, dead on the moors near where she lived, buried by the snow for some days – and Jessica, the poor little mite, left all alone. And the person who could have helped her – your mother, Ben – actually forgot her, in her haste to protect her precious boy. There is little wonder her imagination trespassed down such terrible roads. Does that sound like the basis for a settled adulthood to you?

'She wasn't settled. She was, in fact, most decidedly unsettled.'

He jabbed a finger towards the laptop and Ben turned to it, reading further down the screen. '"I want it to stop",' he said. 'The answer was, "You have nothing to trade."'

'No! Well, she didn't, did she, Ashley? And after all, you wanted to see her, so very, very badly. You did see her, didn't you? You'd turn up at her door in her darkest moments, and after those awful nights – well, she needed you, didn't she? A friend. She needed a *friend*.'

Ashley passed a hand across his face. It was his right hand, his whole hand; he slid the other across the desk, drawing it in towards him, and it left a streak of blood behind it.

'Then you started to ask for more, didn't you, Ashley? But I'm rushing ahead. Onward, please, Benjamin.'

'"Please make it stop. There are ghosts. I can hear them all around me. Make it stop." Again – nothing to trade, nothing to trade. Wait—' Ben frowned, reading without speaking, and then said: '"I want it all to stop." And it says: "Request accepted". What does that mean?'

Jones' lip twitched. 'What do you take it to mean, dear boy? What would anyone?'

'There's no price written here. You just agreed to it.' He thought. '*I want it* all *to stop.* That was when she killed herself.' He looked at Jones. 'The game accepted her request. So – what, you agreed to it? You made her kill herself on purpose?'

'Whatever are you suggesting – that the Devil would twist anyone's words? Why, if that were the case, what kind of Devil would I be?' Jones winked. 'You cannot deny that she received what she asked for.'

'But that wasn't—'

'How do you know? You cannot know what was in her heart of hearts. Lying there, night after night, terrified. She would stare up at the ceiling, her eyes wide open in the dark, just listening for what might come. And after a time she started hearing other sounds, things that weren't even there. She always was a little – *unsettled*, as I said. It occurred to her, you see, that her poor dear mother had come back. She had returned from the icy moor to find out why her little girl had never come to find her, where she lay half buried in the snow, the cold seeping into her bones. Yes – she thought her own mother had come back, but changed somehow; her mother in some terrible form. She cried about that so hard, didn't she, Ashley? All of her fears, her innermost sorrows, she told them all to you. And you held her in your arms, I believe. You offered her comfort.' His countenance darkened. 'What a goodly fellow. What a – what a *friend*.'

Ashley began to cry again. No one approached; no one offered to comfort him.

'You give me too much credit, you see.' Jones smiled around at them. 'I did nothing of this. You were the architects. Yours were the hands, yours the hearts. I simply facilitated. Isn't that what they call it these days?' He waved a hand around the office, as if he could make it all disappear, revealing what lay beneath. Ben had the sudden image of something rotting under the floors, behind the walls.

Jones gave a laugh. 'Ah, Ashley, you thought it meant something, didn't you? The things you shared with her. Those most intimate moments. You actually thought it might lead to something. You had your picture taken together, presented it to her in a silver frame. Beautiful! There you were, stuck in some dead-end village, and you thought you'd found a path, didn't you? A narrow and difficult path, but one that led out. One that would lead to something else: sunny skies and picket fences and kisses. Oh, yes, you dreamed of those, didn't you?'

Ashley shook his head, more in despair than denial.

'But Jessica didn't ask for friendship, did she, Ben? She didn't ask for any of the usual things. She didn't want money'

– he looked at Simon – 'or power, or health, or the return of a loved one. Or, indeed, their removal. She only wanted one more thing from me, didn't she? Just one last request. But you've seen that before, of course. You know what it is already. What you don't know is what happened before that.' He gestured towards the screen.

Ben read down, though of course Jones was right. He already knew what Jessica had asked for. But what was written there was something else.

INFORMATION: ASHLEY BOLTON

I want to be with her can you make her want to be with me too

He blinked. Why was this under Jessica's account?

INFORMATION: ASHLEY BOLTON

I want us to be together. I want us to be more than friends

And another: INFORMATION, and a paperclip symbol next to it, indicating an attachment. Ben clicked on it and a box appeared on the screen, nothing but a blank white space, and then blackness filled it. It took him a moment to realise it was a photograph. The quality was poor, the texture grainy. It had been taken at night.

At first he thought the subject was a pale cross, but then he made out the wooden frame of a window, its panes filled with darkness. He blinked. There was something else there, not seen through them, but beneath them. Someone was crouching below the window, just out of sight. It was a man wearing dark clothing, and he was holding something against the wall. Ben thought it was a short piece of wood. He imagined the sound it would make, a dry scraping against the stone. He wondered how that would seem to anyone inside the building, someone who was trying to find sleep, to forget their strange imaginings.

He looked up, puzzled. He couldn't work out why the photograph was there, in the record of Jessica's game and not Ashley's. Then he did. 'You *told* her? You let Jessica know what Ashley had done?'

Ashley sniffed miserably.

Jones made a brief gesture, a magician revealing his trick.

'But how? You knew where he was going to be, I suppose. So you followed him, took this picture—'

Jones laughed. 'Why have a dog and bark yourself? No, I did not creep about in the dark with a camera, Benjamin. Don't be silly. Do you really imagine me doing that?' He winked. 'But I had other players, many of them, all wanting this or that. It wasn't difficult to give one of them a price, and quite an easy one, in comparison to some.' His eyes flicked to the cupboard at the back of the room.

'So, Ben, Jessica sees the photograph and she understands what her good friend, now her closest friend, has done. She hears all about his little antics. She remembers the way he held her while she sobbed, the way she told him her every fear; she remembers the terror she felt at the thought of her mother. The way *he'd* made her think that she had come for her. The way he made her believe that her own mother must have hated her. So why don't you tell us what it all means?'

Ben's mouth was dry. He found he couldn't speak.

'Cat got your tongue, boy? Anyone else?'

Gaila answered. 'She asked for revenge. But it wasn't—'

'It wasn't, was it!' Jones grinned.

'She wanted revenge on *him*,' Damon said quietly. 'On Ashley. Not on you. Not on the company.'

'It doesn't matter,' Ben said. 'The company was still behind it. It drove her to it. It made Ashley do the things he did. He might have been stupid, but his heart was in the right place. He wanted to be there for her.'

Jones screeched with laughter. 'Was it? Why don't you tell them, Ashley?' He jabbed a finger towards Ben. 'There's something you've missed, isn't there, Ben? Rather a lot, actually. You're really not doing a very good job. Dates and times, dear boy. You really should pay attention to dates!'

Ben looked back at the screen. The information had been transmitted to Jessica on the twelfth of April. And there it was, Jessica's last request, that single word REVENGE looming large on the screen. He scanned it again. She hadn't submitted it until two days afterwards: the fourteenth. 'There was a delay,' he said. 'You told her about Ashley two days before she asked for revenge. But that doesn't mean anything. She'd had time to think about it, that's all.'

'Is it? Really, Ashley, the time has come for you to speak. You can't leave all of this to me. The truth will out, dear boy; the truth will out. Why don't you, too, start with a date?'

Everyone waited. Slowly, Ashley raised his head. His cheeks were reddened, his eyes wet. 'Thirteen,' he whispered.

'What's that, Ashley? I can't hear you.'

'The thirteenth. I said I wanted to – see 'er, and the game told me when. It gave me a place – Jessica's apartment – and a time. Eleven oh-three, it said, and I was surprised. Not just because it were exact when it hadn't been bang on about times before, but because it was so late.' He drew a long breath. 'But I knew – I knew how we felt about each other. I thought it meant—'

Jones gave a mocking laugh and Ashley glared at him, hatred in his eyes. 'It was private,' he said. 'It was between the two of us. You said—'

'I never said anything of the sort. I do not lie, as I have told you. Do not make me tell you that again. Now, what happened on the thirteenth?'

'I was there, outside 'er door, just like you said. Just like you set it up. I waited there. I watched the second hand on my watch until it was the exact time and I knocked.'

'And she answered, didn't she?'

'Aye, she answered. She looked terrible, like she 'adn't slept. I knew as soon as I saw 'er 'ow much she needed me. 'Er face were white. 'Er eyes 'ad these dark circles underneath. But she were still beautiful.' He faltered. 'She tried to shut the door in my face, but I got there in time. I wedged my arm in the gap. It 'urt, but I din't care.'

'Of course you didn't.' Jones' voice was soft. 'Because you cared for her, didn't you? You only wanted to help.'

Ashley nodded. 'She started cryin'. She told me to get out, but I couldn't leave 'er like that. Then she let go of the door. I knew what she wanted. I – I'd asked the game, and it said yes.' He looked up, his eyes hardening. 'It wouldn't 'ave said yes if—'

'Of course it wouldn't. What then, my child?'

'She started yellin' at me. At first I couldn't tell what she was sayin'. Then I realised, and it were like—'

'Everything stopped, didn't it?' Jones prompted.

'Yes. Everythin' stopped. On the inside, anyway. She said somethin' about me being outside 'er window. I thought she must 'ave seen me; I thought she'd looked out.' His eyes narrowed. 'If I'd known what you'd done, I would 'ave found you sooner. I'd 'ave cut your throat.' He stayed where he was. He didn't move to attack Jones or anything else; he started to cry again, his breath coming in hitches.

'She said she din't want to see me any more,' he whispered. 'I – I din't even understand. I loved 'er so much. It weren't what I'd asked for, what the game *agreed*. It din't even seem like it could be happenin'. I reckon, in some part of my mind, I'd talked meself into thinkin' it weren't. I told her, I said I did it all for 'er, so I could be with 'er. An' then she slapped me. No, she – she flew at me. She hit me wi' 'er fists and she clawed at me, on'y she din't scratch me 'cause I grabbed her hands.

'I din't understand, don't you see?' He turned his eyes, full of tears, upward, as if asking for forgiveness.

'I told her it was all right, that it was all for the two of us. That we were s'posed to be together. The game said so. And we 'ad been, you know? I knew everythin' about her by then. I – I loved her. I thought she loved me. I couldn't see why she was bein' that way. She was playin' the game too, wan't she? And then I realised, that's what it was, and I laughed. She just stared at me, like she got it too.

'I kissed her.' He closed his eyes.

Jones gestured, a jab of his index finger towards Ben. Ben understood at once. He looked back at the screen, typing in Ashley's name. He scrolled down the list of the requests he'd made. 'I want us to be together,' he read. 'I want us to be more than friends.'

'And you were, weren't you, Ashley?' Jones said. 'You had asked to be friends, and you were. Then you were more than that, if only for a short time. And then – you weren't friends any longer, just as you had asked.'

Ash fought back a sob. 'She wanted me too,' he said, and then he didn't say anything else, and they stared at him. He shrunk under their gaze.

'She din't fight,' he whispered. 'Not really. It was all – pretend. The game said it would 'appen. It *gave* 'er to me.'

Gaila's mouth fell open. 'What? You fucking bastard. You

think the game can give you a person? It can't. Nothing can.'

'Quite right.' Jones made a clicking sound with his tongue. 'I think you overstepped the mark there, young man.'

'Overstepped the *mark*?' Gaila said.

'Be careful, little girl. Next I'll be thinking you don't want to be with your old dad. That might not be so good for you. It might not be good at all.' His voice lowered to a growl.

Gaila subsided, glaring at him.

Damon addressed Ashley. 'You raped her,' he said. 'You'd been tricking her all that time, and then you forced yourself on her.'

'No. It weren't like that.'

'Then how was it?'

'She cared about me too. When things 'appened to her, when she 'eard them sounds, who'd she turn to?'

'You made those sounds.'

'No, the game made them. I were just—'

'*You* made them.'

Ashley shook his head. 'It made me believe. It made 'er believe too. I thought – I thought it 'ad given us both to each other. She had me right where she wanted me, din't she? Whenever she wanted me, I was there. I loved her. We loved each other. It wan't like – it wan't what you said.'

'She hated you,' said Damon.

'No! No, she din't. That were the game too, all of it.'

'You said you didn't believe in the game.'

Jones gave a low laugh. 'That was part of it, don't you see?

Of course Ashley believed.' He held up his left hand, touching the fingers one by one, as if counting them off. 'Ashley did nasty things to her. He made her think she was haunted. He pretended to be her friend, while carrying out the worst possible deception. And all the time she turned to him, didn't she? Ah, all the myriad ways the betrayer and betrayed are bound together, one in Hell and one in Heaven. But we couldn't have that, could we? That could never last. And then he goes and has his wicked way with her. The one person she has decided to despise more than any other. In her bed. In *her*.'

Ashley made a choking sound.

'You see, the game *had* to be real, didn't it? Or what terrible thing was it that this young man had done? Ladies and gentlemen, we make our own games. We create our own devils. Otherwise, what does that say about us? About our guilt?'

He leaned over to Ashley, half closing his eyes. 'You are damned, Ashley Bolton,' he said. 'You belong to me.' He reached out and stroked his hair, mock-lovingly. 'It does not matter why, don't you see?'

'Jesus.' Ben felt sick. 'That was why she did it. She'd had one friend and he betrayed her. That was why she killed herself. But you – you're acting like your game had nothing to do with it. Like you're not culpable.'

'I'm behaving just like a Golden Boy, is that it?' Jones winked. Then he gave a smile, guileless and open. 'Not at all, dear boy. You know why? Because *that's not how it happened*.'

Ashley looked up, his face dark.

'He made a request,' Jones said, 'and if you're keeping up, it's obvious what the price was. And yet it's not quite so simple, is it, Ashley? What are we missing here, do you think?'

Ashley didn't move.

It was Ben who shook his head. The price? You took his *hand*.'

'Actually, I think you'll find I took his finger. Cheap at the price, don't you think? I should have asked for his head. But that's not quite right, is it, Ashley? Not quite. IF, it said. IF your response is granted, the price will be the little finger of your left hand. Do you accept? Well, clearly he did, didn't you, Ashley? And cut it off yourself, too. I'm almost impressed by that. Of course, he would have been feeling pretty wretched about it all by then, wouldn't you, Ashley? You probably felt you deserved it.'

'Christ,' Gaila spat.

'Not at all.' Jones smiled.

'So that was why she did it.'

'Ah – picture it. Can you? The poor girl, all alone, betrayed. She takes the only recourse she has left – runs herself a bath, a warm, foamy bath – it is her last, after all – and she climbs into it. Perhaps she was even grateful, at the end, because at least she knew those sounds would not come creeping through the walls, to haunt her endless sleep. Perhaps she even thought of her mother restored at last to her old sweet form. Who knows? Perhaps we should not ask. Some things are sacred, after all.'

Ben stared in disbelief.

Jones saw his face. 'No?'

'Her final request,' Ben said. 'Not just the date of it, but the *time*.' He studied the screen. 'It was the next day, the fourteenth, but not long after midnight. She hadn't just given up. She didn't feel there was no recourse. She believed in the game too by then, so she asked for revenge.'

'Ah.' Jones smiled. 'Well, perhaps Ashley here could shed a little light on that. Ashley? Nothing to say? Then perhaps I'll try.

'Jessica, distraught and unable to make Ashley leave, heads for the door. Ashley, protesting his lack of understanding – no defence in the eyes of the law, by the way, dear boy – prevents her from going. Isn't that the way it went?'

Ashley's face was like stone.

'So she retreats further into the apartment. And what does she see but her laptop, sitting on the desk. She runs to it and what does she find but that eternal question – *What do you want?* – how am I doing, Ashley?'

'You, of course, had followed her. Isn't that what you always did? Following, just like a little puppy, eager for a stroke. You saw what she was doing. You tried to wrest the laptop from her, but it was too late: the word was there on the screen, plain to see. You couldn't stop her in time. And then what – Ben?'

Ben scrolled down. 'It doesn't say her request was accepted.'

'What does it say, pray tell?'

'It says, "End of Record". It's – it's hidden.'

'And what did you find on the screen in Jessica's apartment?'

Ben blinked. Did Jones know about that too? Did he see everything? 'It looked like a picture of a darkened room,' he said. 'There was only one word on it: END.'

'She'd reached the end of her game,' Jones said. 'It knew, you see? I always know.' He winked at Ashley. 'But we haven't finished this night's confessional. Because Jessica said she'd tell, didn't she?'

'No,' Ashley whispered.

'Now, don't lie. I do so dislike lies. She said that she would tell, and you snapped, didn't you? You had done it all for *her*, after all. Never a thought for yourself. Now she was going to betray you. And a little part of you shut down, didn't it?'

Jones looked around the room. 'He pushed her away from the desk. She backed away and then she ran. He caught her by the bathroom. She went into it, trying to lock the door, but she was too slow. And there he found the reason for her being half dressed when she answered the door to him; late as was the hour, she had been about to take a bath. Perhaps she was going to wash away the thought of his betrayal. Perhaps she was merely trying to put off the time when she'd have to lie awake in the dark, trying to sleep, knowing that no sounds would come because it was Ashley, her *friend*, who had made them.

'And Ashley saw the bath and pushed her into it. He caught

her head as she fell, a little act of love. Or was it that you didn't want her to bruise, Ashley?'

Ben looked at the others. They were frozen; stunned.

'Still, he didn't grab the bottle and break it. She did that all by herself, didn't she, Ashley? That was your saving grace. The police would have been mighty puzzled if they'd found your fingerprints on the glass. They were puzzled anyway, of course, but then, she was a little unhinged. Her aunt had heard her wild tales of ghosts; she corroborated that. And there was nothing else very sharp in her apartment: a couple of knives in the kitchen in need of grinding, a few safety razors, no use to anyone. Nothing to cut with. Nothing to *open*. But she saw the bottle on the side of the bath and she broke it – the act of a desperate woman, a woman in despair – and she *did* try to cut, didn't she, Ashley? But she didn't try to cut herself. She tried to cut you, to make her escape, but you caught her hand and you turned the glass inward. You put it to her wrist. You're a strong fellow, aren't you? You had to be, didn't you, to make the cut so clean? There was only one misstep, but the police accepted that; they thought it was her first hesitant attempt. She improved after that, didn't she?'

Jones paused, then asked: 'What did it look like as the blood drained from her?' He licked his lips. 'Did it discolour the water all at once, or did it gradually bloom? Delicate shades of rose perhaps, deepening to pink, until at last it was incarnadine?' His eyes went distant, seeing it all. Then his eyes flicked to Milo. 'It is time,' he said.

Milo looked startled. Then he leaped forward, grabbing the blade from the table; the one Ashley had used to cut off his finger. It came away from the drying blood with a sucking sound. Its handle as well as its blade was edged with gore, but Milo didn't hesitate. He adjusted his grip on it as he moved and he raised it over his head and he swung.

Ben opened his mouth to shout but there was no time. The blade seemed to move slowly, so slowly, yet a split second later it was buried in Ashley's neck.

Blood foamed across the desk, thickly red, the flow strong and pulsing. Raffie shrieked and leaped towards the door. Everyone moved back like an ebbing tide. Ben gasped, but it was drowned by the sound Ashley made: a high *uh-uh-uh*.

He knows, was the thought that passed through Ben's mind – *he knows he's dying* – and then Ashley tried to stand.

There were more shrieks, more surging away as his life-blood gouted. Ben thought about stepping in, pressing his hands to the wound to try to staunch the fountaining blood, but he couldn't move. Then Ashley let out a wail that went on and on, and suddenly his legs buckled and he fell. He landed half across one of the chairs, and it tipped. Ashley sprawled, spilling more blood across the floor, his slick-wet hands clutching at his neck. He couldn't get a grip on the blade, didn't have the strength. His eyes widened. He fixed them on Ben, kept on looking into his face as the light started to go out of them.

When it had, Ashley went limp. He fell face down with

a crunching sound and an acrid smell filled the room. Ben covered his mouth with his sleeve. He couldn't help it; he wanted to block it all out: Ashley's death, this night, Jones' words, the horror that had come to find him.

A tutting noise broke into his thoughts. He knew who it was even before Jones spoke. 'Dear, dear me,' he said. 'Ashley always did have such trouble articulating his feelings.' And he laughed.

Rage rose inside Ben. He felt it must burst from him, but then the laughter stopped and Jones turned towards Milo.

The young man had straightened. He had a half-smile on his lips; he had triumph in his eyes. 'I did it,' he said. 'I did it! I paid the price. Now you have to do your part. You have to show me everything.'

Jones breathed in, savouring the scent that had come to fill the room. 'I have to make you just like me,' he said. 'Is that it?'

'Yes.'

'I have to make you understand the game. How it works. Show you – everything?'

Milo nodded. His arms were crossed in front of him, speckled with blood. The watch that was too big for his wrist hung from it, snatching at the light.

'That is what I want.'

'Very well,' Jones said. His eyes snapped to Damon and he nodded once. A second later, the gun was in Damon's hand.

Ben glanced at the floor where he'd dropped it, but

of course, it had gone. He didn't know when Damon had snatched it; there had only been confusion, and blood, and he couldn't think. But there was no time. Ben opened his mouth to shout a warning but Damon swung the gun towards Milo and everything exploded. White light blinded Ben and he couldn't hear; there was only a ringing in his ears, high and endless. He didn't hear the shot, but he saw Milo's head disintegrate into droplets and clumps that spattered across the wall. There was screaming too, somewhere beneath the ringing sound, but it was a long way away.

He saw people pressing back against the walls; Raffie pulling on a door handle that wouldn't open; blood on his sister's face. A sudden flashback: Gaila as a child, a rough stone lying at her feet. Her hand pressed to her cheek, bright blood smeared beneath her fingers.

He couldn't look at what was in the centre of the room, the thing that had once been a man. A man who had done awful things, but a man nonetheless, and the blasphemy of it struck him; this thing that should not have been, this transformation of humanity into flesh, into wet meat. And he realised there was another sound: laughter. Laughter that grew, that was all around him, not fading but getting stronger, louder, until it became everything; the echo of an eternity that didn't care and didn't stop.

Ben looked at Jones. The man stood quite still. He wasn't laughing now, wasn't even smiling, but he looked back at Ben with amusement still on his face. Ben suddenly wanted to hit that face, more than anything. Then Jones waved a hand and the ringing in his ears stopped, just like that. All of it stopped. Utter, black silence took its place; the silence of the tomb. The dead, cold sound of nothing at all.

THE SIXTH CIRCLE

ONE

When Ben was a boy, there was a time he'd lost all faith that his dad would ever come home. Pete had been in Afghanistan. They had used all kinds of names for what he was: *lost*. *Missing*. They had never used the word *dead*. They never said *destroyed*. They'd had so little faith – his mother most of all – that she'd moved her son miles and miles away, to a strange place she wanted him to call home: Darnshaw, a tiny village miles from anywhere. She'd told him there would be children to play with and long, sunny days, but when he got there, there had been nothing but snow. He didn't realise, not until long after his dad had been found again, that he'd been waiting all along for Pete to come striding in and sweep him up and rescue him.

Now Ben felt old inside. He knew that no one was going to rescue anybody else. They were each alone, and strangers to each other, all of them as shocked and hopeless as the next.

He didn't even know who they were. He no longer knew who *he* was.

When his dad had come back, Ben hadn't known what to do, not really. He hadn't understood all of the things that had happened to him and his mother while they were in Darnshaw. For a long time afterwards, she seemed to believe that she had met the Devil there. She said he had played with them for a time and told them what to think and what to do. She thought he had swept her along, taken her in; she thought he had fathered her daughter.

At times she had become more and more convinced about what had happened, while Ben only became more confused. In the end, he had not been sure if he even remembered the place or only her image of it. Then it had faded altogether, smudging like an unfixed charcoal drawing until nothing was left.

The memories were closer than ever, but what he remembered the most weren't the things that had happened, or the people they had happened to, but the *cold*. It had settled on his skin, but it wasn't content with that. It had wanted to possess him, to creep inside him, to eat his bones. To nestle close to his heart until he couldn't even feel any longer.

When Ben was young, he had decided he hated the snow. He hated the taste of it on the air, at once metallic and clean. He could taste it now. He was standing in a room full of blood. He couldn't get away from it and no one was going to come, to take him away. It was up to them, the people that had been thrust together – no, *gathered*, by Damon, the man who now stood tall, his arm stretched out, still holding the gun.

Ben found himself wondering if the chill inside him was the first sign of panic or shock – like something his dad might have felt, crouching in his outpost, plaster flaking from the walls as it all came down. What did they used to call it – shellshock? But Ben wasn't sure there was a name for what he felt.

The walls didn't shake. The gun held in Damon's hand was quite steady. Damon's face was steady too, his dark hair lank over his pale skin, his eyes unblinking. There was no shock on his face at all.

'You said you wanted out,' Ben whispered. 'You said – I thought you regretted it all, giving over your soul, that you wanted another chance. I thought you'd – *repented*.' It felt odd, the old-fashioned word on his lips.

The corner of Damon's mouth twisted into a sneer. Then he said, 'There *is* no out. Don't you see?'

Jones moved around the desk. Damon didn't flinch when he clapped him on the shoulder. Ben looked down at Milo. He was a crumpled ruin. His limbs were splayed like a broken doll's and his face was gone. His head was shattered, his brains blown out, spread across the walls and the floor and the desk and their faces. Ben put his hand to the bridge of his nose. The skin there was sticky. He whipped his hand away; he couldn't bring himself to look at the blood on his fingers.

'Loyalty,' Jones said. 'Once mine, always mine, isn't that so, Damon?'

Ben knew, quite suddenly and clearly, that none of them was getting out. Perhaps, he thought, this was Jessica's true revenge. The people here had known her, however slightly, and they could have helped her, but they did not. They had left her all alone. Ben had pushed her face into the snow when she was nothing but a child. He hadn't listened to her call. Damon had said he had come here for her, but Ben wasn't sure Damon really had feelings, not any more. He hadn't cared, not the way he'd pretended to; he'd only used the girl's death to manipulate them, to bring them to this place. None of them had helped her. Now she would be revenged on them all. At any moment, Jones would tell Damon to turn the gun on them. One at a time, he would finish them off. At least, then, it would be over. The whole thing would be gone, buried by deep, indifferent snow.

But Ben was overwhelmed; not by Damon's betrayal – someone who had been his friend, once – but by his own stupidity. *Of course* Damon had sided with Jones. He'd been with him from the beginning. It was Damon who'd gathered them in, reaping them like corn. Now the two of them had won, and all of it would end, and it would serve them right. A fleeting image: he saw for a moment Cass' face, her sorrow, black-veiled and hidden from the world. She would have to attend a funeral after all. He found himself wondering if she would cry for Gaila or only for him, and bitterness flooded his mouth.

'Put the gun away, Damon,' Jones said.

After a moment, Damon did. He appeared neither relieved nor angry. He simply did as he was told, slipping it into his jacket.

'That was why,' Ben said. 'You never told us what the game asked of you, or what you wanted. It was because you belonged to it already. You were never in a position to make bargains.' His voice dropped to a whisper. 'What the hell *is* it that you want?'

'Enough,' said Jones.

'What was it that he promised you?'

'He didn't have to promise me anything,' Damon muttered. 'I serve.'

'You *serve*? That's it?'

'I said enough!' Jones snapped out.

They fell silent and looked at him, but Jones' eyes went distant. 'Jessica was supposed to be a sacrifice to me, did you know that?' he said. 'When she was a child, we brought her to the moor. Your mother was there, Ben, and you were too. Do you remember?' He half smiled. 'I demanded a sacrifice. And she was, wasn't she? She was.' He stirred, shrugged. 'Ah, the good old days. The Darnshaw days. You *do* remember, don't you, Ben? My followers took her to the moor, the white moor, where the stones stood watch. She was to be mine, and you were the one who held the knife. You failed me then. You and your mother both. You thought you'd saved her.' He grinned. 'But no one ever gets away. Once tasted . . .' He gestured towards Damon. 'He made a promise to me when he was yet a child, but he didn't try to reverse it. He didn't fight it. He knew what he was doing and he did it. One has to have a certain respect for that.'

'For evil?' Ben said. 'For not even trying to be—'

'To be good?' Jones sputtered into laughter. 'Oh, that's fine. That's rich. Goodness is easy, didn't you know? Go along. Don't rock the boat. Be unassuming and quiet and don't act, don't do anything, just drift along with the great unwashed and don't *be* anything. Oh yes, it's easy to be good, Ben – until it all comes crashing down. You should know that more than anyone.

'Your mother tried to be good, didn't she? She tried to protect you. Everything she ever did was for you. Yet some would call what she did evil. And what was it to you, her son? Tedium. Ropes around your ankles. A tether, a noose. What did it mean to you, her goodness?'

Ben frowned. This man *knew*. He knew all about them, as if he'd been there and seen it all. Perhaps he really was the man his mother had thought was the Devil. What had Jones called it? One of his *iterations*.

The life slumped out of him. He looked at the wreckage of what they had tried to do, the way they had tried to fight. He had thought that was good, hadn't he? Trying to stop the game from destroying anyone else. Now, there was this: a room full of the stench of death and two lifeless men slumped on the floor. That was what had come of his aims. And all the time, he'd been doing exactly what Jones had intended. He was probably standing, right at this moment, exactly where he wanted him to be. Jones had known what he was thinking all along and he probably knew what he was thinking now. It didn't matter if Ben hadn't played his game. Jones didn't need to see the desires of his heart written in black and white. He *knew*.

Ben looked at him and Jones looked back. They regarded each other.

'Such a shame,' Jones said at last. 'So much lost time. All that heartache, Ben. The protestations and confusion of your mother, the vacillating over every opportunity I've given you. The sad, compromised life you chose to lead. All of it is such a waste.' He smiled. 'Do you know the meaning of your name, Ben?'

Ben started.

'We know your sister's. How about yours?' He looked down, then gazed up through his eyelashes with those clear blue eyes. It was coquettish and horrible; Ben wanted to look away, but he found he could not.

'I thought not!' Jones was all eagerness. 'It has several meanings, Ben. Son of the South – well, you could have been that, couldn't you? Before you went running back to your mother's skirts.

'It has other meanings too: Son of my Sorrow is the next. And I have sorrowed over you, Ben. You will never know how much.' He paused. Tears had actually risen to Jones' eyes. Ben had no idea if they were real or a new kind of sham, but in his heart, he felt certain they were real. Perhaps it was only because of Jones' voice; the way it sounded in his ear, like honey.

Jones drew a long sigh. 'But the meaning of your name I want you to think about today is – Son of the Right Hand.' He held out his own hand, palm upward.

'You could be at my side, Ben,' he said. 'You and your sister together. Three of us. A family. Gaila at my left hand, you at my right. Oh – that would be sweet.'

Ben glanced at Gaila; he couldn't help it. He had seen her expression from the corner of his eye when she heard Jones' words. Something was dawning on her face, and it wasn't a good thing. It wasn't anything he wanted to see.

'Ah – she is my child, of course. But you – you are the one who escaped me, aren't you, Ben? What so nearly was – it was beautiful. And you've heard the story of the prodigal son, haven't you? It's the child who wanders, the child who turns his back, whose return is all the more celebrated.' He bowed his head towards Gaila. 'You wouldn't mind, would you, dear? Not when it's your own darling brother.'

Ben turned and looked Gaila full in the face. He could see something happening inside of her: anger. Sorrow. Resignation. She was always the second child, always the naughty one, the one in disgrace. The one with bad blood inside her, something rotten. Not like Ben. Not like the Golden Boy. He could see the thoughts working inside her, embedding themselves like splinters. And Jones knew that; of course he did. He had always known.

Ben shifted his gaze to Jones. He couldn't even blink. Jones' eyes drew him in. They were rimmed with light. Everything was there, every lie and every truth he had ever been told. Every tear his mother had shed; every one of his sister's. The future and the past were there, every time he had tried to do the right thing; every time he'd known it was worthless. And there was love there too, deep, warm, compelling. It was the love he'd craved when he'd been nothing but a lost boy in Darnshaw, trying to find a home in his games and his friends; not the love of a dad who didn't save him, the love of a mother who forced him to kneel on hard stones. It was a father's love, and he couldn't bear it. He squeezed his eyes tight shut and found they were wet.

'I'll always be there for you, Ben,' Jones whispered. 'Always.' His hand was still outstretched. An offering; an invitation.

Ben still didn't take it. He couldn't move. He had to *try*, didn't he? It may mean nothing and he might fail, but someone still had to try to do the right thing, to be – *uncorrupted*, that was the word that surfaced in his mind. His mother had tried to protect him. He had been ungrateful. He wouldn't be ungrateful now. He would do what he thought she would want; he would do what he believed to be the right thing. He shook his head, uttering something under his breath, one simple word.

'No.'

'Why, Ben? Because it's wrong?'

Ben nodded.

'Because I am evil? And because you want to do the right thing, the *good* thing?'

Again, a nod.

'Because you *believe*.'

Ben looked up.

'Well – do you believe, Ben?'

Emotions fought within Ben's mind. The old voice was still there, the stony, pragmatic voice that said it was all nonsense, all a game, but it was weaker now. He had seen things since that voice last spoke. He had *felt* things. He felt them now. He knew it was true that Jones was evil. He could feel it – a heaviness in the room that drew everything towards it. He had seen how it had worked on Milo and Damon and Raffie and his sister. He had felt how it worked upon *him*. He'd been seeing it all his days, the way it had surrounded his mother while she battled against it, the way it had ruined the course of their lives.

'I believe,' he whispered. 'I do. But I still say no. To all of it.'

Jones inhaled, long and slow, savouring Ben's words. 'Why, that,' he said, 'is all that matters. You don't know what that means to me, Ben. Your belief. Your faith.'

'It doesn't matter at all. Whatever this game is – you lose.'

Jones bowed his head and smiled. He went over to the desk. He pulled the chair aside. Save for the way he avoided touching the thick layer of blood that lay glossy across the desk, he was a company man once more. He looked like an ordinary worker on an ordinary day, someone who would soon drink a cup of coffee and start up the computer. He pulled open the desk drawer and reached inside it, reinforcing the image. When he withdrew his hand, he was holding a perfectly ordinary file. Ben felt a wave of disorientation; were they back at the beginning? Jones nearly set it down in the blood, stopping himself at the last moment with a little bob of his eyebrows, almost like someone making a joke. Instead, he held it out.

It was a plain file with a beige cardboard cover, just like the one in which he'd kept Gaila's photographs. It had no markings to betray its contents. It was just a plain office file and the thought of that made Ben want to scream. He could not ask, *What is it?* Jones thrust it towards him, prompting him to take it, to look, and Ben reached out and he did take it.

At first, he didn't open it. He just scanned the surface, looking for – what? Blood? A logo – the cross of confusion perhaps, or some other sign? There was none. And the game was over, wasn't it? He was walking away. He thought about throwing it down onto the desk, into all that blood, and yet somehow he couldn't. He took hold of the edge of the cover between his thumb and forefinger.

'I warn you,' Jones said. 'Once seen, nothing can ever be unseen.'

Fuck you, Ben thought, and opened the file.

He didn't know what he'd expected to see. Pictures,

perhaps. His sister, doing something else; his mother, maybe. Him. He didn't expect the sheets of plain white paper, with words printed neatly in black on some office printer. He ran his eyes over the lines written there and blinked. For a moment they were meaningless, nothing but marks that he couldn't decipher; and then he knew what it was. He had seen it before.

To make sure, he turned the page. The paper was printed quite densely, front and back. He flipped through to the next page, and the next. He scanned the text as he went along, making sure it was what he thought. He *had* seen it before, had scanned it just like this, catching a sentence here, a heading there. Yes, he thought he had. He wondered if it had meant any more to him then, the first time, than it did now.

He looked up at Jones.

The man sat back in his chair, his head tilted to one side. 'Your employment contract,' he said. 'You really should read it, Benjamin.'

Ben stared. For a moment, he couldn't breathe.

'Particularly page six. You should look at that quite carefully.'

Ben wanted to dive across the desk and take Jones by the throat. He wanted to push his face into the blood on his desk, to lift his head and smash it down again and again. Instead he reached out, quite deliberately, and turned to page six. He began to read. The words were meaningless, something about grievance procedures and discipline, the usual stuff, and then he reached the lines that shouldn't have been there, that didn't belong in any employment contract he'd ever seen.

I, the undersigned, irrevocably and without question, hereby surrender my immortal soul to the Company, condemning my immortal being of light to the environs of Hell, upon my death for evermore . . .

The paper shook in his hand. It could not be true. It *wasn't* true. It was nothing but a lie, the invention of this man, this *monster* sitting before him.

But he knew it wasn't a lie. He remembered the day he'd signed the contract. He had been sitting in an outer office, one that was bright and cheerful, with padded leather seats in fashionable colours. Orange. Blue. Pink. It had all been incredibly modern. He had kept looking around to take it all in. And grinning, he remembered that too; he'd had to make an effort to straighten his expression when the Human Resources person came in, a woman with long auburn hair and a white smile, her pencil skirt revealing fabulous legs. He didn't want her to think he was an idiot, grinning like that, but it had been difficult to stop all the same. She told him he had got the job. They'd had over a hundred applicants and they had chosen him over them all.

She passed him the document without glancing at it and he'd taken it the same way, without really noticing. She'd handed him a pen. He'd signed it, and just like that, he'd become a member of staff. The images spooled out in his mind as Jones began to utter the words of his promise, just as if he were reading it from the page Ben still held before him.

I, the undersigned, irrevocably and without question . . .

He looked down at the words. He let the folder fall, holding on to the stapled sheets. He flicked to the back page. The signature, written in plain office Biro, was a little crooked, but it was his.

'So sweet,' Jones said. 'And so much sweeter, now that you *feel* it. So much better now that you believe.' When he spoke again, there was a smile in his voice. 'I forgot to say, son. Welcome to the family.'

TWO

Ben had loved computer games when he was a young boy. He had especially liked the ones that made him feel like a smaller version of his dad – the games where he got to be a soldier, stalking through dunes or makeshift structures, checking around each corner before he moved. Most of all, he liked it when he sat cross-legged before the screen, the controller in his hands, and his dad came and sat down next to him. Pete wouldn't say anything at those times. He'd simply grin. Sometimes he rubbed his son's hair. Ben would duck, but he wouldn't look away from the game. If he did, the enemy might get him. Ben was quick to spot them, quick to shoot. His fingers danced over the buttons while pixelated heads turned to neat red clouds.

He was good at the game. His scores were always higher than Pete's. Later, when Pete had gone, Ben buried himself in it. He felt that, if he let it envelop him, if he could stare hard enough into its world, if he could only *kill* enough, that the game might let him in. He would be a real soldier then, instead of pretending. He might even meet his dad there. Even if that didn't happen, if he didn't believe enough, if he didn't have *faith* enough, they had still been soldiers together, hadn't they? If only for a little while.

Ben knew that his mother didn't understand. Sometimes he would be jerked out of the game, not by her hands but by one of her looks. One moment there was nothing but the waiting enemy, and the next he'd feel her eyes boring into his back, and he'd become aware of it all: the room in which he sat, the carpeted floor, the building in which they lived, the long hall, the red stair, the door to outside and all the miles of snow around him. And he'd remember the distance that separated him from Pete. He'd remember that he wasn't a soldier, he was only a kid whose dad was gone, and he'd want to scream at his mother to just stop looking at him like that.

He wanted to scream now. He could feel eyes on him, dragging him back into the room, making it all real once more. It wasn't just Jones. He knew without turning that Gaila was watching him too. She had seen the knowledge bloom across Ben's face. Raffie was there, and Damon and Simon, but it was his sister he cared about. Her dark eyes had always looked deeper. They had always known what was passing through his mind.

Golden Boy. It was never a name he'd wanted for himself.

He wondered if she would ever use it again, and he realised he missed it, now that it was behind him.

When he'd been older, Ben had decided he didn't like computer games any more. After all, his dad had come back by then. He didn't need them any longer. It helped that Pete didn't like them any longer either. Ben would try to play sometimes, just to see if Pete would come and sit beside him as he'd used to, but it didn't happen. Instead his dad would gaze at the screen, his face waxen, and he would say something in a flat voice about how it didn't measure up, that it wasn't even real.

He'd never played. He had had the opportunity to try *Acheron,* many times, but he had always turned away. He had thought, somehow, that put him above everything that had happened; that it would pass over his head and leave him untouched. He stared down at the papers in front of him, seeing them and yet not seeing. He'd refused to play and yet he'd lost everything after all.

Jones didn't speak. He didn't have to. He simply waited, and there was no triumph in his eyes, only an understanding tinged with sadness, as if he felt Ben's sorrow. Ben did not respond. He had become something loose and light that could, at any moment, simply let go, leaving everything that he had been somewhere far behind him.

THE SEVENTH CIRCLE

ONE

'Now, let me tell you what it is that I want,' Jones didn't look triumphant any longer and he did not look sorrowful. He looked like he had something unpleasant to impart. He steepled his fingers in front of him, his elbows resting on the desk, one of them just touching the skin that had formed on the surface of the blood that had been spilled. It clung to him, flexing with his movements. Jones didn't notice or didn't care.

They waited. At first he did not speak, only raised his head and examined them one by one with those sharp blue eyes. 'Not here,' he said.

It struck Ben that he had once thought Jones looked like an ordinary man. He did not think he was ordinary now.

'We have a journey to complete, you and I,' Jones said to Ben. 'I have such things to show you.' He pushed himself up from the desk. 'Gaila, Damon. Raffie and Simon, you may come too. You shall be our witnesses. Six. We shall go.'

Ben stared down at the contract in his hands. His mind was in freefall, his skin prickling. He did not know if he were hot or cold or even if it mattered. *He had signed.* He hadn't even read the fucking papers because he'd been looking at the Human Resource manager's legs and at the room, that fashionable, expensive, *London* room. He'd just flicked through the contract in a manner that he'd imagined was at once worldly and casual, and the woman hadn't glanced at it either, as if it didn't even matter. As if it wasn't important. Had she understood what it was she'd asked him to do? Or was she just another one of Jones' dupes?

'The big city,' Jones whispered, as if he could read every thought passing through Ben's head. 'Come, Ben. See it with me.'

Ben roused himself. He realised that Jones was holding out his hand. Jones' skin was pale and dry-looking, the palm unmarked. He turned over his own hand and words passed through his mind, the ones he'd thought of when he'd been planning his trip to Darnshaw, the small betrayal that had begun it all:

How much could one promise matter?

'Everything.' Jones reached out and took the papers from Ben's hand. 'I'll show you everything.' Ben twitched, then looked up once more. There was a light in Jones' eyes. It was greedy; rapacious.

Ben's shoulders slumped. When Jones pulled on an old black coat and strode towards the door, Ben didn't say a word.

He simply followed. The sound of the others' footsteps filled the corridor behind him.

Theodore Jones led them out into the night. It had grown clearer and colder since they'd been inside. Ben felt the presence of the city around him. The light streaming from street lamps and windows was hard. The blocky buildings cutting out the faintly orange-lit sky were sharp-edged and brutal.

Jones didn't look around and he did not speak. He turned down a narrow cutting and strode ahead until everything opened out around them and Ben realised where he was: Paternoster Square, the wide space behind London's great cathedral, fringed by investment banks and cafes. Its pale paving was smooth and gleaming. A tramp was attempting to sleep on one of the studded stone benches; he did not move as they rounded the monument at the centre of the square, a single column topped by what looked like an illuminated torch.

Ahead of them, there was only the looming magnificence of Saint Paul's. Its huge dome looked unreal against the sky. Jones strode straight towards it.

Ben followed at his heels, as did all of the others, and none of them questioned where he led. His stride spoke of purpose, and no one crossed it. He went past the Chapter House and then there was nothing between them and the soaring grandeur of columns and arches and sheer overwhelming stature. And then they were in front of the smooth stone steps leading up to the tourist entrance, long since closed, and still Jones did not pause until they were in front of the door. Words were etched into the glass; over Jones' shoulder, Ben caught something about the *Gate of Heaven*.

Jones muttered something in a low voice: 'Behold. I stand at the door and knock,' and he let out a low laugh, the meaning of which Ben could not fathom. He opened his mouth to say something about the place being closed, the doors locked against them, and then Jones put out his hand and pushed and he heard the low *thunk* of a lock disengaging. The revolving door began to move.

'One at a time, please.' Jones' words were those of a tour guide, but his tone was mocking. Ben stepped forward and the door swallowed him. Then it spat him into the cool, dark interior, the space cavernous and empty all around him.

Ben passed the signs meant for sightseers: no photography, pre-booked tickets only, guidebooks for sale, audio tours. Beyond that was the cathedral in all its hollow vastness: simple wooden chairs perfectly aligned on the black and white chequered floor. Thick columns soaring into shadow. Golden chandeliers, not burning now. Nothing moved and for a moment there was no sound, none at all.

Ben remembered coming here, years ago. The place had been full of tourists and school trips. Everywhere people were staring upward, and it had struck him as odd that no one appeared to be speaking, everyone struck into near-silence, and yet everywhere was the constant underwater burble of voices, echoing and indecipherable.

Jones led the way, not down the side of the structure, but down the nave, the wide central aisle. Ben walked after him, Gaila at his side, as if on the way to some dark wedding. Simon and Raffie trailed behind and he heard Raffie's protest, her voice caught by the alcoves and chapels and arches: 'Why . . .'

Ben pulled a face. He wasn't sure he cared *why*, any longer. There was only this. There was only now. They were once again in a place they didn't belong and shouldn't be, led by a man – or a devil – they didn't know. At any moment, security would come. The light of the world he knew would shine in their faces and they would awake from their nightmare, to more trouble than any of them knew how to handle.

Images flashed across his eyes: Mephistopheles, lying dead in a spill of blood. Ashley raising a barbaric blade over his own hand. Gaila, her dark eyes fixed on Jones, their expression impossible to read.

Jones led them to the centre of the cross that formed the cathedral, so that they were standing immediately beneath its huge central dome. Ben couldn't help it; he looked upward. He remembered a glowing thing of paintings and carvings and of gold, but now, everything was dark. There was only a faint glow in a perfect circle coming from the Whispering Gallery, and above that, the merest glimmer of windows. He wanted to cry. He had been here before when he had had no worries, no fears, before he had signed that terrible contract.

He found himself staring down at his palm, and remembered: an old black book, smelling of dust and something spicy and sweet, a little like cinnamon. A knife. A pen – the old-fashioned kind that could be dipped in ink. A list of names, crimson at the bottom, the older ones towards the top of the page dried to a deep red-brown.

He came back to himself; he felt certain that Jones was watching him, a wry smile on his face, but when he looked around he saw the man was staring down at a circle of brass inlaid at the very centre of the cathedral floor. And in his eyes was unutterable sadness.

Ben saw what Jones saw. The circle was surrounded by a grand sunburst, hemmed in by a ring of Latin text. He caught the words *Christophorus Wren*. The brass glimmered as of gold.

Jones let out a long sigh. 'This place has been torn down,' he said, 'and built again. Not just one cathedral has stood here, but five, each grander than the last.' His voice went so low that Ben could hardly make out the words. 'Is it the same, do you think? Was each one of them still Saint Paul's, or something else?'

For a while, he didn't speak. Then Jones looked up, scanning the darkness, the empty space above their heads. He stared for a while and Ben followed his gaze, saw what appeared to be a mosaic glimmering from the shadows: a cherubic face, outspread wings.

'I was one of them once,' Jones said, his voice bitter, and then he straightened and barked, 'Onward!'

He strode away, all brisk efficiency, and headed away to the right, where another door stood open.

TWO

The spiral staircase was wide, the steps shallow, each stone riser topped neatly with wood. Wall lights at intervals gave out a muted glow and windows, each heavily barred, showed the dull orange of street lights somewhere outside. The sound of a siren intruded momentarily from somewhere in the city and then was gone. Only silence remained, and the cold, and then came the sound of Jones' footsteps leading upward, steady and implacable.

Raffie whispered, somewhere behind Ben. 'I'm not going up there. I'm not going to follow him.'

Damon responded with a snort, perhaps to remind them of the gun concealed in his jacket. Gaila, unhesitating, started up, her shadow dancing around her as she went. Ben followed. He knew the others would too. It wasn't long until the sound of their quickened breath surrounded him. Around and around they went, Jones not waiting for anyone. The endless rhythm began to take on its own sense of unreality, the steps seeming to shift under Ben's gaze. It was better when he fixed his eyes on his sister's straight back, her form so slight she looked little more than the child he had once known.

I want to go with my dad, she'd said.

Ben pushed away the thought. They had reached a landing. Above their heads, the ceiling was no longer the underside of stone risers, but wooden beams. Jones led them through a twisting passageway, narrow and dark, Ben skimming the wall with his fingers. After that were more narrow stairs – Gaila stumbled and Ben put out a hand, but she had steadied herself – and Jones opened a door onto a vertiginous drop.

Ben knew this place. The Whispering Gallery had always stuck in his mind as one of the gems of London. All was splendour. The dome was above them, reaching into the dark, and the gallery lined its base with a narrow stone walkway guarded by a high railing. Far, far below, he could just make out the cathedral's chessboard floor. They did not pause to look at it, but squeezed along the narrow space – Ben could feel the channel worn in the stone by the passage of countless feet – and the sound of their steps was loud, echoing back and amplified by the walls so that they were surrounded. Surely there were security guards who would hear? But then Ben remembered the way the sealed doors had opened at Jones' touch, the way the place had been *waiting* for him, and suddenly he knew that no one was coming. This would be between them and them alone. The thought made him feel all the emptiness around him, the silence that lay beneath the rustling of their footsteps.

Jones pushed open one of the mysterious arched doors set into the circumference of the dome. Beyond it were more steps. He went through it and began to climb.

In here, the air was colder still. Ben was glad to be moving, generating heat to keep that cold at bay. Below him he could feel Damon's stare on his back, and behind him, hear Raffie and Simon's low complaints. He didn't pay attention to the words. Gaila was practically skipping along, the only one keeping pace with Jones, who did not seem troubled by the exertion. The passageway forced them into single file, keeping them separate. Pipework and wiring jutted from the walls. It was interminable, and as they went they blocked out the light, sending shadows darting, making each step one of faith.

Another door and they stepped into the night sky, a cold wind blasting Ben full in the face. There were murmurs of dismay, rustling as everyone pulled their clothing tighter. Damon stood holding the door, his face a blank. Raffie and Simon gazed out at London, its lights and towers and siren wails, and Ben caught a glimpse of the Gherkin and the Shard before he realised they hadn't stopped their ascent, that Jones was taking them higher still. He strode up a short metal stair, caught hold of another door and Ben heard the distinct *click* as it unlocked under his hand.

They passed inside once more, into a darkness deeper still.

Only faint panels glowed, their light catching on railings everywhere; there were struts all around them, giving the impression of being in a cage. The walls were either painted white or were the dull black of soot. Another metal stair, a tight, narrow spiral, soared upward. Ben tilted his head back, at once feeling dizzy. Another wave of disbelief washed over him. What were they doing here? But there was no time to wonder. Jones started upward once more, Simon leaning against the wall, drawing in a ragged breath. He grimaced at Ben, but he had no time to worry about Simon. He nodded at Gaila as she started after Jones, and he followed close behind her.

It was not an easy stair to climb. It was steep and the black railings did nothing to shield them from the sight of the spaces all around. They were suspended in the air, somewhere beneath the dome, rising ever upward. The handrail was now on the right, then on the left as they reached a landing and the spiral reversed. Ben clawed for it and pulled himself up. He started to count the steps, lost track at around seventy and still they headed towards the sky. His legs were burning.

Then another door opened and they stepped outside and saw what Jones had wanted them to see.

London from here was tiny, faded and softened by the distance, like a city in a dream. And yet it was alive, full of light and the sound of late-night traffic and revelry, which hung over it like a shroud.

They were at the lantern, the very top of Saint Paul's dome, and below them was everything. Above, there was very little left.

Ben stepped onto the narrow stone walkway between a tall iron railing and the pale stone of the cathedral at his back. It was carved into alcoves with narrow stone benches, their surfaces worn into soft curves. Jones was ahead of him. They squeezed along one at a time. Then they reached an alcove where two benches faced each other, and Jones indicated that Gaila and Ben should sit. They did, their knees almost touching, and at once gained some blessed shelter from the wind. Damon stood at their side, his face turned away, though Ben could still see the waxy pallor of his cheek. Raffie and Simon were somewhere behind him. Ben could not see their faces.

Jones leaned back against the railing and smiled. The cold did not seem to trouble him. He closed his eyes and drew in a long breath. Ben smelled the air, caught the merest hint of exhaust fumes and smoke and old stone and time.

'This is it,' Jones said. He waved a hand, indicating the city spread beneath their feet.

All this can be yours, Ben thought.

Jones smiled at him. 'Yes,' he said, 'it can. And so it should be.'

'And you?'

Jones shot a questioning look at Ben, then raised his eyebrows. 'Ah – just so, Ben, just so. I promised to tell you what it is that I want; and now I shall. You and your sister must be with me. We are family. You will stay here and work with me and do my bidding. That is what you wanted anyway, isn't it?'

He shifted his gaze to Gaila. 'You are my daughter and your place is by my side. You asked me something once, do you remember? Another request you made of the game – you see, you want so much, the need is in you – and yet *Acheron* did not answer, until now.

'You shall have all, Gaila. Everything you can see and more. You asked me for the world, didn't you? How did you put it? You wanted a face that could break a million hearts.' The laughter started somewhere deep inside of him and burst into the cold sky. 'Why, you already do, of course. All you need is for me to show you how. But you shall have it, my dear. Of course you shall.'

He shifted his gaze once more and grinned, wolf-like. 'Now you, Ben. You were promised to me once and yet you escaped. I think we can see how that worked out. My mark is still there, on the palm of your hand, is it not? Now you will come home.'

Ben did not reply. Damon, standing at his side, shifted uneasily.

'I have your souls. Now I want your hands and your hearts. Give them to me, with everything you are, and you shall have everything. My gratitude. My care. My love. You will see how valuable such things can be.' He waved a hand again, over everything, and he gave Gaila a sweet smile. 'My dear child. I cannot offer this chance again. Come to me.'

Gaila stared at her hands, pressed together between her knees. She stirred, that old knowing look returning to her, and Ben thought: *She has her father's eyes.*

'My father is joy,' Jones said, echoing Ben's thoughts. 'It was all decided before you were even born. And you can share in that joy, my dear, as was always meant to be. Did you think you belonged with your mother? Did it feel that way to you? Did it feel natural? Of course it did not. You always knew that you were meant for other things, didn't you? You felt it. That was me, Abigail, that was my call, sounding in your blood. Now you can be whole, if you will only put your hand in mine. Do you imagine that you have seen success already? You will be magnificent! You have seen only one small part of what I can do for you. Ask me, my dear, and I will show you: a boon. Anything you wish.'

His focus was on Gaila, all on her, as she passed a hand across her eyes. Then she looked up and began to stretch out her hand, slowly, towards Jones.

'Gaila!' Ben snatched for it, realising what she was about to do. She started, as if she had forgotten he was there.

'Gaila, please. You can't go to him. Think of Cass.'

She did not move.

'This is what Cass has been fighting her whole life. This, Gaila, for you and me. If you do this – it will kill her.'

His sister's eyes widened, but he realised it was not in shock at the idea. It was not in horror. It was more like the dawning of realisation.

Jones chuckled. 'It will! Of course, it will kill her. The knowledge of what you both have done – is that not perfect, my dear? The thing you asked for, delivered so neatly. Ah, do not try to pretend it isn't truly what you want. That's all in the past. You don't need to pretend any longer. You don't need to be anything other than the glorious, perfect thing you are.'

'She wouldn't,' said Ben. 'She'll never do it.'

Gaila's head snapped around to him, her face twisted with fury. 'You don't speak for me.'

'Gaila, please—'

'Fucking Golden Boy. All your life . . .'

He hadn't thought to hear those words again. Now he was stung by them. 'Gaila, it isn't like that. You're my sister.'

'Am I?'

'Of course you are.' Ben reached out towards her, gesturing towards her pocket, and he saw that she understood. She put her hand to it and took out his gift, the pendant.

'I know that things weren't perfect, Gaila. I know *I* wasn't perfect. But at least we can try, can't we? We can get by together, without him. We don't need him. We don't want to go to any place he wants to lead us, or have anything he wants to give us. We can be a family for each other. He says he has our souls. Well, does he? Maybe we don't have to accept that. It was all nothing but a trick, after all. Only a game. We don't have to believe in it; we don't even have to believe in *him*.'

Jones tilted his head, considering.

A muffled voice said: 'You do. You do have to.'

Ben turned to see a figure pushing past Damon, who sneered down at them, contempt written across his face. It was Raffie, forgotten and yet listening to everything that passed. She looked somehow diminished since he'd first seen her; not the person she had been when they'd set out on this blighted evening.

Ben did not ask what she meant. This wasn't about Raffie. He could feel the threads that tied him to Gaila stretching between them through the cold air. They had grown thin, and at any moment they might break. He did not know what he would do if that happened. He was her brother, and he was the eldest. He should have prevented any of this from happening. Instead he had led her here, first to Damon's lair and then to this place of – what? Testing? Temptation? He should have taken her to the airport and made sure she caught her flight. He should never have opened the door; he should never have been the key.

But she had asked him to come to London first.

Gaila wasn't looking at her brother. She was listening, waiting for whatever Raffie had to say. Jones didn't withdraw his outstretched hand, didn't do anything at all. He only muttered something under his breath: 'Tick-tock—'

'You have to,' Raffie repeated. She held out her hands and Ben realised he could still see Mephistopheles' blood on them. 'He won't help me,' she said. 'But you could.'

Ben scowled. 'I don't know what you mean, Raffie. I can't

do anything. I can't *undo* anything. Anyway, it doesn't work like that.'

Jones snorted. 'Of course it does!' He beamed, leaned forward and clapped Ben on the shoulder. 'You'll grasp it soon enough, my son. She did!' He nodded towards Raffie, who clung to the thin railings as if they could save her. The woman's eyes were open wide and her face was coated in moisture – clothed in mist. She mouthed something at Ben.

He narrowed his eyes.

'Anything at all!' said Jones.

'If you work for him, you can change it,' Raffie said. 'You could help me. You could make the game help my daughter. You can make it do anything. It'll be yours too, won't it?' She glanced at Jones, who nodded.

'Quite right, quite right! Let's say it will. I knew I brought you here for a reason, Raffie. Well done! All it takes is one little handshake.'

'It's nothing you haven't given him already,' Raffie said.

'Nothing at all!' Jones rubbed his hands together.

'It can't count for anything.'

'Anything!'

Ben covered his eyes. His own face felt numb. He couldn't be hearing this. He could hear the pain in Raffie's voice and he hurt for her, but this wasn't about her. Thousands of people must have the same problems as her, but the burden of it didn't rest on Ben's shoulders. He hadn't asked for it. He couldn't accept it.

'I'll do it,' Gaila said.

'Ah, at last! Good girl. You finally see sense – which side you're on, which way the bread's buttered, et cetera, et cetera. Wonderful!'

'But I do want something in return.'

'Something in return, she says! And I'm about to give her everything!'

Gaila repeated the word that Jones had spoken, and that, a few moments ago, Raffie had mouthed at Ben. 'A boon,' she said. Now it was her turn to smile upon Jones. 'Just one little thing. Easy for you to give, nothing you're going to miss.'

He raised his eyebrows, waiting.

'It's like she said. You let Raffie go, completely. You have no claim on her life or her soul. What she did to Mephistopheles – that should never have happened. You *made* it happen. You said you'd make sure there's no blood on her hands, nothing to come back to her, to any of us – you have to do that. But also, you have to make her child better.'

Raffie made an inarticulate sound. She flung herself forward, sliding along the rail and throwing herself down. Ben heard the sound of her knees striking the stone at Gaila's feet. She clutched at his sister's legs and Ben watched in dismay. It should have been demeaning, but somehow it wasn't. The woman was broken; not by her pain, but by the hope Gaila had given her. As he watched, she started crying – no, *keening* – in great gulping breaths.

The woman was cast low in this high place, and what Ben

felt, then, was a crushing sadness, born not only of pity, but of disappointment in himself. He had failed, hadn't he? He had told himself he couldn't help, that it wasn't his concern; it was his sister who had leaped in and acted. Ben had done nothing and she hadn't needed to think twice. She had offered everything that she had and all that she was to save a child she had never met for a woman she didn't really know.

He remembered what Jones had said about Cass, when he'd compared her to Raffie. He'd said that she would have used the knife without hesitation, if by doing so she thought she could save her child. And Ben had known he was telling the truth. That was exactly what his mother would have done. Now this: Gaila leaping in where Ben had done nothing. All of those times she had called him Golden Boy, and he knew that there was some small, smug part of himself that had thought she was right. Now, which of them was right and which wrong? Nothing was clear to him any longer. A sudden image came to him: Gaila and Cass on one of their good days, their faces pressed close together as they laughed; their smiles, so different and yet the same. At that moment, he could believe that Gaila was more their mother's child than he had ever been.

His sister was waiting for a response. 'Well?' she said.

'Goodness.' Jones frowned. 'What mighty conditions you place on me indeed.' He put his hands together, ready for binding. 'Perhaps you don't trust me at all, daughter?'

'Nevertheless,' she said, her voice steady, 'that is what I

want. That is my price. And then I'll come here and I'll work for you. I'll stay at your side. I'll be loyal to the company. I'll do whatever you ask. Isn't that what you want?'

He inclined his head.

'So shake my hand.' She thrust it out in front of her and, after a moment, Jones leaned forward and took it.

The air *shifted* around them. It felt lighter. *That's not right*, Ben thought. *It should be darker now.* She *should be darker.* But when Gaila turned towards him, her mood had lifted too. Her eyes shone and she smiled, dimpling her cheek. The old scar was barely visible at all.

Ben couldn't move. He realised they were all watching him. Only Raffie didn't look; she crouched on the floor, shaking with her tears, her hands still clinging to Gaila's legs.

'You may go,' Jones said.

Ben was startled. Was he being dismissed? He imagined for a moment stepping out into the dark, cold London night and walking away. He would be alone. He would hear his footsteps echoing along the quiet streets and none would answer them. He would be alone *for ever.*

Jones pointed towards the door. It swung wider in the breeze.

'Raffie, you may go. It seems you have something to trade after all. Leave this place and do not think of it or speak of it again. You are free. Find your daughter well.' Jones bowed, a magnanimous smile on his face: a saint granting a supplicant a miracle.

And all Ben could feel was relief that Jones had meant Raffie and not himself. His head swam. He did not know what that could mean. He found himself wondering, once more, who he really was.

Raffie stood and brushed tears away with her hand. She embraced Gaila, who leaned away, seeking to vanish into the stone at her back. Then Raffie shuffled along the narrow space, squeezing past Damon and Simon towards the door.

'You too,' Jones said.

Simon's eyes were clouded. He looked angry for a moment, looking at Gaila and then Ben – maybe wondering why he too had not been granted a gift. He opened his mouth, perhaps to protest about the way he'd made this climb for nothing.

'You know the way,' Jones said. 'Down.'

Simon couldn't meet his eyes. Now he only looked afraid. He turned hurriedly and scurried after Raffie, worried that Jones would change his mind; that he might at any moment be called back again.

Theodore Jones closed his eyes. He stood there for a moment before stirring. 'And now we shall follow our friends,' he said, 'for there is one more thing to be done. Is there not, Ben?' He gazed at him and smiled, and there was no mockery or greed in his expression, only sadness.

Ben screwed his hands into fists, started to protest, and Jones held out a hand to stop him. 'Please,' he said, 'no more. Not yet. I shall lead us. Please: after me. Watch your step. Damon, kindly follow.'

Damon scowled but said nothing, only waited for Ben to pass him, followed by Gaila. Ben couldn't meet his sister's dark eyes. He no longer knew what he should do, but he knew they had to leave this place. At least then he would have time to think.

As they crept down the steep metal stair, he thought he could hear the rattle of Raffie and Simon's progress somewhere below. He couldn't see them; they were swallowed by shadows. He wondered if he would ever see either of them again. He wondered what Raffie would find when she got home. He knew it was not really possible that she would find her daughter healed and well and waiting for her, everything bright and happy and with a future once again, and yet he somehow could not bring himself to doubt it.

THREE

When they reached the Whispering Gallery once more, all the life slumped out of Jones. He grasped the balcony rail that ran at shoulder height, followed it a short way and then sat on the stone bench. He did not look up.

Ben did. The great dome above them was still dark, only a little light coming through the windows to illuminate the grand paintings he knew were there. He caught the suggestion of statues, their pale faces gazing down in stern judgement. The railing around them was of wrought iron, and Ben could see where it curved around the space that it was painted in gold, but only on the outside. In front of his face, it was black.

He stared at Jones. The man showed no sign of being conscious of his presence. Now that they had stopped moving there was no sound at all. He found himself thinking once more of his visit here, years ago. He had sat on that same cold bench. He remembered being startled by a noise away to his right; the colossal sound of someone opening a packet of crisps, too loud, and he had been disconcerted to find the space empty. It had taken him a while to see the source of the sound, across the vertiginous drop and on the opposite side of the gallery: a small boy sitting next to his mother and smiling.

The Whispering Gallery was aptly named. It had strange acoustic properties; by accident or design, Ben didn't know. He remembered hearing of it before his trip. He had been told to put his ear to the wall, to have someone on the opposite side of the gallery whisper something into it. The words would come back to him, he had been told, and he remembered the thrill he had felt at the idea. He had imagined pressing his ear into the waxy old stone, striving for those words. When he had finally stood in this place, he understood how wrong he had been. There was no need to strive. The words were there, no longer whispered but loud, frighteningly so.

Now there was nothing. Only a soft rushing, like a distant breeze rustling in a treetop; that, and the faint suggestion of someone singing.

'What are we doing?' Gaila snapped, too suddenly, and the sound flashed back at them from across the void. *Doing? Doing?*

'Please,' Jones said, and Ben waited for the echo, but somehow did not hear it. 'Sit.' He indicated the bench next to him and they sat, sinking onto stone that looked pocked and roughened but was smooth as glass to the touch. The cold sank into him, went deep.

Other sounds came to them out of the dark. At first he thought it was the echo of the rustling they'd made, amplified and distorted, but then they changed and Ben realised they weren't diminishing, but growing louder: metallic clattering and dry scraping and the sharp *click* of a switch.

He closed his eyes. He knew the sounds had no place here because he recognised them: they were kitchen sounds. He pictured Cass, picking up after her children, piling the pots in the sink, switching on the hob.

But that wasn't right, was it? He glanced at Jones who was sitting with his eyes closed, leaning back against the encircling wall, wearing a peaceful smile.

The hiss of heat sparked and spat. Ben started, looking at the place it was coming from. There was nothing there.

Jones opened his eyes a slit. His eyes were pinpricks of light. 'You hear it too,' he said. 'Don't you?'

Ben scowled, shifting away from him. 'It's just one of your tricks.'

Tricks . . . tricks . . .

'As you like,' Jones mouthed, and closed his eyes again.

Ben felt Gaila watching him, but he did not look around. He leaned forward, listening. Reaching for the words. There were none. There was only the murmur of someone's voice, so distorted there were no words in it, and yet he recognised it. The voice was dear to him. It was his mother's voice, the first one he had heard in this world.

Then there was a harsh *tsssssss* and he jumped from his seat, leaning over the rail. He knew that sound too, but didn't want to think of it, didn't want to hear it. It did not fade. Instead it grew louder, filling his mind until it was deafening, blending and changing into his mother's scream.

'I heard it back then, too,' Jones murmured, and Ben whirled to see him, still with his eyes closed, still wearing that smile. 'She made a promise to me once. It was all about you, Ben. I'm sorry, Gaila, but it's true. I made her think you had signed away your soul, Ben. It wasn't true – not then, anyway. How eager she was; how willing, to give her own in its place. And she gave to me so much more.' He waved his hands in the air, an echo of Cass' form, her embrace.

Ben stepped towards him. He felt Gaila clinging to his arm.

'And then! To think she could take it back. With one simple act: burning away the scar left behind when she signed her name in blood.'

Jones looked up at last, his eyes shining with amusement. 'We did it the old way then. In a way, it was rather more fun. Now it's just one little click. So quick, so clean an excision.' He grinned.

Gaila pulled harder and Ben tried to shake her off, but she wouldn't budge. 'Ben, it doesn't matter. You don't have to listen to him. You should go.'

Go . . . go . . .

Damon snorted with laughter. It rang in Ben's ears, full of mockery and contempt.

'I'm not leaving.'

Leaving . . .

'Ben, please. You should go back home. Be with Mum. She'll be all right, as long as you're there. She needs you. I'll be fine.'

He hung his head, drew a deep breath, and said: 'No.' He spoke quietly. There was no echo. He still knew that they had heard. 'There's something I want too. I'm staying.'

Jones' expression held new interest. He gestured for Ben to go on.

'I want Mum to be all right. That's part of my bargain.'

Jones slowly shook his head. 'You know I can't do that. A prior commitment, my boy. I made a promise to your sister, and a deal is a deal. Unless—' He raised his eyebrows at Gaila.

'Of course!' she snapped. 'I never really meant what I asked. I didn't know . . . I mean, I want her to be all right too. Just leave Cass alone.'

'Done.' Jones brought his hands together. It clapped back from the walls, louder: once, twice, thrice. He held out a hand to shake.

'Wait,' Ben said. 'That isn't all. When I say I want Cass to be all right – I want her to be *really* all right. The way she thought she'd signed away her soul—'

'She did! For you, Ben. Of course, she did.' Jones leered.

'Well, whatever happened, whatever she did, I want it to be undone. You say she did it to help me, or she thought she did. Now I—' He swallowed. 'I'll do the same for her. I want my mother to be free of all this. I want her soul to be her own again. And there is to be no going back for her, playing more tricks or anything else.'

'My, you two *are* careful. You'll go far, my boy! All right.' Jones spat on his palm and held it out once more.

This time, after a long moment, Ben took it. His hand jerked involuntarily, but Jones did not let go. An arrow-point of coldness pierced Ben's palm, shooting up through his arm and into him. It felt like he'd damaged a nerve. It entered his chest and lodged there, close to his heart, and it didn't feel as cold any longer. It felt like something to be cherished, something to nurture within him; something to be held close, to allow to grow.

When at last Jones let go of his hand and Ben turned towards his sister, he saw that she was crying. Tears ran silently down her cheeks. She was beautiful; more so than she had been in any photograph. Ben could see the scar on her cheek, the imperfection that somehow made the perfect complete, the thing that had bound them together. She was his sister, his family. They all were, the three of them. Only Damon was separate, still sitting a short distance away, a dark shape staring into the abyss.

'Now,' Jones said, standing, 'we have work to do.' He was no longer smiling. Ben wondered how he ever could have thought the man looked ordinary. Here, his face gleaming in the dull light, his face appeared longer, his cheeks more hollow. He looked predatory. A trace of the scent from his office returned to him; it was the smell of blood, but Ben suddenly doubted its source. The man in front of him was a monster. He wanted only to devour, to rend and tear, if not flesh then hearts and minds; souls. Perhaps, one day, Ben would be like that too. He would become inured to whatever work this man set before him. He might even grow to like it.

'No, we don't,' Gaila said. There was no echo, but her words hung in the air between them.

Jones leaned forward, putting his hand behind his ear. 'Beg pardon? Not quite ready, young lady? Then make yourself ready. For you shall be the busiest of all.'

'Oh, I am ready,' she whispered. 'But not for you.'

She took something from her pocket. It was a knife. It was the knife Raffie had used to kill Mephistopheles and Gaila had not cleaned the blood away. Scraps of meat clung to its edge. It looked evil. It looked hungry.

Gaila blinked back tears. 'Ben, I said you should go. I'm not sure I can do this with you watching.'

'Gaila, what are you doing?'

'Ah,' Jones said, slowly. 'I believe your sister is in rebellion.'

'It's the only way, Ben.' She shot him a frightened glance. 'We're a part of this now. He'll make us do anything he wants, if we let him. But we don't just have one choice, do we? We can choose over and over again. Every day, we can choose – as long as Jones is gone.'

'But we signed – and you, you promised—'

'Now I'm promising something else. I'm not going to let him ruin us, Ben. It could be too late for me. I've been ruined all my life, by his blood in my veins if he's telling the truth. I think he probably is. But I can try, can't I?' She paused. 'You still don't get it, do you, brother? We sold our souls to *the company*.'

Ben's eyes widened. Jones *was* the company, wasn't he? None of it would exist without him. None of it would *work* without him.

'Not if he's dead.' It was as if Gaila read his thoughts. And perhaps she had; after all, Jones' blood flowed in her veins. She had always been able to see through her brother, to understand just what he was thinking, to see what he *was*. She probably knew that better than he did.

He felt a wave of lightness, as if he were falling. One day, perhaps he would land; he hoped it would be somewhere solid and comforting and ordinary.

His sister pushed her way to his side. He tried to lift his hands to stop her, but he couldn't move. Gaila was standing in a cathedral in the dead of night, holding the Devil at bay with a blade covered in human meat. It was surreal, and yet Gaila seemed to be the most real thing in his world.

Then he remembered Damon, the gun he possessed. He whirled, but Damon hadn't moved. He was still sitting with his head down, staring into the dark.

'Don't look, Ben,' Gaila said. 'Get out. Walk out of here and keep on going. Get on a train and go home. Say hi to Mum for me, if she ever – if she cares.' Her voice broke over the words and she took an unsteady breath, steeling herself as she shifted her grip on the knife's black handle. She wrapped one hand around the other, ready to raise it above her head.

Jones laughed.

At last, his voice had found an echo. His laughter rang around the empty spaces. It sang from the walls. It echoed in Ben's mind until it was everything, until he wanted to press his hands over his ears and scream. Jones laughed until Ben felt his mind must give way before the onslaught. He realised he was muttering something under his breath: *No*, over and over, although he couldn't hear his own whisper.

Gaila was not troubled by the sound. She stood firm, though Ben could feel her arm shaking where it was pressed against his side. His sister. He felt a rush of love for her. She was strong, he knew that; the only thing that had made her falter was the thought of his mother.

I never really meant what I asked. I didn't know— I mean, I want her to be all right too.

'Gaila—'

Jones cut him off. 'Your sister believes she can finish me, Benjamin. I have to confess, that does make me somewhat angry. There we were, a nice little family unit, one-two-three of us, and already this – this black sheep, this bad egg, thinks she can disrupt everything. Thinks she can forget her promises.' His eyes narrowed as he straightened. Every shadow, every well of darkness in the place was centred in him. 'Promises such as those you made are sacred. They are binding. Nothing can release them, save that I will it.' He jabbed a finger towards Gaila. 'Do you wish for dear sweet Raffie to get home and find her child a withered husk? Do you, Ben, wish for your mother to scream in the fire for all eternity?'

Ben opened his mouth, but it was Gaila who spoke. 'I promised to stay with you,' she said. 'I promised to work for you. And I am going to do that, Jones, as long as you exist.' A lighter sound cut through the air; she was laughing. 'A promise is a promise, and I'm going to keep mine. Our bargain stands.'

'You damn yourself, girl. You think you can free yourself from me? You'll have blood on your hands. You'll never be free of it. You'll be a murderer. Think of that; it's something to live with. To die with.'

'Yes,' she whispered, 'I will. And that is what I choose. I choose it all.'

Ben reached out at last and grabbed her shoulder. 'Gaila, don't. Remember Cass – all the things she did for you.'

She half turned to him, astonishment written across her face.

'I mean it. I know she worried about what you are, about your birth. But all her odd ideas about you – they were the truth, weren't they? But she still worried. She still *cared*. You say she doesn't, but you know that isn't true. She worried over you more than anyone, don't you see? Because she was responsible for you. The fact that you were half his – she always knew it was her fault. But she was still your mother.'

The tears shone on her face.

'Gaila, you can't do this.'

She let out a bitter laugh. 'Can't? You think so? Think, Ben. We sold our souls to the company. And I'm his *daughter*. When he's gone, the company's ours. We can disband it. We can release all of its contracts. We can delete every last stupid request anyone ever made in their worst moments, the ones that no one else should ever have seen. We can forgive them all.' She turned to face him. 'Can't? Oh, Ben. I have to, don't you see? It's not just about us. It's about everyone he ever touched, about anyone who agreed to play his stupid game. We can do so much good.'

'Gaila, no. Not like this. You'll be a—'

'A killer. A murderer. I know. But someone has to, so that others can be free.' So that *you* can be free, is what her eyes told him.

'I can't let you do this.'

She laughed. 'Oh, Ben. You never listened to our mother at all, did you? Sometimes you have to do the right thing by doing the wrong thing. Don't you see that?' She smiled. 'Did Cass teach you nothing? She did anything she had to do, to keep you safe. To protect you. And if you'd been my kid, I'd have done the same. Do you really think she deserved damnation for that? Do you think she deserved the years of guilt she put herself through? Sometimes – sometimes, we just do what we have to do. And then we forgive ourselves, Ben, if we can.'

He could think of nothing to say. All he could think was: *their smiles were the same.*

'The thing is, I thought that everything Cass did was for you. I thought you were the one who got all the good, who'd follow in her footsteps.' She took a step backwards, towards Jones, who was staring out over the gallery, his eyes soft, focused on nothing, or perhaps on everything.

Gaila let out a sharp laugh. 'Perhaps Cass had an influence on me after all. Every time she made me out to be bad or wrong or nasty – maybe she was actually teaching me something good.'

She turned again, hefted the blade, raised it. Ben snatched for her, a wild movement, and his hand closed on nothing.

'Very touching,' Jones murmured into the dark. 'But you are my daughter, Abigail, have you forgotten that? My soul is in your flesh. My words were whispered to your bones before you were born. My name is written in your heart. *My father is joy* – have you forgotten?'

The knife in her hands shook. 'You're not my dad.'

'Ah. So you say. But do you know it to be the truth? I do so like the truth, Abigail. Do you really think you can destroy me? Others before you have tried. Others thought they succeeded. I have – *iterations*, Gaila. We are legion.'

'Not this time. Not any longer.' She raised the blade higher. Ben saw that the blood it had been bathed in was dripping from it, droplets soaking into her T-shirt, running down her arms. She stepped forward and Jones did not move. He let her come; he did not raise his hands to defend himself. He did not call on Damon to help him.

Gaila held the blade high. Everything was focused on its point: their past, their future, everything that they could be, the best and the worst of it. All of it was held there, in perfect balance.

'You see.' Jones smiled. 'You cannot. Maybe one day, Gaila, when we've cured you of such sanctimonious passions . . . And we *will* cure you, don't you see?'

The blade began to shake. She made a sound of effort or despair, and she did not move. 'Ben, I—'

'Can't,' Jones finished for her. 'Of course she can't. She hasn't had the right training. She hasn't yet had the light burned out of her soul.'

He put out his hand and touched his index finger to the tip of the weapon. Then he put it to his lips and tasted it. 'So sweet,' he said, and Gaila slumped and Ben stepped forward, reaching for the blade that would finish this man, this *devil*, for ever.

Something hit him from behind, sending him into the railings, and Gaila staggered too. He caught hold of her arms, feeling the angularity of her bones beneath the skin, and he looked up to see Damon pushing past them both. For a moment, everything was confusion. Damon had reached his mentor. Their two shapes were locked together, struggling, and then Damon gripped Jones' arms, bending and pulling him half across his shoulders. Then Damon fell, but Ben realised it was deliberate, that he had Jones trapped against the railings. Damon pushed, forcing him higher, so that his face was suspended over the drop.

For a moment, Jones twisted his head and met Ben's eyes. He smiled, and then his expression changed. There was love in that look, and sadness, and knowledge; he looked as if he knew something that no one else did.

He did not struggle when Damon bent and wrapped his arms around his legs. Then Damon straightened and in one smooth movement, surely too fast, Jones fell.

He did not cry out. Ben rushed to the railing in time to see his fall, his black coat flying behind him like charred and broken wings. It took too long and yet no time at all and then he was lying in the glimmer below, his body spread across the golden disc at the heart of the cathedral. Ben could see from the shape he made that he would not rise again, and yet a part of him still expected Jones to stand, to call out something mocking about how he'd fooled them all. It didn't happen. The only thing that moved was the blood that slowly spread from him, shockingly bright against the shadows all around, and there was no sound, none at all.

FOUR

It was Damon who moved first. His face a mask, he leaned out over the railing. He looked down for a long time and then he turned away and murmured a single word: 'Bastard.'

Ben was ready to pull Gaila back, away from Damon, but Damon didn't move; all the fight had gone out of him. When he looked up, he seemed confused to see them there. 'I wanted my soul back,' he whispered. 'I told you that once, and it was true. He liked the truth, didn't he?'

'He said he did,' Ben replied.

Damon swallowed. 'All right, then. I'll say it: fuck my soul. I've been worrying about my soul ever since I was a kid.' He paused. 'All I wanted was my fucking *life* back.'

Ben and Gaila glanced at each other. There was nothing left for them here, not now. Their hands had been spared from spilling blood. Later, the police would come. There would be consequences; they would have to answer. But for now, there was nothing.

Damon shook his head and his face darkened. 'He said he'd give me everything, just like he offered to you. He promised. I was supposed to be the one, don't you see? His right hand. But there were only ever three chairs in his office, weren't there? For him and for the two of you. There was none for me. It was you he wanted.'

His face contorted into an ugly sneer. 'It was you and Ben all along. It was always about Ben, even when we were kids.' He bowed his head. 'Get out.'

They did not move.

'Go on. This is all about me now. I destroyed him. And I'll stay with him.'

Gaila reached out towards him and he flailed, knocking her hand away. 'I said go! Can't you give me the one thing I'm asking for? This is for *me*.' A tear slid down his cheek. 'He was my father too. Even if he forgot me, in the end.'

Ben reached for Gaila. Damon was lost in his own crazed thoughts, his twisted memories, and Ben did not know how to call him back. He wasn't sure he wanted to. Gaila grabbed for him too, seizing his wrist. They held on to each other. They did not need to speak. At first they backed away, fearing that Damon would come for them, finish all of them, but he did not follow. He simply stood there, his head hanging, mourning his mentor and his god, his *father*, and the tears poured down his cheeks.

They stepped into the corridor that led downward and they pulled the door closed behind them. Ben realised the passageway was not as dark as it had been before. A faint glow came from a heavily barred window, one that spoke of early morning skies, of a pale sun rising; of a new day being born over the city.

They did not speak. They hurried on until they reached the spiral stair, and they gripped one another's hands a little more tightly as they started down.

Ben's feet flew over the shallow steps, around and around. They seemed to shift under him and he began to wonder how far they would have to go before they were free of the place. Surely they had been descending for ever? Perhaps they would simply keep on going; perhaps they wouldn't emerge onto the cathedral floor at all. Perhaps they would just keep on heading further and further down, until they were beyond such things; until they descended into Hell itself.

But eventually the door was before them and he realised they had found the right way after all. The black and white chequered floor was there, just as solid and sure as it had always been. They spilled through and he pulled Gaila towards the entrance and he felt a tug on his hand.

'No,' she said. 'First—'

He knew at once what she meant. He could tell by the way she looked; he had always known his sister so well. He nodded in assent and followed where she led.

She took him back to the centre of the cathedral, the

crossing place, the golden disc at the heart of it all. There her father lay, unmoving, his blood already darkening. Ben remembered the way Jones had gazed down upon that floor; he remembered the expression on his face. He was glad that it was turned away from him now, so that he did not have to look into it. He didn't want to see his eyes. Most of all, he didn't want to see his smile.

For there is one more thing to be done. Is there not, Ben?

Now there was nothing left to be done at all. Without speaking, they turned and walked away.

THE EIGHTH CIRCLE

ONE

Ben sat on the low wall. The traffic was behind him and the noise of it was constantly in his ears. He had his back turned to a large junction, the meeting of Bradford Road and Abbey Road, and he could hear the squeaking brakes and ragged acceleration as motorists stopped at the traffic lights then hurried on their way. It was not a pretty place in which to stop. Uninspiring shop fronts were overshadowed by the bright promises of advertising hoardings. He had alighted from his bus a little further down the road – delaying his arrival, maybe? He wasn't sure and didn't care. He only knew that he'd been drawn to this small and oddly positioned patch of garden, a place of easement on the journey.

He had left Gaila in London the day before. She hadn't accompanied him to King's Cross Station; that wasn't the kind of thing Gaila did.

He stared across the thin, mean stretch of greenery at an

old monument that was the reason for the garden's existence. The monument was squat and toad-like, topped with a row of wide arches whose shape was echoed by the stone bowl beneath. Above that, the words *drink and be grateful* had been carved deep. The stone bowl had long since run dry.

Ben's lip twitched and he pushed himself to his feet. He turned to walk towards his mother's house. He followed the main road, not looking right or left at the tributary roads that led onto it; he wasn't interested in their names. The surface was hard and cold and unforgiving, and his feet made no echo, only a faint gritting sound that he soon ceased to notice. Cars sped past, people on their way to appointments or jobs or the airport or the supermarkets dotted further down the valley. Then white flakes drifted into his face and he stopped, disorientated.

For one brief moment, he thought it was snow. Then he realised: it was springtime after all. Somewhere, the first blossom was drifting from a tree. Small white petals, tainted with traffic fumes and dust, floated in the air. He couldn't see their source. There was only this; something once beautiful and pure that had now fallen.

He began to walk once more. He didn't want to think, didn't want to do anything except let his mind empty, and just keep on moving forward the best way he knew how. He had only stayed long enough in London to talk to the police. It hadn't been a pleasant interview, but Damon had been determined to bring everything down on his own head; it was as if he wanted that whole night to belong to him. Ben found himself wondering if it was the first thing Damon had done in a very long time that hadn't been under a compulsion. It hadn't been a pleasant thing, but it was his own. Ben doubted it would bring him joy.

Soon the familiar street came into view. Ben wasn't sure how he had reached it so quickly. The place he had once lived looked so exactly the same as it always had, it brought tears to his eyes. There were the narrow faces of the houses, pocked with satellite dishes, topped by the reaching claws of TV aerials. There were the small paved gardens fronted by low gates, full of the crooked-teeth rows of wheelie bins. It was all red brick and faded paint under a formless grey sky. This was the road where he and Gaila had run and played. It seemed like centuries ago and yet he could see the shadows of who they had been, chasing each other down the hill, all knees and elbows and careless glee, full of excitement at some forgotten scheme. It made him want to touch the ground, to feel it under his hand, to know it was really there, not just some illusion designed to fool him into doing – what?

But that time was over. No one was trying to trick him; he didn't need to think that way any longer. He started to walk up the hill, his calf muscles stretching, and he wondered when it had begun to be such an effort. He was sure he'd never thought about the hill as a child; it wasn't something he'd even noticed.

He went up to his mother's house and pushed on the gate,

and at the same moment Cass opened the front door. Her appearance startled him, and he wasn't sure what it was that was odd about her; then he realised that she was smiling, a real smile, a happy-to-see-him smile. Ben smiled back; he couldn't help it. He walked up to the door and she held out her hand and drew him inside, leading her child. 'Come on,' she said. 'There's something I want to show you.'

The pictures had gone from the walls. Cass didn't need to point it out to him. The whole room was lighter without their presence, despite the overpowering pattern of the wallpaper. She waved a hand around, indicating that he should look.

'I gave it up,' she said. 'I didn't feel the need any more. I think – oh, you know, Ben, sometimes I felt like I was still there. I made a promise once, something that was wrong, and yet – it's all right now. It's gone, or forgiven, or something like that.' She glanced down at the palm of her hand, the one that was melted and burned from the day she'd tried to sear an old scar away. She looked as if she could scarcely believe what she'd done.

Ben opened his mouth to speak, but she hushed him and spoke first. 'I'd do it again, you know.'

'But—'

'Sh.' She put her hand to his cheek. 'Look at you, Ben. You're a good man. You always try to do the right thing.'

'But I don't. I *don't* always do the right thing.'

'Nor do I.' She smiled. 'But I'm not sure that's important

any more. You know, what I did – it was for love. Because I love you, Ben. And look how it turned out. I – I'm proud of you.'

'But I'm not—'

She stroked his cheek. 'You're my sweet boy, Ben. You're safe. I don't know why I feel that, but I do. And that's enough. Because acting out of love – that can't be so bad, can it? It has to mean more than – oh, I don't know. A dry old set of rules that we don't even understand.'

Her voice fell to a whisper. 'When I look at you, the person I helped make – that's when I know I did the right thing. And I would do anything for you, Ben. You know that. Anything.'

She thought about what she'd said, then shrugged. 'I don't mean – I mean, I know I've been a worry to you, but all that's going to change. I suppose we always show our worst side to those we love the most. But you don't have to take care of me any longer. It's enough, knowing that you're out there, that you are who you are. I feel like that's all behind me now. I'm going to start again.'

Ben closed his eyes. Everything that Cass said to him was sweet. They were the kind of words he had wanted to hear from her for such a long time, and yet—

Whatever she did, I want it undone. She did it to help me . . . Now I – I'll do the same for her. I want her to be free of all this. I want her soul to be her own.

His promise to Jones felt a long time ago and a long way away, like a story he'd once been told, something he didn't really believe in. It was as if it had happened to someone else, a person he wasn't sure he even knew any longer.

But he had asked for his mother to be free. Now she was.

He thought of Gaila thrusting out her hand for Jones to shake, of the deal his sister had made. He didn't know if Raffie's daughter had been cured. Raffie hadn't contacted them again and Ben hadn't enquired after her. He hadn't wanted to know. He liked to think of them anyway: a mother holding her child in her arms, stroking her healthy hair, her healthy, glowing skin, rocking her to sleep, unable to keep the smile from her face as she felt the warm weight in her arms.

Of course, Ben had replaced his mother's promise with one of his own, but wasn't that dissolved now, too? His contract had been with the company and that would pass to his sister. Jones had offered it to both of them, but Gaila was his daughter. If anyone had a claim upon it, she did. It was too early for anything to be made official, but he knew it was going to happen – it was written in his blood; or rather, in his sister's. And all the promises and contracts it held would belong to her, his own among them. It would be safe with her, he knew that. Like Cass, he was master of his soul: he was free.

'That brings me to something else,' Cass said. 'Come with me a minute.'

She took him by the hand and Ben allowed himself to be led. She went further into the house, opening a door onto the stairs. She started up them and he followed. She didn't tell him where they were going or why, just opened the door onto a narrow bedroom. It hadn't been used in a long time. Ben knew that, because it was his. He had slept in it when he'd been a boy.

Some of his old books, fantastical tales adorned with lurid covers, torn and peeling, were still there on the shelf in the corner. His old teddy bear sat next to them, its eyes glassy and blank. He found himself wondering whether, if he opened the wardrobe, his old clothes would be there too: his white school shirts pressed and ready, his trousers ironed with a sharp crease down the front.

Cass tugged him further inside. It was like stepping back in time, into old shoes that no longer fit. The room was narrow, the walls too close. She led him to the window. 'Never mind all this,' she said. 'It's time I cleared it away. I can't think why I kept it.' When Ben was standing beside her, she slipped her arm into his. 'Do you see?'

Ben looked out. There was a line of red-brick back-to-backs across the road, very like the one in which they stood. If he peered down, he could just see a dull line of tarmac, an old takeaway carton half open in the gutter. After that the street sloped down towards the main road. He could just see the large blocky premises of a shop on the opposite side. Beyond that were more streets, their colours fading to grey, the windows growing smaller, the rooftops blending into one as they receded. And above it all was the sky, a grey lid keeping everything inside.

'Do you see?' Cass asked again. She sounded worried.

Ben shook his head.

'*There.*' She pointed, and Ben saw there was something else after all. Between the rooftops and the sky, somewhere out beyond the edges of the city, was a thin dark line.

'Would you mind, do you think?'

'Mum, I'm sorry, I have no idea what you mean.'

She dug him in the ribs. 'Me moving, of course. I think I've had enough of the city, Ben. This house – it was only ever chosen for me, you know. By your granddad, when he left me this place. And I never really felt like I could change it, but now – I feel like I can make my own choices. Choices that actually matter.'

'Mum – of course, you should move. That would be perfect. I always thought you should. And you know I'll come and see you.' He paused. 'Gaila will.'

She smiled, and Ben was startled to see a tear spring to her eye. 'I hope so, Ben. I was never – I wasn't really a good mother to your sister, was I? I tried so hard. But there were so many things to think about, and I'm afraid I never really gave her a chance. But she's my blood too, isn't she?' She half smiled, waved the words away. 'I can only try to make it up to her. But what about the move?' She laughed and gestured towards that distant line of green. 'The problem is, when you suddenly have the whole world to choose from – where do you go?'

'You can go anywhere, Mum. Like you said, you're free.

Maybe you should travel for a bit, until you've thought about it.'

She looked more serious. 'Actually, Ben, I've been doing a *lot* of thinking. And it may sound odd, but I might go back to Darnshaw. I thought, if only – well, it would show that the past doesn't matter any longer, wouldn't it? That it's gone for good. I envisioned a certain kind of life for you there once. I thought it would be the perfect childhood. You running and playing with all the other kids, and there would be fields and woods to play in, and it would always be sunshine. I imagined something innocent, you know? Well, maybe I could have that now. Not for you – you have your own life to build – but for me this time.' She closed her eyes and took a deep breath. 'Yes, I really think I could.'

'Of course.' Ben put his arm around her. 'It's beautiful there. Of course you should go.'

They stayed like that for a while, staring out of the window at that green line, so very far away. He wasn't sure what had happened. His mother *was* free, and he didn't know how it had come about, whether it was something he had done or because she'd finally decided to cast off the shadow of the past. He didn't even care any longer; he only knew that his mother had decided to *live*.

Perhaps that was what Raffie was doing now. Perhaps Simon was. Maybe even Damon was too, in his own way. Ben had seen a piece in the newspaper about the man who'd broken into Saint Paul's and jumped to his death. It had been seen as suspicious, especially as no one could find out how he'd got inside; more so when they'd discovered Ashley's and Milo's bodies at the offices of Acheron. But in the end they had decided it was a suicide. Mephistopheles' body had never been found. Perhaps what had taken place needn't haunt them after all. Perhaps it wouldn't haunt Gaila. But then, his sister had always lived without fear. It struck him that he could do that too and he closed his eyes, remembering the way that Jones had fallen, becoming boneless, his coat flapping behind him. The way he had looked at them before he fell. The man who'd proclaimed himself a devil; what was it that he had said? *We create our own devils.* Is that what they had done – created not a god but the Devil, one they'd all deserved? If so, it was a devil that preyed upon fear: fear of Hell and damnation and punishment and the flame. Perhaps the way to truly destroy whatever Jones had been was to cut that thread of fear and never look back.

Ben closed his eyes and found himself thinking of something else that Jones had said:

If you gaze long enough into the abyss, the abyss will gaze back into you. But what if it didn't? What if there was only silence? A long, cold silence, and nothing more, for ever and ever.

Perhaps that was what it came to, in the end: to face nothingness alone. But that happened to everyone, didn't it? Some day.

He felt Cass take his hand. Hers felt warm against his skin and he squeezed her fingers. *No*, he thought: *not alone.* And he knew that it wouldn't be dark, because if he stared hard enough into the abyss, long and without flinching, he knew there was light there too.

Cass spoke again. Her voice was breathy, excited, childlike. He turned and watched her forming the words and it came to him as something of a surprise that his mother was still young. All the years that had lain so heavily upon her were falling away.

'The hills are beautiful,' she said. 'Do you remember them in winter, Ben? Just whiteness, all around. The stone buildings, all honey-coloured, the way they glowed at sunset. And the trees by the river, the sound the water makes . . . the song of the birds – oh, for all I've seen, it's the closest thing to hearing the voice of God, or whatever's out there, don't you think? Do you understand, Ben – do you remember any of it?'

He smiled. He felt now that he could barely remember being a child at all, but still, he did know what she meant. He remembered what he had seen of the place when he'd gone there with Damon. The little houses set into the valley, the wildness rising all around them, the long arc of the sky reaching over everything.

Now he simply held her hand and let her talk. And for the first time in a long time, it seemed as if the future was going to be a beautiful thing.

THE NINTH CIRCLE

ONE

The launch was at the centre of a media feeding frenzy and yet nothing had happened for hours. Ben had looked for word of it at midday, but nothing appeared until the news at six, when a live report began.

It was reminiscent of a film premiere. The street was crammed with news vans. Men and women clutching microphones spoke into cameras or simply waited, brandishing them like weapons. Crowds lined the roadside, leaning over barricades to see better. Judging by their pale faces and the rolled sleeping bags some of them clutched, the more determined had been waiting for a very long time.

In the background was a simple black door that Ben knew well. He should. For a while he had entered by it every weekday morning, full of the enthusiasm of youth and ignorance. He could have been there now if he'd chosen it; but he hadn't chosen it.

Theodore Jones had left a will, and it had been upheld. The company now belonged in its entirety to his sister. The first thing she had done was to ask Ben to move down to London and help her run it, but he didn't feel that was where he belonged any longer.

He remembered the telephone call when he'd told Gaila that he wasn't coming. The thing he had really wanted to say had been left unsaid; that he wanted to stay as far away from the game as he possibly could. Her reply had been disappointed and resigned and a little sad, tinged with just the faintest hint of anger, and then she had mastered it. He had sensed her swallowing it down. She'd been gracious; she had wished him well. He wished her well too, and he had told her that he was sure she was doing the right thing. He knew that because of the way she had pushed that anger down, burying it so completely; it augured well.

Gaila had always been better than him, he knew that now. Despite all the misgivings he'd ever felt at her plans, he knew that she would steer the right course. He had faith in her.

The screen erupted with popping flashbulbs and a surge of movement, a tide pressing towards the shore. Its focus was a long black car with two black flags flapping on its bonnet. Ben squinted. He could read what was written on those flags: one single letter – an *A*, in the same gothic font used in *Acheron*, and beneath it: *666 Protocol*.

A voice-over began. 'It's not often that the launch of a new computer game hits the headlines. But 666 *Protocol* isn't any ordinary game.'

The black car edged along the road and drew to a silent halt at the kerb.

'A spate of deaths at these very offices infamously demonstrated its ability to make its players believe in its supernatural powers. Sometimes that belief had disastrous effects.

'A combination of web search algorithms, spyware planted on the user's hard drive and photo analysis software means the game can appear to know more about the player than is, in reality, possible.

'Those same deaths have in turn wrapped *Acheron* in more than its share of notoriety . . .'

The car door opened.

'. . . which has made this the most hotly anticipated new release on the market.'

For a moment the crowd drowned out the correspondent's voice with their cheers. The sound rose in pitch, then became less ragged. Ben wasn't sure when the formless shouting evolved into a chant: 'I believe! I believe! *I believe!*'

Onlookers surged forward. Thickset men in plain black T-shirts marked with a single symbol – a cross, ending in a curve – linked arms to keep the horde back.

Someone stepped out of the car.

Ben recognised his sister at once, though she had changed her hair for the occasion; it was tied up in a series of knots. The tufts, haphazard and spiked, were each tipped with a fiery red. Her face was pale and clear against the press of bodies at her back, and she was as beautiful as ever, perhaps more so. Ben couldn't see the scar on her cheek, but he could see her eyes, and they were dark. Still, they shone; there was a light in them. There was a light in her face.

Ben realised that his sister was wearing a cloak. The black silk enveloped her slight form, rising high around her neck.

He pushed away the images that presented themselves. He told himself that his sister had done the right thing. This was a publicity stunt, that was all. She had to go along with it, the image of the company, its heritage, in order to put it right. Those had been her words. And yet it was something Theodore Jones had said that echoed through his mind: *not just one cathedral has stood here, but five, each grander than the last . . . Is it the same, do you think? Was each one of them still Saint Paul's, or something else?*

He shook his head, concentrating on the television. Of course, his sister was right. Without *666 Protocol*, people would keep on playing the old game. And even after poaching some of the best programmers from rival companies, no one had been able to analyse how that had worked, not in its entirety. They weren't even sure if it would continue to work. No: it had to be stopped, and Gaila, he had to admit, was doing it in style. She was poised like a starlet; like someone who had spent time in front of a camera, learning her angles, perfecting her art. But of course, she had.

'The new CEO of the company,' the voice-over said, 'is

ex-model Gaila Cassidy, heiress of Theodore Jones. Still just eighteen years old, she was present at the offices on the night that several protesters were found dead and the previous owner killed himself, leaving her everything.

'Cassidy was cleared of all charges, but in the eyes of fans and detractors alike, she retains a certain air of notoriety; or perhaps, in some circles, allure. She's about to make her announcement. We'll go over to her now.'

Gaila had stepped up onto the roof of the car. She knew that the world was watching and she made it wait. The camera zoomed in and she stared directly into the lens. Now Ben could see the scar on her cheek. She had made no attempt to cover it. She did not look like she was wearing make-up, save for her painted, blood-red lips. He thought she was looking straight at him, but that had always been her skill, hadn't it? To make people think that she was seeing into them, reading their innermost thoughts; learning their secrets.

She winked and the connection was broken. When she spoke, her voice was amplified. It carried easily, though Ben couldn't see a microphone.

'Welcome,' she said, 'to *666 Protocol!*'

The crowd screamed and she paused until they quieted. She looked up at just the right moment, but again she made them wait for her words. Instead, her hand went to her neck, loosening a tie, and she let the cloak fall. It caught the air and spread itself, drifting towards the crowd; their clawing fingers grasped for it.

Beneath the cloak she wore skinny black jeans and a black T-shirt. She wore no jewellery. Her top, unlike those of the bodyguards, did not bear the cross of confusion. Instead there were two simple words: PLAY AGAIN?

She spun slowly, her hands on her hips, and eager cries spread across the crowd as they read the words. Gaila gave an arch smile. 'Well?' she asked, 'will you?'

Again, her words were lost amid the screams of assent. Then, other voices rose up from the melee, surfacing before being subsumed:

'My wife is sick. Please . . .'

'Will it give money? I need . . .'

And then, simply: '*Help me*, Gaila.'

For a moment her smile faltered. Then it spread across her face once more, but to Ben, it no longer looked like a real smile; it looked like a smile put on for the cameras.

'There have been certain rumours,' she said. 'Well, there's only one way to find out, isn't there? But that's not what I came here to say.'

In an instant, all was silence.

'This is our best game yet,' she said. 'I promise you that. But anyone who has – at any time – purchased any previous incarnation – *iteration* – of the game, may trade it in for the new one free of charge.'

She gave a sweeping bow as the crowd erupted and Ben had the impression that she was still wearing a cloak after all, something to swirl around her in an invisible flourish.

She leaped down from the car in one light movement and headed towards the waiting black door without another word. The dense crowd parted for her easily, as if she'd commanded them, and yet she looked neither to right nor left as she skipped up the steps. The door opened to an unseen hand. She passed inside and it closed behind her, cutting her off from sight.

'Well, there you have it,' the correspondent said. The view switched back to the presenter; a perfectly coiffed blonde woman, her make-up immaculate, a scarf draped around her jacket collar. 'The somewhat abrupt departure of Gaila Cassidy – new CEO of the company behind *Acheron* – following an announcement set to send shockwaves through the industry, even while filling any eager gamer with joy. Now, back to the studio . . .'

Ben flicked off the television and sat back in his chair, a smile playing about his lips. He had known that she could do it, handle the media and the limelight and everything else. He had told her she could, even when she had called him in the night, her voice shaking with uncertainty. He had assured her that she was doing the right thing.

Still, he couldn't push her parting words from his mind as he stared at the empty television screen. At the time, he'd barely heard them. It was after they'd said their goodbyes and just before she'd hung up, and her voice had been little more than the sound of a dead line: *Power is temptation, though, isn't it Ben?*

And then she'd been gone, hundreds of miles away, as far out of reach as the little sister she once had been.

EPILOGUE

THE FIRST CIRCLE

He had navigated the Slough of Despond, had successfully located the entrance to the underworld. He had gathered a golden coin to present to Charon, the ferryman, to pay his passage across Acheron, the River of Woe. Once he was across, he knew where he must go: to the Fields of Punishment, en route to the central rings of Hell. Along his journey he had opened chests and found the lost sword, the magical emerald diadem and potions guaranteed to send the drinker straight to oblivion.

So far, so dull.

He sighed as the ferryman's oar stirred the dark waters of his computer screen and turned instead to another screen, a laptop sitting next to his gaming computer, and the words he'd written there.

My experience confirms that of other review sites, and makes me rather wish I'd put off my trial of 666 Protocol even longer – or

indeed, indefinitely. What began with fire and brimstone is likely
to end with a sad little puff of smoke, and a mutter about how
what's given away for free is generally of no value.

Clichés abound in this, the latest release of Acheron, *or*
just The Game *in some quarters, so desperately awaited by*
deluded souls everywhere. The drama around its inception,
sadly, far outweighs that delivered in its ponderous and out-
dated format.

He paused long enough to lean over and, with an outstretched
index finger, contemptuously tap a key. On the screen, his
character – the avatars in the game were supposed to look
just like the player, weren't they? This looked more like a
lumbering figure made of a child's building blocks – began
to move along a boulder-strewn path.

It is a pity that so many discarded their older versions of the
game in order to obtain their 'freebie'. A sad day it must have
been when they actually began to play. When does a freebie
become daylight robbery? That is the question.

His character stopped its lumbering procession. In front of
him was a rough-hewn wooden door. It was marked only
with a single character: a cross, ending in a curve a little like
a question mark. Another desultory press on the keyboard
revealed that the door was locked.

The myth surrounding this game, the stories of dreams coming true, are sadly much more exciting than the gaming experience. Gather treasures, keys and coins, wander around a maze that borrows its names from a hotchpotch of diabolical mythology, and what do you have?

He leaned over and this time tapped several keys. Pop-up boxes of options flew past, almost too quickly to be read. It took a little longer for the figure on the screen to respond. It suddenly had an axe in its hand.

Another sigh, lean, click. The figure raised the axe above its head and rough sound effects, a little too high and tinny, began to beat out a steady rhythm.

Even my hardware is too sophisticated for this dross. The sound quality isn't worthy of my speakers.

He sat back, pushing himself away from his desk.

At least the view from my window is good.
Actually, no it isn't.

He waited until the pounding of the axe against the door had stopped, leaned over and deleted the last two lines he'd written. 'Christ,' he muttered, under his breath.

In short, no one is recommending this to anybody. Word has it, on gaming forums and blogs everywhere, that Acheron has had its day. On the other hand, if you want your kids to relegate their fancy new toy to the back of the cupboard by Boxing Day, get hold of a copy. (In case you don't get sarcasm: no, you won't thank me.)

The door on the screen opened. Blackness yawned.

I could add something about the most blatant over-hyping of a game in the history of games, but I'm not sure I've escaped with enough will to live.

One of the oh-so-thrilling slogans for this piece of tripe was, 'If the Devil didn't exist, you'd have to invent him.' It's a pity they couldn't be arsed. It might have made it a little bit more exciting.

I can only conclude by adding the words repeated by gaming souls everywhere – JUST DON'T DO IT. Save your time, your sanity, your self-respect, and most definitely your old versions, if anyone has one left. Steer clear of this like the pile of burning sulphur it is.

He stared at the screen, which remained full of darkness. He twitched in irritation.

And if you just can't help yourself – well, don't come running to me when you're weeping at all the hours you'll never get back.

He pressed a key; the game's forward command. Nothing happened. He frowned and hit it again. He muttered something aloud about shoddy goods that didn't even work.

Then something did happen.

In the centre of the screen, a single pixel shone. He squinted, peering at it. It made him think of an antique television being switched off, the picture shrinking to a single light in the middle of the screen. He leaned in closer. Perhaps he'd been premature, blaming the game; maybe it was his screen that had a fault. He let out a spurt of air. It wasn't likely. Still, he reached out, carrying out the manoeuvre guaranteed to fix screens everywhere: he slapped it, hard, on the side. The picture didn't change.

But the light, slowly, began to grow.

He stared. The light on the screen wasn't steady. It flickered. It took him a few moments to realise it was a candle. It took longer still to see that it was cradled in someone's hands. The inner curves of their palms shone. The hands ended in long sleeves reminiscent of the kind of robe a monk would wear.

The graphics had improved, but the game hadn't. Like its advertising, it promised more than it delivered. His confusion had made it interesting, if only for a second, but if confusion was all it could offer . . .

He leaned over to the laptop once more, scathing words spinning through his brain. He never typed them.

He could see the face now, hovering in the darkness. He

had heard stories about this, hadn't he? About reaching a point where a guide would appear. Sometimes that guide wore the face of the player, didn't it? People spoke about it with wonder. They were never quite sure how the game carried off the trick.

Confusion gave way to curiosity. He hunched over, leaning towards the screen as the figure grew closer. The underside of its features were lit by the light it carried. They shifted and flowed with the flicker of the candle. He could make out a nose, the trace of lips. The eyes, though, remained in darkness. At least now the graphics were good; he had to give them that.

The figure glided towards him and he pushed away from the screen, knocking his mug with his elbow, slopping coffee across the desk. He didn't care; he couldn't take his eyes away from the face that was revealed.

It wasn't him, after all; not even a clumsy simulacrum. It was a girl standing there, and he didn't know when he had seen anything more lovely.

She wore a heavy cloak, but her form was slight beneath it. Dark spikes of hair protruded from the hood. Her features were small and neat, almost elfin. Her eyes, though, were what held him. They were black, but a light shone inside them. Her expression was amused, playful. She did not look away from him and she did not blink and he felt those eyes taking in his form, his surface; probing what lay beneath.

He couldn't take his gaze from the screen. He wanted to

know what came next. He could see that something would. He needed to know what it was. There was a promise in the girl's eyes. He suddenly felt he was standing at the edge of a precipice, looking out at a great vista of opportunities; his life had opened out instead of closing inward, to this room, his laptop, his own scathing words. He put his hand to his head. For a moment he felt dizzy.

A part of him thought the girl's expression hadn't changed. Another part of him thought he had seen her smile. He would do anything to see that smile again.

He gripped the edge of his desk, tightly, and forced himself to look away. This was stupid, wasn't it? He knew the game wasn't any good. He glanced at his laptop. He'd said so, quite candidly, in black and white.

The laptop screen was blank.

He blinked. The words did not reappear. He reached out, rubbing the mouse-pad with his finger. Nothing happened. There was only an empty page, waiting to be filled.

Irritation ripped through him, and then he looked back into the girl's eyes and it faded. She was beautiful. Her lips, like her eyes, were dark. Moisture shone from them as the candlelight shifted in her hands. They were a deep, rich purple. *The colour of poison*, he found himself thinking, and did not know why; he only knew that the girl had a face that could break his heart.

He focused on the light she held and he frowned. He had thought there would be some candlestick in her hands, but there was not. Instead, she simply held them out, cupped together in offering. The candle flickered above them, but there *was* no candle, only the flame, dancing and writhing in the air. For a moment, that's all there was: a small light, wavering against the darkness. So delicate, so ready to fail.

He saw the light reflected in her eyes. He wondered if it was reflected in his.

And then he realised; nothing was happening. For all the effect her appearance had had on him, still, nothing was happening.

Promises much, he thought. *Offers little.*

The girl on the screen shook her head and laughed. Then she turned, glancing back over her shoulder. She started to walk away, into the dark.

He found himself reaching out, trying to catch her shoulder, to draw her back. Watching her walk away from him like that – it was like a physical pain. He couldn't understand the effect it had on him, didn't know why he was so affected by seeing her face, her eyes – *her eyes* – but he did know that he never wanted it to end.

He felt something settle into the centre of him as he reached for her, something just like that pixel of light, and he recognised it: it was loss. It felt cold, like a tiny sliver of ice.

He frowned and rubbed at his chest. What was happening to him?

Then, across the bottom of the screen, words began to form.

Do you want to make it interesting?

They shone more brightly before fading, as if they had never been. There was nothing more. He didn't know what that was supposed to mean. He was no longer sure he was playing the same game at all.

He sat there staring at the blankness before him, and then he stirred. He leaned out and, slowly, pressed the Y key.

The screen was still dark, but somehow it gave the impression that he was moving. He squinted. He had no idea how it was doing that, but he knew that he was right when a grainy silvering began to take the place of the blankness. He narrowed his eyes, trying to make out what it was.

He realised it was a small, shabby room. He was looking down on it from above. It contained a desk that was far too large for it, the walls made even more cave-like by rows of shelves that were stuffed with files, DVDs, books. With a start, he realised it was *his* room.

And there he was, sitting in his chair, the thinning patch at the top of his scalp quite visible. He was carrying too much weight, he knew that, but it was different to see it from this angle. The way he sprawled in his chair wasn't flattering, his posture doubling the folds of his belly. He pushed himself straighter, sitting back in his chair, smoothing down his T-shirt. His counterpart on the screen did not move. That version of him simply sat there, one hand resting near the keyboard, tapping one finger against the desk. He realised he could hear it, a soft *tap-tap-tap* coming through the speakers.

Feeling a wave of disorientation, he looked down at his own hand. He was surprised when he saw that it was curled in his lap, a dead and useless thing.

He turned and looked up at the ceiling. He half expected to see a camera there, a joke perhaps, set up by – whom? He knew no one who would do such a thing. Anyway, there was no camera, only a blank section of wall hiding nothing.

More words began to unfurl across the screen. He squinted, leaning in closer. Something happened in his chest. He felt as if someone had opened a door. He could almost feel the breeze on his skin.

What do you want?

Those words. He had heard about those words, the source of so many stories. Wild stories. Sad stories and tragic stories and magical and murderous and cruel, all of them together, spiralling around the game like smoke around a candle. He stared at them for a long time.

Then he leaned over and he began to type.

ACKNOWLEDGEMENTS

Huge thanks are due, as ever, to Jo Fletcher and the fabulous team at Jo Fletcher Books, as well as to my agent Oli Munson. You are all heroes.

This book wouldn't exist without the readers of *A Cold Season* who wanted to know what happened next. Thank you so much for your kindness and support, and for turning my mind to Darnshaw and its characters again. My appreciation also goes to the Richard and Judy book club, for helping launch *A Cold Season* into the world.

A shout out to Martin Littler and the gang at Inclusive Technology for harnessing technology for rather more worthy purposes than *Acheron*, and for first taking me to Saddleworth. A big thank you to Wayne McManus for keeping my website looking shiny.

Finally, deepest thanks and love go to my family, and of course to Fergus.

Alison Littlewood is the author of *A Cold Season*, published by Jo Fletcher Books. The novel was selected for the Richard and Judy Book Club, where it was described as 'perfect reading for a dark winter's night.' Her second novel, *Path of Needles* – a dark blend of fairy tales and crime fiction – was shortlisted for a British Fantasy Award. Her third, *The Unquiet House*, is a ghost story set in the Yorkshire countryside; it has been nominated for a Shirley Jackson Award.

Alison's short stories have been picked for *Best British Horror*, *The Best Horror of the Year* and *The Mammoth Book of Best New Horror* anthologies, as well as *The Best British Fantasy 2013* and *The Mammoth Book of Best British Crime 10*. Other publication credits include the anthologies *Terror Tales of Yorkshire*, *The Spectral Book of Horror Stories*, *Where Are We Going?* and *Never Again*.

Alison lives in Yorkshire with her partner Fergus, in a house full of creaking doors and crooked walls. You can talk to her on twitter @Ali__L and visit her at www.alisonlittlewood.co.uk.

Also by Alison Littlewood

A BROKEN FAMILY

Cass is trying to rebuild her life after the loss of her soldier husband, and a renovated mill in the picture-perfect village of Darnshaw looks to be the idyllic spot to bring up her traumatised son, Ben.

A DARK SECRET

But the locals aren't as friendly as Cass had hoped, and Ben is beginning to display a hostility she can't understand. Then the blizzards blow in, and Darnshaw is marooned in a sea of snow.

ISOLATED

Now, threatened on all sides, Cass finds herself pitted against forces she can barely comprehend.

The cold season has begun.

AVAILABLE NOW

PATH OF
NEEDLES

Some fairy tales are born of dreams . . . and some are born of nightmares.

A murderer is on the loose, but the gruesome way in which the bodies are being posed has the police at a loss. Until, on a hunch, Alice Hyland, an expert in fairy tales, is called in. And it is Alice who finds the connection between the body of Chrissie Farrell and an obscure Italian version of Snow White.

Then, when a second body is found, Alice is dragged further into the investigation – until she herself becomes a suspect.

Now Alice must fight, not just to prove her innocence, but to protect herself, because it's looking like she might well be next.

AVAILABLE NOW

THE
UNQUIET
HOUSE

Mire House is dreary, cold and isolated. But when Emma Dean inherits it from a distant relation, she immediately feels a sense of belonging.

It isn't long before Charlie Mitchell, grandson of the original owner, appears, claiming that he wants to get to know her as they are the last of the family. But Emma suspects he's more interested in the house than his long-lost relatives.

And when she starts seeing ghostly figures, Emma begins to wonder: is Charlie trying to scare her away, or are there darker secrets lurking in the corners of Mire House?

AVAILABLE NOW